# TRANSPLANTED

## ᵀᴼ:RED CLAY

# TRANSPLANTED

## TO RED CLAY

### APPALACHIAN ROOTS – BOOK FOUR

JANICE COLE HOPKINS

Ambassador International
GREENVILLE, SOUTH CAROLINA & BELFAST, NORTHERN IRELAND

www.ambassador-international.com

# Transplanted to Red Clay

Appalachian Roots – Book 4

Printed in the United States of America

ISBN: 978-1-62020-573-0
eISBN: 978-1-62020-597-6

All Scripture taken from the King James Version, the Authorized Version.

Cover Design and Page Layout by Hannah Nichols
Ebook Conversion by Anna Riebe Raats

AMBASSADOR INTERNATIONAL
Emerald House
411 University Ridge, Suite B14
Greenville, SC 29601, USA
www.ambassador-international.com

AMBASSADOR BOOKS
The Mount
2 Woodstock Link
Belfast, BT6 8DD, Northern Ireland, UK
www.ambassadormedia.co.uk

*The colophon is a trademark of Ambassador*

*For I will set mine eyes upon them for good,*
*and I will bring them again to this land:*
*and I will build them, and not pull them down;*
*and I will plant them, and not pluck them up.*

—Jeremiah 24:6

# CHAPTER ONE

# Down the Mountain

## APRIL 14, 1879

"WILL I BE ABLE TO go, Mama?"

Rachel Moretz leaned over her mother's shoulder to better see the letter from her aunt. They hadn't seen Aunt Ivy since she'd married Sam and left the farm just after the war ended about fourteen years ago.

Mama looked up at her. "Do you want to go and leave our mountains?"

Rachel sat down at the kitchen table. "I do love the mountains, but I would like to have an opportunity to socialize more. About the only time I get to see anyone off the farm is when the circuit rider comes or sometimes when we go to Boone. The trips to see Grandfather in Salisbury are too few and far between to really count. I wish we lived closer to one of the churches." She thought for a moment. "What did Papa say about me going? I'm sure you two have already discussed it."

"Yes, and we're still thinking. This is too important to make a hasty decision."

"Aunt Ivy did say she needed me to help with Hope."

"I don't know what you could do to keep Hope from her wild ways if her family isn't able to handle her. Ivy and Sam are both strong-willed people, so I can't see Hope having her way too much. Even Patrick seemed very responsible, and he's her older brother. I'm not sure it would be wise to put you in the middle of this."

"Aunt Ivy is asking that I become Hope's companion. That's all."

"She says she thinks you will be a good influence. I'd think Patrick would be as good an influence as anyone could be."

"I wish I could remember Patrick better. I have a vague impression and remember I liked him, but nothing's very clear. I don't remember Aunt Ivy or Uncle Sam at all."

"Well, you were only two when they left here. You missed Patrick for the longest time. He was eight when he left. He spoiled you worse than anyone, but I never had to worry about your care when he was around. He watched after you like a mother hawk and kept you entertained as well. He would ask, 'Who's your best friend, Rachel?' and you'd always say, 'Paddy' and grin at him."

"Why have we never gone to see them? They've invited us often enough."

"I don't really know. Time's just slipped away. It's hard to believe it's been fourteen years since I've seen Ivy. We've written each other, however, and kept in touch that way."

"Do you not want me to go, Mama?" Rachel asked tentatively.

Mama looked at her. "It's hard for me to believe you are now this beautiful young woman. Where's my little girl? Personally, I certainly don't want you that far away from me. I know I'll miss you terribly. However, I want what's best for you. That's what makes this so hard. Your father and I really don't know what's best."

"I could attend school to see how good my education is compared to those students who've attended a regular school."

"Are you implying your father and I aren't good teachers?" Leah teased.

"No, Mama." Rachel laughed. "I was thinking I'd probably stun everyone with my vast knowledge." Her voice held the same teasing tone her mother's had.

Mama's expression turned serious. "Are you hoping to meet someone you'd like to court you?"

"That would be nice, but it's not the main reason I want to go. Besides you don't have to worry about who I might choose. I'm going to be extremely picky. If the fellow can't offer me a love like yours and Papa's, I don't want him. I plan to hold out for the best."

"I hope you will, Rachel. I'd like to see you happily married someday, but I'm in no hurry for that day to come."

"Is this a woman-to-woman discussion, or am I welcome?" Papa came into the kitchen.

"You're always welcome, dear." Leah smiled up at him, and he kissed her forehead. "Where are the boys?"

"They're finishing up some chores. They'll be in shortly."

The twins burst into the house like thunderstorms. They must've been racing.

"I won!" John announced.

"No, you didn't," Mark argued. "You know I got to the door first. Papa, who won?"

"I'd say it was a tie," Luke told them.

"You always say that," John complained.

At thirteen the twins were identical in looks. Their personalities were very different, however. John was the laughing daredevil, while Mark was more serious and studious.

Papa looked around. "Where's Matt?"

"He's down by the creek looking for frogs with Josh," John answered.

"Go tell him to come in for dinner," Leah said. "It's still too cool to be playing in the creek."

"Race you to the creek," John said as he took off with Mark right behind him.

"Were you talking about Ivy's letter?" Papa asked.

"Yes, Rachel wants to go," Leah told him.

"Let's pray about it and see what God leads us to do."

"Luke, you and Leah don't need to worry about anything here," Aaron Carter told Papa as he helped load their belongings in the wagon. "You won't be gone over a month, and you've already plowed and planted your early garden. We can get the fields planted as soon as you return."

The Carters had come over for breakfast this morning, and they would stay with the boys while Papa, Mama, and Rachel traveled down the mountain to Stanly County, where the Whitleys lived.

"You make sure you behave for Aaron and Maggie," Papa told the twins and ten-year-old Matthew. "You're expected to do your chores and help out too."

"Aw, Pa," John complained.

"You know we will, Papa," Mark agreed.

Mama gave Maggie, Aaron's wife, a hug and hugged the boys, even though John acted embarrassed. Rachel hugged them also, as well as Josh and Amy Carter. Rachel had tended the Carter children almost as much as she had Matt. Josh had just turned eleven, and Amy was eight.

While Papa checked the team, Rachel looked over the farm one more time. The Carters had lived with them at first, but now they had their own house across the road and down from the meadow, but well within sight. When they'd built a clapboard, Papa had told Mama they could clapboard theirs, if she wanted, but Mama had always liked the logs. "It fits here better," she'd said.

The two-story log house had been built by her great-great-grandpa Moretz, but it had been a small cabin at first. Great-grandpa

Edgar and Great-granny Em had added the second story to give three more bedrooms. Rachel was thankful, because it allowed her to have her own room.

It would be a while before Rachel would see the farm again. She planned to stay with the Whitleys through the winter, so she'd be gone about a year.

They all bowed their heads, and Papa said a prayer before they started out. He asked for God's protection and blessings on their journey and for those who were staying behind.

All too soon, the wagon headed down the mountain toward Boone, but they would turn south before reaching the town. Before they got to Charlotte, they'd turn east. This time, they wouldn't go through Wilkesboro or spend the night with Grandfather in Salisbury. Rachel didn't know how many times they'd have to stay overnight going this way. She just knew it would be a long trip.

This was the first time Rachel had gone somewhere alone with Mama and Papa since the twins were born. She didn't remember much about their birth, because she'd been only three at the time. They were born less than a year after Papa came home from the war. He'd been held a prisoner at Salisbury and Andersonville prisons, but he didn't like to talk about that time.

Rachel looked at her parents. She'd always been fascinated by their relationship. Even after being married all these years, they were still very much in love. Aaron and Maggie were, too, but there was something about her parents' relationship that went much deeper. She knew their story well. She had asked Mama to tell it to her often enough.

Ivy and Mama had lived on a plantation in Anson County. Papa had been visiting a friend and had thought he'd fallen in love with Ivy. Since their mother wanted them to get married to men they didn't want, Ivy talked Mama into running away with her to the mountains, where she planned to marry Papa.

At the time, Ivy acted spoiled and selfish, and she became contentious. Papa began to have second thoughts, but he felt bound to live up to his promise. Ivy hated the mountain farm from the very beginning, and she secretly met Sam Whitley at a church in Boone and ran away with him.

That didn't work out so well either, because Ivy and Sam began to quarrel. He left her stranded in South Carolina, just below Charlotte. Papa and Mama had fallen in love by this time, and they rescued Ivy, who was by then in a "family way."

Papa arranged for Ivy to marry Lawrence Nance, who had another plantation in Anson and had always had feelings for her. Ivy fell in love with Lawrence and he claimed Patrick as his own. Mama and Papa were then able to marry, and they lived happily ever after. Well, not really. They lost twin babies before Rachel was born, and the war was awfully hard on them both.

Rachel looked at her parents again. She did intend to find someone who would love her as much as Papa loved Mama, and he would have to be someone she could love as much as Mama loved Papa. If she couldn't find that, she'd prefer to be on her own. She had that independent spirit of the mountain people, and she would be fine. She sighed. She'd much prefer to have a husband, however. She'd just do as Mama and Papa had always taught her. She'd depend on God to direct her path. Then, she wouldn't go wrong.

Exhaustion hovered around Rachel as they pulled up to the Whitley farm. The trip had been too hurried to get much rest. She wasn't accustomed to this piedmont heat either, and it would only get worse with summer.

No one must have heard them come up, because no one came out to greet them. Perhaps they were eating supper, because the time grew late.

"Are you sure this is the right place?" Rachel asked.

"I think so," Papa said. "We'll just go knock on the door and see."

"Oh, you're here!" Aunt Ivy opened the door and rushed to hug Mama. "Come in, come in." She stepped out of the way for them to enter.

Uncle Sam came up with a huge smile, shook Papa's hand, and gave Mama and Rachel a brief hug. He welcomed them warmly.

"Let me introduce the children," Ivy said. "You remember Patrick of course."

"I remember a wonderful boy of eight," Mama said, "not this handsome man before me."

Rachel looked at Patrick and realized he'd been staring at her. He stood tall and handsome with rich blond hair and sparkling blue eyes. He shook his head slightly, as if he were trying to wake himself up from a trance.

"It's good to see you again Aunt Leah and to finally meet you, Uncle Luke." His eyes turned back to Rachel. "I can't believe this is Rachel. You've certainly done some growing up too. I don't guess you remember me, do you?" His voice sounded almost hopeful.

"I do have some sort of memory, but it's not very clear."

"Well, I don't think Patrick has ever forgotten you, Rachel," Aunt Ivy said. "I thought he would never quit pining for you after we left. He was your champion when we stayed there."

"So Mama tells me." She glanced back at Patrick. He didn't seem at all embarrassed by his mother's words. That surprised her, but then Patrick had turned twenty-four now. Perhaps he'd passed the stage of being easily embarrassed.

"Here's Hope and Sammy," Ivy announced.

Rachel looked at her cousins as the introductions were made. Hope could be called pretty, but she didn't have the beauty her mother possessed. Although Aunt Ivy seemed to have put on a little weight from what Mama had described, she was still a very attractive woman. Hope had darker blonde hair and dull blue eyes. At fourteen, she might continue to develop.

Sammy had the lightest blond hair of any of them, and his blue eyes looked full of mischief. He reminded Rachel of John, except in coloring. Sammy was only eight.

Papa, Uncle Sam, and Patrick went to unload the wagon and take care of the team. Mama and Aunt Ivy went to the kitchen while Rachel and Hope sat in the parlor.

"I'm excited you've come to visit," Hope said. "It'll be fun to introduce you around. I hope you're planning to attend school with me."

"I've thought about it. Are there other sixteen-year-olds there?"

Hope nodded. "The oldest girl is fifteen, but some of the boys are sixteen. Many of them aren't attending now due to planting, but maybe they'll get most of it done this week, when we're out for spring break. It's usually the week after Easter."

"When will school be over?"

"There's only another month, but you could go and see if you'd like to attend next year. Besides, it'll be a good way for you to meet some other young people." Hope's expression pleaded.

"I doubt if I'll want to go next year, but I might go after Mama and Papa leave to go home. I want to spend time with them, while they're here."

Everyone came back inside and they sat down to supper. Sam said the blessing and thanked God for the family now with them. Rachel ate enough, because she had gotten hungry, but the food didn't taste as good as Mama's did.

"I used to have a colored woman who came in to help me through the week, and she cooked dinner and supper," Ivy said. "But she became sick, and I haven't been able to find anyone else who suits."

"Maybe I can help you some," Rachel offered. "Mama began teaching me to cook years ago."

"Why, thank you, Rachel. Leah is the best cook I know. How she managed to have edible food with all the shortages we endured during the war is beyond me."

Rachel looked around the table. Papa had a frown on his face, which was something he rarely did. Mention of the war always brought up bad memories for him. He looked at Mama, and she smiled at him. That smile seemed to carry a lot of love and understanding. He smiled back.

She looked away to find Patrick watching her again, but he didn't make her as nervous as someone else would have. He didn't try to hide the fact, for one thing, and maybe she subconsciously remembered more of him than she'd thought. He almost had a look that said he felt proud of her, although Rachel couldn't understand why.

Patrick turned to his sister. "Maybe Rachel can teach you how to cook."

"I'll pass," Hope said. "Mama tried that already, and I'm not interested."

"Hope, you may need to be able to cook for a family someday," Aunt Ivy said. "It would be easier to learn now."

"I'll just have to marry someone who can afford to hire help then, won't I?" Hope looked defiant.

"From what I could see, you have a nice-looking farm here," Papa said to Sam. Rachel knew he hoped to lead the conversation to more pleasant grounds.

"We've been blessed. We have enough fields I have to hire help during the harvest, but I wouldn't be able to farm as extensively if it wasn't for Patrick. He has worked alongside me from the very beginning. Of course, Sammy is beginning to help some too. He has enough energy, that's for sure."

"You can thank my time in the mountains for that," Patrick said. He looked at Rachel and smiled. "I knew nothing of working on a farm until Hawk and Moses got me interested. I loved helping them."

"Speaking of Moses," Aunt Ivy said. "Have you heard from him and Patsy? How are they doing?"

"They write about once or twice a year," Mama answered. "Things seem to be going well for them. You remember Luke and I went back to the plantation with them when they moved. It was sad to see how it was left—just a scorched shell. The house had been burned."

"It was good of you to give them the land," Uncle Sam said.

"He and Patsy sure helped us out," Mama said. "Patsy worked with me from the time we first went to the mountains, and we would have never made it after Hawk died if it hadn't been for Moses."

"They were slaves, weren't they?" Hope asked.

Mama shook her head. "They were our friends."

Papa said, "We helped them sell the back side of the plantation to get enough money to build them a house and make their first planting."

Aunt Ivy looked over at Patrick. "We kept Fair Oaks in case Patrick or one of the children ever needed it. Sometimes I wonder if it's worth all the taxes we've paid on it."

"Land will always be worth something." Sam smiled tenderly at his wife.

"They're not making any more of it, are they, Papa?" Hope had a haughty tone.

Rachel looked over at her parents. They would stay here with her for two weeks. She was glad. She needed their presence until she adjusted better, and it would still be hard to see them go.

Uncle Sam stood up. "Come into the parlor and join us for our family devotion."

CHAPTER TWO

# The Whitley Farm

RACHEL AWOKE THE NEXT MORNING to bright sunshine spilling through the window. It took a moment to realize where she was. When she remembered, it felt strange to be in someone else's room. Even the morning noises sounded different here. On top of the odd feeling of being somewhat misplaced, Patrick also caused confused thoughts. Somehow, she felt drawn to Patrick and not to Hope, who lay next to her, still asleep.

When she and Hope had talked the night before, before falling asleep, Rachel realized how different their values were. Hope wanted to talk about fashion, socializing, boys, and impressing others. Rachel wanted to socialize more and find the right man, but she didn't put those things first.

She didn't know what drew her to Patrick. Maybe it was the way he looked into her eyes with such honesty. Perhaps it was the way he seemed to accept and appreciate her. Whatever the reason, their connection came as an unexpected surprise.

Rachel had washed up last night to get rid of the travel grime, so she eased out of bed and quietly put on her clothes. She tiptoed out into the hall and headed for the stairs.

The house had four bedrooms upstairs. Patrick and Sammy were sharing one now, so Mama and Papa could have Patrick's room. It was located directly across the hall from Hope's, where

Rachel would also be. The door stood open, and the bed had been made. She found her mother in the kitchen cooking breakfast, and Rachel fell into helping.

"The men went outside to milk and do chores," Mama said, "and Ivy is getting dressed. Everyone should be ready for breakfast soon."

"Don't you just love the stove?" Aunt Ivy came in. "It's so much easier to regulate the temperature and cooks so much better than a fireplace. Where did you put yours?"

"We sealed up the kitchen fireplace and set it where the fireplace was, using the same chimney," Mama said. "I hated to lose that fireplace, but I do like cooking on the stove better."

"We still have the fireplace in the sitting room," Rachel added.

Aunt Ivy set the table while Rachel and Mama finished cooking. Mama dished up the eggs and grits, and Aunt Ivy added the bacon and put the plates on the table. Rachel had just taken the biscuits from the oven when the men came in.

Patrick inhaled a deep breath. "It smells awfully good in here."

"Come and sit down," Aunt Ivy said. "Leah and Rachel did the cooking, so we're in for a treat."

"Hope isn't going to join us?" Rachel asked.

"We've found she's grumpy if we don't let her sleep," Aunt Ivy said. "I'll fix her a plate and set it on the warming shelf."

Uncle Sam said grace and they began to eat. Conversation ceased as everyone enjoyed their food.

"These biscuits are wonderful," Patrick said. "To whom do I owe the thanks?"

"Rachel made those," Mama said. "I taught her how, but hers always seems lighter and fluffier than mine—more like Granny Em's, if you remember."

"I think you've just predetermined yours aren't good," Papa said. "You've always complained about them, but I've never seen a thing wrong with your biscuits."

"You've always thought anything Leah did was perfect." Aunt Ivy laughed. "And I see things haven't changed one bit. But I have to agree with you on the biscuits. Leah's have always been better than mine."

Ivy set out some strawberry jam, and everyone had at least one buttered biscuit with jam. Sam and Patrick had several. Aunt Ivy put the last biscuit on a plate for Hope, or it would have been eaten too.

"That was delicious, ladies," Patrick said, but he looked straight at Rachel. "The biscuits were heavenly. The only suggestion I would have is make a few more of them next time."

"Careful, son," Aunt Ivy said. "You don't want to get fat."

Uncle Sam laughed. "The way Patrick works, there's little danger of that."

He did look fit. He stood almost a head higher than Leah and had a healthy glow about him. He must surely be courting someone. In fact, Rachel wondered why he wasn't already married, because he was as handsome as anyone Rachel had ever seen. He also conducted himself well and acted the gentleman.

"Did you gather the eggs this morning?" Aunt Ivy looked at the Moretzes to explain. "If the rooster's around he likes to attack Hope or me."

"No, we thought it was time to eat." Patrick grinned.

"I'll get them," Rachel volunteered.

"I'll go with you and show you some of the farm, then," Patrick said.

Rachel took the basket Aunt Ivy handed her, then turned for the door. She stopped when Patrick began to say something.

"I need to slop the hogs. Do you mind if I take the bucket with us?"

"Not at all. Remember, I've grown up on a farm. You don't need to be concerned about offending me with something like that."

"Not like Blanche," she heard Aunt Ivy say as they went outside.

"Who is Blanche? Is she the girl you're courting?"

"No. There could hardly be someone less suited to me than Blanche Furr. She's attractive enough, I guess. At least others seem to think so, although she appears rather washed out to me. The problem is, she's conceited, selfish, and seems to think she's better than everyone else. She tries to put on airs too. I pity the man who ends up married to her. And, to further answer your question, I'm not courting anyone." He said it softly and smiled at her with laughter in his eyes.

Rachel wanted to ask him why not, but she didn't want to be so forward and possibly offend. He must have noticed a questioning look, however.

"I've yet to meet a woman I wanted to court for long. I've associated with several at church events and even some when I was still in school, but I've never found one I thought would make me a good wife."

"I think it's wise to take your time and choose wisely. I plan to do the same. Just before we came, I told Mama I wanted to find a love as great as she and Papa have. Otherwise, I'd just as soon stay single."

A strange look came over Patrick's face.

Rachel wondered if she had gotten too personal. Well, she could change that. "Your fields look good," she said, changing the subject. The land spread out much flatter here, and the fields looked as if someone had rolled them out with a giant rolling pin. "What all have you planted?"

"You can see the beginnings of our large garden from here and also the start of the corn and cotton. Besides that, we have a field of sugar cane, another of corn, and two fields of hay. We have about forty-five head of beef cattle pastured, besides our milk cows."

"I'm impressed. It's going to take me a while to get use to the large stretches of land and no mountains."

"We didn't always have this much planted. We started much smaller, but we've gradually expanded. The improvements to the farm machinery have also helped. When Sammy gets old enough to do more, maybe we can even add to this." He looked at her as if he were searching for something. "I hope you'll like it here."

"Do you like the mountains or here better?" she asked to avoid replying. It was too soon for her to tell how she would feel about this area.

"I like them both. I think I'd be happy living almost any place, as long as I could farm."

"I can agree with you there. I'll always be a country girl at heart. I don't think I'd ever be as happy in a big city. I enjoy visiting Grandfather in Salisbury, but I'm always happy to get back to the farm. How far is it from here into town? I didn't notice when we came in yesterday."

"The big town of Big Lick?" He laughed. "We're only about three miles out. Big Lick may not be a big town, but it's actually the second biggest in Stanly County. Only Albemarle, the county seat, is larger, although I guess Norwood is running a close third."

Patrick slopped the hogs as they talked. Rachel looked in the pigpen. There were two huge hogs and eight pigs, which must have been born recently.

They moved to the chicken coop. The door had already been opened, and the chickens milled about. As soon as the rooster saw Rachel he flapped his wings and made a beeline toward her. Patrick moved in front of her and gently pushed her behind him to shield her from the attack.

"You just try to flog me and see what happens," he told the bird.

The rooster drew up short, stopped, and looked around. Seeing his prey had disappeared, he turned and went back toward the hens.

"Let's get in the chicken coop before he sees you again," Patrick told her. He placed his hand lightly on her back to direct her. He still stood between Rachel and the rooster in case the fowl returned. "He only attacks those in skirts."

"Perhaps I should wear pants, then." Rachel said it before she thought of how scandalous that would be. What would Patrick think of her?

"I'd like to see that." Patrick laughed again.

She could tell he knew she was teasing, and she relaxed.

"We have one hen setting in the last box," he said.

"How many eggs do you usually gather?"

"Usually a little over a dozen a day. If we get too many on hand, we sell some to one of the stores in town. With five people, we can use most of them, though."

"I understand. We have six in just our family, and we often get together with the Carters too."

"Did your brothers not want to come? Sammy had hoped they would."

"Mark would have been fine, but John and Matt don't travel as well. They get bored with having to sit in the wagon. Since my parents plan to leave me for several months, they wanted this to be our time together."

"So you've definitely decided to stay? For how long?"

"Well, my parents said I could still decide to return with them if I want. I think they're dreading being apart from me, but I think this is a good opportunity. I've been rather secluded most of my life, so it would probably be good for me to be in a place where there's more people my age. I'm guessing I'll return home sometime next spring."

"Then you'll miss the harsh mountain winter and leave here before another hot, humid summer. I'm glad you want to stay."

"I'm thankful for your family having me, and I hope you and I can be friends." Rachel stopped. Sometimes she had a tendency to say too much.

Patrick didn't seem to mind, though. "Oh, I think we've always been friends, ever since you were born, and I'm sure that will continue. I find you very easy to talk with, and that's refreshing."

"Really?"

"Yes, you are open and honest. Most of the females I've encountered are full of social rules, subterfuge, and silly games. They use confidences against you and would betray a friend without a thought if there's something in it for them."

"Are you warning me to beware?" She gave him a smile that she hoped let him know she just teased.

"That might be wise, but you seem very rational and sensible. I'm confident you'll do just fine. As pretty as you are, though, you may have to deal with some of their jealousy, especially from Blanche. She's never had any real competition before."

Rachel looked at him, and he didn't seem to be teasing. She wasn't sure what to say. She'd never thought of herself as pretty. Mama and Aunt Ivy were pretty, not her. "When they find out I'm an eighth Cherokee, they won't care about my looks. They'll have enough to use against me."

"I don't think that'll matter much here. No one in this area remembers any accounts of Indian raids. If anyone does bother you, you just let me know."

"Still my protector?" Rachel teased.

"Always and forever." He gave her that melting smile of his.

"Ready to get to work, son?" Uncle Sam asked as he met them. "We're getting a late start this morning, but we've got an extra pair of hands today. Luke says he wants to help us."

"That's great. Maybe we can finish up a little earlier then."

"We'll see."

Hope stood before the sink when Rachel went inside. Hope smiled and nodded, but said nothing.

Rachel picked up the towel to dry dishes while her cousin washed. "Patrick and I slopped the hogs and gathered the eggs this morning."

"I see." Hope looked at the basket of eggs on the table. "I think Patrick has been more excited about your coming than anyone. He's reminisced about the things he remembered when he and Mama lived with you. I think you surprised him when you walked in last night all grown up, though."

"Surely he didn't think I'd still be two years old."

"No, but I don't think he or I was prepared for how mature and attractive you look."

"Thank you, Hope." Rachel didn't know quite what to make of the two compliments she'd been given on her appearance this morning.

Hope shrugged. "I'm not sure I'm going to like being compared with you, but I guess if we stick together, we'll receive a lot of attention. The young men will probably flock around you—a new pretty face and all."

"I'm not sure I'd like that."

"Why not? I would love it, and Blanche certainly does."

"Tell me about Blanche. Patrick doesn't seem very impressed with her."

"I don't know what's wrong with Patrick. Blanche is gorgeous. She has platinum blonde hair, violet eyes, and a luscious figure. Her parents dote on her, and she has the most fashionable dresses. She's been courted by most of the eligible men around, but she eventually tires of them and starts seeing another. She's almost like a queen holding court. Just wait until you see her."

"Was Patrick one of the ones she tired of?"

"No. He's never courted much at all. I've noticed him watching Blanche from a distance, but he appears to be watching a performance more than anything else. Blanche flirts with Patrick every chance she gets, but he pays her little attention. Blanche isn't going to take kindly to you."

"Why do you think that? She's never even met me."

"You are much too pretty. She wants all the attention, and I'm sure you're going to cut into that."

If this was what being around people her own age would be like, Rachel didn't know if she wanted it. It also bothered her that Hope seemed to value popularity and material things so highly. But instead of voicing these concerns she merely asked, "Is Blanche a Christian?"

"I suppose. She goes to church every Sunday, but she definitely doesn't live by the Golden Rule. Her rule is more 'do unto others whatever will give you the most.'"

"How sad."

———

Patrick found himself working too far away from his father and uncle to be able to carry on a conversation with them, so he let his mind drift. He couldn't keep from thinking about Rachel. She had stunned him. He knew she was sixteen, not two, but the beautiful young woman who walked through the front door last night had almost taken his breath away.

Although she'd worn her hair up last night, he saw at breakfast she had straight hair, which was so dark it appeared almost black as it cascaded down her back, yet it had highlights of mahogany, especially when she stood in a light. Her eyes were brown, not as dark as her father's, but a warm chocolate that melted his heart. Her skin was creamy with the lightest touch of a peachy tan. In his eyes, she was perfect.

His emotions were so jumbled he had a hard time sorting them out. He'd expected to feel like her big brother. After all, that's what Mama had always told him he had been to Rachel. But, what he felt now had nothing to do with her being a sister to him.

They were only half cousins, since their mothers were half sisters, and even full cousins married. He knew he'd let his mind run ahead way too far, but he didn't know what to think about these new feelings? What would Rachel think? She'd said she wanted to be friends with him. Well, that would be a good start. What did he want? He didn't know the answer to that, and his train of thought scared him.

Patrick went back over everything she'd said in his presence since yesterday, especially their conversation this morning. He'd never talked with anyone who made him feel so complete and alive. In a way, she touched some inner place deep within him. It made no sense to him, and he would never have thought such a thing possible.

*Lord, You're going to need to help me on this one. I feel lost.*

When they went in for dinner, Patrick had decided to try to be more distant, but with the first smile Rachel gave him, that resolve dissipated. He connected to her in a way he couldn't explain, even to himself.

Papa said grace, and Aunt Leah asked Uncle Luke what he'd done that morning. He gave an amused laugh. "Not as much as I normally would, I forgot how hot it is here, even in the spring. I once vowed never to come to the flatlands in July or August, if I could help it. I don't see how Sam and Patrick stand it."

"Rachel and I understand," Aunt Leah said. "She and I have been in the kitchen with the cookstove going most of the morning."

"I didn't think this tasted like Mama's cooking," Sammy stated, and they all laughed.

"It is good," Patrick agreed. "The kraut is sweetened perfectly, and I like these potatoes for a change."

"This is the best cornbread I've had in a long time, too," Papa added.

"The way you two talk, you'd think I've been starving you," Mama teased. "I thought I would get Leah to cook a good German meal while she is here, and I still have sauerkraut left from last fall."

"Well, I'm no more German than you are Ivy," Aunt Leah said. "Besides, Rachel can cook anything I can, and she doesn't mind cooking."

"You may not be German," Mama said to Aunt Leah, "but you've lived in a predominantly German household for more years than not. Tell me again how you fix these potatoes?"

"They may be more French than German, since they have a white sauce, but I'm not sure. Don't you remember? You just peel, cut up, and boil the potatoes and add some butter. Take some milk and beat in a little flour, salt, and pepper. Add it to the potatoes and bring to a boil until it thickens."

"I love how you never give amounts."

Aunt Leah winked. "I just make it until it looks right. I don't measure."

Mama laughed, then turned to Rachel. "If you're willing, you may be doing a lot of the cooking. Is it true that you enjoy it?"

"If you're this appreciative, I'd love it." Rachel laughed.

Patrick smiled at her. He'd love to know what she was thinking. Was she as confused too? Probably not. She just wanted him to be her friend. Hopefully, he could be a good one.

———————

This time Rachel washed the dishes from dinner, while Hope dried them and put them away. "Is something wrong?" Rachel finally asked.

"Not really. I just feel rather left out."

"How's that?"

"Well, you came here to be my companion, but I feel you and Patrick are getting along better than you and I are."

Rachel looked at her cousin. "I can be friends with both of you."

"I guess."

Patrick did seem easier to talk with and be around than Hope, but Rachel would never tell her so. With Patrick, Rachel could just relax and be herself. With Hope, she felt she needed to be alert and on her guard.

Somehow she knew Patrick would do anything he could to help or protect her. This morning's encounter with the rooster proved that. If she ever needed anything or had any problems, she felt she could turn to Patrick. If she'd had an older brother, she would want him to be just like him. How could she feel this way in only a day? She guessed the relationship they'd had as children must've laid the groundwork. How else would such a thing be possible?

Leah and Rachel fixed pinto beans, cabbage, fried potatoes and onions, and cornbread for supper. All the Whitleys raved about the food again. Surely they would grow accustomed to it soon. Rachel didn't see anything out of the ordinary anyway.

Patrick did the family devotion after supper. Apparently Uncle Sam and he took turns. He read the Bible in a strong sure voice and then they discussed it. Rachel was struck by how deep Patrick's faith seemed to be.

Her faith had always been very important to her too. Papa and Mama had seen to that. Rachel had been taught to put God first at an early age. She still found having a personal relationship with such an awesome God truly amazing. She couldn't fathom how God could love someone like her so completely and even want a personal relationship, but she praised Him that He did.

"Would you like to lead the devotion tomorrow night, Luke?" Uncle Sam asked Papa. "The three of us could take turns while you're here."

"I'd be honored," Papa said.

"Why don't the women get a turn?" Hope asked.

"I do the devotions when Luke is away," Leah told her, "but I don't think who leads it matters to God. What matters is that each one of us worships Him and learns His truths."

"You are welcome to take a turn, if you'd like, Hope," Uncle Sam said. "In fact, I think that would be good."

"Oh, never mind," Hope replied.

"I think it's the man's responsibility to see to the spiritual well-being of his family," Patrick added, "but it should be something shared with his wife."

The others agreed. Hope just shrugged.

After the devotion, Hope went to her room and brought down a dress she was making, so she could sit with the family and finish the handwork on it. Rachel liked the royal blue polished cotton trimmed in white lace.

"That's a very pretty dress," Rachel told her. "Is it for you?"

"Anything Rachel makes is usually for her," Aunt Ivy said. "She does like to sew. Now, if I could only get her to sew some shirts or do some mending."

"At least it's easier and faster than it used to be," Mama said. "Isn't a sewing machine wonderful?"

"I can't even imagine sewing one totally by hand," Hope said. "That would take forever."

"Lots of inventions have made life easier," Mama said. "I appreciate canning in a jar too. Foods keep so much better, and we can preserve so much more."

"Wouldn't Granny Em have loved the newer developments? Do you still miss her?" Aunt Ivy asked.

"I do miss her and Hawk both. They were very special people. And, yes, Granny Em would have loved to can, sew on a sewing machine, and cook on a stove."

"I wish I could have known her," Rachel said. "Mama and Papa have told me so much about her, I almost think I do."

"She sure loved you," Aunt Ivy said. "Hawk, Luke, Leah, and you were everything to her."

"She loved Grandpa too," Papa added, getting in on the conversation.

"I'm sure she did," Aunt Ivy said, "but Leah and I never knew Edgar, since he died before we came. I guess she was like me in that way. She was blessed to love two wonderful men."

Rachel hoped she'd be blessed enough to love only one man. She didn't want to lose the first one. She couldn't imagine what Mama and Papa had gone through when the war separated them for over three years. When Papa was in prison, they weren't able to write each other, and Mama didn't even know what had happened to him. Knowing how deeply they loved each other, Rachel hurt for them.

Did all couples go through such hard times? All the couples she knew seemed to. Maggie and Aaron had it about as easy as anyone she knew, and even they were unsure of each other at the start. Then, Aaron didn't think he could ask Maggie to marry him, because he didn't know how he would support her.

Maybe Rachel would be better off to just go home and live with Mama and Papa on the farm and forget about ever getting married. No. That would be cowardly of her, and Rachel Moretz was not a coward. Besides, life on this earth seemed to always come with sets of problems. There was no escaping it. The secret to rising above them was to let God take your hand. Then, you could overcome anything. She just hoped He had someone special planned for her.

CHAPTER THREE

# Mt. Olive Baptist Church

RACHEL WAS GLAD MAMA AND Papa were still there to go to church with her on Sunday. She didn't know what had come over her. She had yearned to attend a church for years, but now that she had the opportunity, she dreaded it so much she felt as if she were going to her own execution.

Part of the problem had to be Blanche. There'd been so much talk of the woman, Rachel felt reluctant to meet her, and that would no doubt happen today. The young lady seemed to hold way too much power over the whole community.

The church would also be holding a dinner on the grounds after the service, which meant it would probably be crowded. Each family would bring dishes of food and their own plates and eating utensils. This meant they would also stay much longer than usual.

"We usually hold a dinner at church at least three times a year," Aunt Ivy told them. "We don't have them in the winter, because the church building is small, and we hold the meals outside."

Although Rachel remained anxious about meeting everyone, especially Blanche, she decided she'd just go to worship and praise God. She would also enjoy the good food and fellowship. She wouldn't let some stranger spoil the day for her, but despite her best intentions, doubts and uncertainties kept creeping back.

31

Rachel got ready slowly, taking her time. She chose to wear her best dress other than her ball gown. This one was fashioned from emerald silk with ecru lace edging. The long Polonaise jacket had pleated sides and a lace-trimmed, softly-bustled back. The princess-style jacket had a front closure of tiny pearl buttons, the exact shade as the lace and no seam at the waist, which made her waist appear tiny and showed off her curves. The turn-back collar was of contrasting ecru cotton, as were the cuffs. The matching skirt had a deep flounce at the back and formed a small gathered train. The two-piece ensemble gave the impression of a dress.

Papa had insisted that she have some new dresses. Now, Rachel appreciated his foresight.

Rachel let Mama put her hair up this morning. It wound around the top of her head to form the latest style, at least according to the ladies' magazine they'd seen.

When Rachel walked downstairs, she knew she had chosen well. Papa's face was filled with pride, and Patrick's was so full of admiration, she would have turned red if she'd been the type who blushed easily.

"Here's my other lovely lady," Papa said with a big smile. "You look stunning, Daughter."

"I agree," Uncle Sam said. "I'll be the envy of everyone at church with four such beautiful women to drive."

"I hope you'll give me the honor of escorting and introducing you around at the meal today," Patrick said to her.

"I'd like that," Rachel said without thinking. Perhaps she should have allowed Hope to introduce her, but she felt much more comfortable with Patrick. Hope seemed to stir up contention, while Patrick preferred to be a peacemaker.

Aunt Ivy and Hope came down together. Aunt Ivy looked pretty in a rose-pink dress, and Hope wore the royal blue one she had just completed. It looked well made, but Hope didn't seem pleased with Rachel's appearance.

"Where did you get the latest fashion?" Hope asked. "I had mine already cut out before I learned of the new cuts."

"We made ours too," Mama told her, "but Rachel's grandfather sent us some magazines from Salisbury to go by."

"Shall we go then?" Patrick asked as he extended Rachel his elbow to lead her out.

The Whitleys had a large surrey with three bench seats, which would carry them all. Rachel had never seen one quite as nice.

"I got an excellent deal on it," Uncle Sam said, "and I couldn't pass it up. Today, I'm glad we have it, so we can all travel together."

They got to church a little early, but people were already pouring in. They left their food in the surrey and would retrieve it after the service to place on the temporary tables set up outside. They'd also brought two quilts to spread under a shade tree.

Rachel looked around as they went inside. The church had been made of logs. The iron church bell had been placed in one of the big oak trees out front. Rachel didn't see anyone who resembled the description of Blanche Furr.

"Blanche usually tries to be fashionably late and make a grand entrance," Patrick whispered, as if he'd read her mind. "I'll never understand why it would be fashionable to be late."

"I agree with you." Rachel smiled.

Patrick dropped the arm she held and put his hand lightly on her back to direct her down the aisle. The gesture comforted her and somehow eased her apprehension.

Uncle Sam introduced them to the pastor, who came up to greet and welcome them, as did many of the deacons. Some of the women also came up to welcome them. At least many of the people were friendly.

Sam and Papa went back outside to talk with some of the men standing around, but Patrick stayed with Rachel. He allowed Mama and her to go into a bench first, and he followed behind Rachel. This put Mama on the far end, and she stopped short, leaving enough room for Papa to sit on the end. Rachel ended up sitting between Mama and Patrick. Hope came next, followed by Aunt Ivy. That didn't leave much room at the aisle end for Uncle Sam and Sammy.

"Don't worry," Patrick said. "Mama usually allows Sammy to sit with one of his friends."

Still, when the men came in, Patrick had to scoot closer to Rachel to make room for his father, and she found herself sitting so close to Patrick they touched. Instead of making her uncomfortable, however, it made her feel secure to be wedged in between him and Mama.

The bell began ringing and grew loudly insistent. It sounded as if it might be heard for miles.

A young lady who could only be Blanche, along with a distinguished-looking couple, came in after everyone else had taken their seats. She walked slowly down the aisle, smiling and nodding at those who looked her way. She then sat on a bench near the front on the opposite side, but Rachel had a good view of her.

Rachel didn't know why Patrick had called her "washed out" looking. She was the most beautiful woman Rachel had ever seen. Aunt Ivy might have been prettier when she was younger, and Mama might have rivaled her, but no one really compared now.

She had beautiful, shiny blonde hair the color of corn silk, so pale, it barely looked yellow. Her light skin looked almost like a china doll's.

She looked back and caught Rachel's eyes. Her amethyst eyes shot daggers. The look was meant to wound and put any competitor in her place, but Rachel held her gaze. Blanche was the first to look away.

Patrick reached over and patted her hand. "Good for you," he whispered.

She hadn't realized he'd been watching, but she should have known. He seemed to always know what was going on with her.

The preacher delivered a good sermon, and the service passed too quickly. Rachel dreaded the encounter with Blanche she knew would come.

Sure enough, at the end of the benediction, Blanche immediately made her way toward Rachel. She stopped in front of her and looked her carefully from head to toe, as if searching for some flaw.

"Blanche, I'd like for you to meet Rachel Moretz from Watauga County," Patrick said. "Her mother is my mother's half sister, and she'll be staying with us for a few months. Rachel, this is Blanche Furr, the belle of Stanly County."

Blanche seemed to gloat at Patrick's last statement. "I don't think I've ever met someone from the mountains before. I hope you don't feel too out of place here, Miss Moretz."

"Ah, we finally get to meet, Miss Furr. I've heard so much about you over the last few days." Rachel had already formed her reply as a way to keep from lying. She couldn't truthfully say she was glad to meet Blanche, who apparently had no such qualms.

"Please call me Blanche, and I'll call you Rachel. It's so good to meet you," she said with a sweetness that never reached her glaring eyes. "I'll be so glad to have a friend with some fashion sense. Wherever did you find that lovely dress? Why, my *Godey's Lady's Book* just arrived this week with that design."

"My mother is quite a talented seamstress, and my grandparents in Salisbury help us keep up with the latest New York fashions." Rachel sensed Blanche would pounce on and try to shred anyone in whom she perceived weakness. "Of course, we still are behind those in Paris." Rachel sighed, as if Paris fashions mattered greatly to her.

"Come with me, dear," Blanche demanded. "You just have to tell me what you know of Paris fashion."

"I'm sorry, Blanche," Patrick interjected. "I promised to show Rachel around, and in turn, she promised to eat dinner with me."

"Well, another time," Blanche fumed and flounced off.

"You did very well," Patrick whispered. From talking with Blanche, they were the last ones left inside. "I'm so proud of you, but I didn't know you were so knowledgeable about the latest fashion."

"I'm not and don't care to be, but I knew I needed to impress Blanche or she'd feed me to the lions."

Patrick laughed heartily. "Oh Rachel, you're a treasure. I think Blanche may have finally met her match."

"I hope you're not insinuating I'm just like her." Rachel smiled. She couldn't help but be pleased by his reaction.

"Certainly not in malicious character, but you may have just as much bravado and determination. I think you must have inherited those from Granny Em, and most likely with a lot of your mama's intelligence thrown in."

She thought a minute. "Thank you, Patrick. From what I've been told of Granny, that's a tremendous compliment."

"Indeed, it is."

Although Rachel and Patrick were near the end of the line for the food, the array of food still made the choices hard. She noticed he chose all the foods she and Mama had prepared, as well as a few others. They filled their plates and went to join Aunt Ivy, Mama, Hope, and Sammy on their quilts. Several people stopped them on the way, and Patrick made the introductions. Most asked Patrick and Rachel to join them, but they declined.

Papa and Uncle Sam came through the line late too. They had stood around to talk with some of the men first. Since four were sitting on the first quilt, Papa and Uncle Sam joined Patrick and Rachel on the second one, and it was a good thing. Men kept coming by wanting to be introduced, but since each side of the quilt was taken, it was okay not to ask anyone else to sit with them.

"Seems you are very popular today, Rachel," Uncle Sam said. "I know these young men aren't coming around to see us men. I'm not surprised, though, as pretty as you are."

Rachel felt heat rush to her face, and she hoped the blush would go unnoticed with her tanner coloring. She'd met so many people that she hadn't really been assessing the young men for a possible suitor. Well, she would see them again, and she could do a better job of that once things settled down a bit.

"I'll expect you to keep an eye on her for me," Papa said before she could think of a reply.

"I'll do that," Uncle Sam said, "and I think we can also count on Patrick to watch out for her. He's done a good job of that today, I think."

"Thank you both," Papa said. "I can leave easier knowing the two of you are looking after her, and I appreciate the way you've stayed by her side today, Patrick. I know it's made Rachel more comfortable."

"I assure you it's been my pleasure, sir," Patrick responded, and he sounded sincere.

Patrick and Rachel were lingering over dessert when Papa and Uncle Sam went to speak to the pastor.

Rachel looked at Patrick. "I do appreciate you staying with me today. It's made things much more pleasant."

"I'm glad you feel that way," he told her. "I can't think of another person I'd rather be with. Somehow, I think we have a special bond, and I can't really explain it. Hawk might have said our spirits share a special connection. Do you feel it too?" He was looking at her intently.

"Yes, I think I do. I feel very close to you. If I'd had a big brother, I'd have wanted him to be just like you."

A pained look flashed across his face, but it left so quickly Rachel thought she must have been mistaken. He looked away and stared at nothing, as if pondering profound problems. She wanted to bring him back and make him smile again.

"You know, I feel I can talk to you about anything and share my deepest thoughts."

Sure enough, it worked. He looked at her and smiled. "That's great, and I feel the same way. You're the easiest person to talk with and to be around I've ever met."

Rachel looked across the way and saw Blanche surrounded by several young men. She looked as if she were holding court. "Blanche has a lot of attention, too, I see."

Patrick turned to observe Blanche. "She just gathers hers around her, instead of sending them away, as you did. Don't think she hasn't noticed yours, though. I'm sure she's kept count of every man who's spoken with you."

"Really? That seems so foolish to me."

"It is. I hope you don't get caught up in her games."

"Is that what you think I've done today?" Perhaps Patrick didn't regard Rachel as highly as she'd thought.

"No, I think you were doing a good job of surviving Blanche Furr today. Don't think you've seen the last of her, though. She's a spider who loves to catch unsuspecting prey in her web."

"Well, I won't challenge her for any of her admirers. She can keep them all."

Patrick nodded in agreement. "That will help, but you may not be able to avoid it. Some of those men will jump ship when they see you. I think you're prettier than she is, and you're a whole lot nicer."

"How does she keep her entourage if she treats them poorly?"

"Oh, she can be sweet and flirtatious. She bestows just enough favors to keep them dangling along hoping for more. She's a challenge, and most men love a challenge. They're also in competition to win her favors. They just haven't stopped to realize what's happening."

Rachel raised her eyebrows. Patrick seemed to know an awfully lot about the woman. "But you're not trying to win her favors?"

"No, not me. I'm not the type to lick my wounds and go back for more. I prefer relationships that are fulfilling, meaningful, and real. I want to find a woman who is kind and cares, not one who finds joy in inflicting pain."

Rachel glanced back over at Blanche. "Does she really do that?"

"I think she does. She seems to like the power it gives her."

"That's scary."

Patrick gave Rachel a penetrating gaze. "Yes, it is, but you don't have to be afraid of Blanche. You have a strength in you that she can't come close to matching."

"What makes you say that? Exactly what do you mean?"

"If I'm not mistaken, you have a strong Christian faith. With the Lord on your side what can Blanche Furr do?"

Rachel smiled. "You're so right."

"Well, what did you think of Blanche?" Hope asked Rachel as they washed the dishes that evening.

"I thought she was beautiful." Rachel hedged, not wanting to disparage Blanche.

"She is, isn't she? I wish I could be one of her friends, but she considers me too young." Hope sighed. "I'll be turning fifteen in May. Maybe that will help."

"I've heard she doesn't treat her friends well, so I wouldn't worry about it if I were you."

Hope almost huffed. "I'm sure you heard that from Patrick. I can't understand what he has against her. She's never done anything to him, as far as I know. I don't really think it was fair of Patrick to hog you all to himself today, either. I didn't see him leave your side for anything."

"He wanted to help me adjust to all the new people. He was being the big brother to me, just like he is for you."

"If you say so, but I still don't understand. I'd feel like dying if he stuck by my side at a church function. No little sister wants her older brother around like that."

Rachel hadn't considered that, but what Hope said made sense. However, if Patrick wasn't acting the big brother to her, then what? Maybe he was just being a good friend. That had to be it.

The days passed much too quickly. Before Rachel knew it, it was almost time for her parents to leave. They planned to head back on Friday. They planned to go by Grandfather's in Salisbury for a few days this time.

Rachel wanted to stay here, but she hated to see her parents go. They must have felt much the same, because a few days before they were to depart, they took her to Big Lick—just the three of them.

It surprised Rachel to find three stores in the small town. Besides the Cagle store, which also housed the post office, there was the Big Lick Store and the Millard Sasser Store. The town also had a livery stable and various other shops and stores, besides all the houses.

They stopped and browsed in each store. Mama found a few things she wanted, but Rachel didn't see anything she needed right now.

"I'll leave you some spending money," Papa said. "You'll probably want some for presents, and you may need some things for yourself too."

After going to the stores, they climbed back into the wagon, and Papa turned left at the well. The community well in the center of the main intersection fascinated Rachel. Wagons and horses had to maneuver around the well, but the people in town had a place to get water. The Whitley's had their own well at the farm, complete with a hand pump.

"I believe Sam said the school is up here on the right," Papa said.

Sure enough, Rachel spotted Big Lick School, a two-story white clapboard building set back off the road behind Hartsell's Casket and Woodwork Shop.

"Have you decided to attend school with Hope?" Mama asked.

"She wants me to, but I'm still undecided. Patrick doubts I'll be able to learn much I don't already know. What do you think?"

"You could always start and see what it's like," Mama said. "If it isn't what you need, you wouldn't have to continue."

"That sounds like a good idea," Rachel agreed.

"I've noticed you and Patrick get along very well," Papa said, "but what about you and Hope?"

"Hope and I get along fine, but she hasn't been as easy to talk with as Patrick."

"You do like Patrick a lot, don't you?" Mama asked.

"Yes, I do. At first, I thought he was like the big brother I never had. Maybe that came from what you'd told me about when I was little, and he and Ivy stayed with us. Now, I just think he's a very good friend. I'm hoping Hope and I can become best friends, too, but that may take longer. Our relationship is still a bit tentative right now."

Mama and Papa looked across at each other. What did that look mean? What were they thinking?

"We're going to miss you terribly," Mama said, voice quivering.

"I'm going to miss you too. Do you realize we've never been apart for more than a day?"

Papa also looked serious. "You don't have to stay. You can return with us."

"I know I could, but something tells me I need to stay. I need to be able to get out and meet other people and learn to get along in the world. I've always been secluded on our beautiful mountain farm. Besides, I'm not leaving forever. I'll be home in a few months."

"I'm not sure about that," Papa said. "None of us know what the future might hold. As pretty and sweet as you are, you may end up on the red clay of Stanly County, instead of on our dark mountain soil."

"Oh Papa! No matter what happens, I'll always be your daughter, and I'll always love you and Mama."

"Would you like to go on a picnic before we leave?" Papa asked as they headed back to the farm.

"Oh yes, that sounds like a good way to spend one of your last days here," Rachel said.

"Would you like to invite Hope?" Mama asked.

"Not really. I'm sure Hope and I will get more comfortable around each other, but right now, I feel I have to be careful with what I say to keep from offending her, and I find it tiring. She'd also have to take a day off from school. I'd much rather invite Patrick, but it would be fine with me if it was just the three of us again."

"I'll see where Sam suggests for us to go, then," Papa said.

"Sam suggested a trip to Morrow Mountain," Papa later told Rachel. "It's on the other side of the county, so it will take all day. We can leave right after breakfast, take our dinner, and be back for a late supper. I understand there's quite a view from up there. We'll probably need to ride horses, however. A wagon may be too slow to make the trip easily in one day, especially if we spend some time on the mountain."

"There's a mountain near here?" Rachel asked in amazement.

Papa laughed. "Well, from what Sam tells me, we may not consider it much of a mountain, not after living in the Appalachians, but I believe it's part of the Uwharrie range. They're not as steep as the western mountains, because they're older and have been worn down over time."

"You're amazing, Luke," Mama said. "I believe I could live with you a million years and still be learning from your wealth of information."

"I wish I could be with you for a million years," Papa told her with a mischievous gleam in his eyes.

"We'll have that and more in eternity," Mama told him.

"Do you know how to get to Morrow Mountain, Papa?" Rachel asked.

"I have a good idea, but Sam suggested Patrick go with us. It seems most of the property belongs to Dr. Francis Kron. Sam and Patrick have met him, and they're sure he won't mind our visiting. We'll go by and ask him first."

# CHAPTER FOUR

# Good-Byes and Hellos

RACHEL GOT UP EARLY, PACKED the picnic dinner to put in their saddle bags, and had breakfast almost ready when her parents came downstairs. Patrick had already gone to the barn to milk. Rachel left Mama to put breakfast on the table and went out to gather the eggs. She picked up Sammy's baseball bat she saw standing beside the door on the porch and carried it with her.

She opened the door to the chicken coop and let them out, so she could get in easier to gather the eggs. The rooster started out with the others but noticed her and turned. He flapped his wings and started to charge. Rachel quickly set her basket down and grasped the bat with both hands. Just as the rooster got near, she hauled back and gave his head a good whack with the bat. The rooster stepped away, shook his head a couple of times, and staggered off in the other direction.

She heard laughter and turned. Patrick had set the milk buckets down and was coming toward her. "Good for you, Rachel. I doubt if he'll mess with you again."

Rachel smiled, picked up the basket, and gathered the eggs while Patrick waited. They walked back to the house together. The rooster still kept his distance.

"I can't believe you're wearing a skirt like that," Aunt Ivy told Mama. "It doesn't seem decent to me to ride astride like a man."

"It's just as decent for a woman as for a man, if you think about it," Mama said. "It is also safer and a lot more comfortable. Look, when I button this front panel, you can hardly tell it's split. This loose panel in the back is just attached at the waist, and it covers the split in the back. It looks like a normal skirt."

"Until you get on a horse," Aunt Ivy said. "You might get by with it in the mountains, but people here will think it's scandalous."

"She designed and made it herself," Papa said. "I think it's ingenious. She was always so tired and worn out when she rode sidesaddle."

Aunt Ivy shrugged. "Well, if you approve, Luke, I guess I have no right to insist she do otherwise, but you all know how I feel."

Rachel wore a skirt just like her mother's, except they'd made hers in a dark brown instead of the dark forest green. They had split the skirt in the back and front and sewn two inserts on the inside of each to form a type of leg. Another panel across the front could be unbuttoned when riding. A second row of buttons balanced the front, but they wouldn't unbutton.

"What do you think of our skirts, Patrick?" Rachel asked. For some reason, what he thought mattered to her.

He'd been watching quietly, but spoke up to answer Rachel's question. "I don't see anything wrong with them. They're long and cover your limbs much better than when riding sidesaddle with a regular skirt. Besides riding a sidesaddle has always seemed awkward to me. I know I wouldn't want to try it."

"I give up." Aunt Ivy threw up her hands and laughed. "Have a good time."

Papa helped Mama into the saddle, and Patrick helped Rachel. He lifted her carefully but with little effort.

"Dr. Kron is an interesting man," Patrick told them as they traveled. "He was born in Prussia, married in France, and immigrated to America in 1823. He was the first doctor in this area, but he's also a noted horticulturist and is interested in education. He has his home, doctor's office, infirmary, and a greenhouse on the mountain. I'd guess he's in his late seventies now."

"Does he have children?" Mama asked.

"I think he has two daughters who never married. I believe they went to school in Raleigh, but that's all I know about them. I've never met them."

They didn't talk much more, but rode at a good pace. Rachel watched the scenery as they traveled east. Farmland and wooded areas comprised most of the landscape. When they got to Albemarle, they took a break and gave the horses some water from the creek.

"Hasn't this town grown, since we came through it with Ivy and Patsy all those years ago?" Mama asked Papa as she looked over Albemarle.

"It sure has," Papa agreed. "I wouldn't have recognized it as the same place."

"When was that?" Patrick asked.

"In 1854," Papa told him. "Ivy and I were engaged, and she'd agreed to run away with me. Leah had agreed to go with us to chaperone."

"Yes, I remember the story," Patrick said. "Mama ran away with Papa when you got to the mountains. You must have been pretty worried."

"We were. It took months to find her, and she was in bad shape when we did."

"Papa told me how he had been making bad choices and wrong decisions, and he abandoned her, but everything turned out okay in the end, didn't it?"

"Indeed it did. We finally got the right couples together, and the four of us have been very happy."

"I still remember Lawrence," Patrick said. "He was a good man."

"Yes, he was," Papa agreed. "Lawrence had always been my best friend, and to think, he died fighting against the side I was fighting on. The war never made much sense to me."

"I've often wondered how Mama could have loved Lawrence so much, and I know she did, and then love Papa just as much."

"I can't really help you with that one, Patrick," Papa said. "I've only really romantically loved one woman, and she's all I'll ever love. I came to realize what I felt for Ivy was only infatuation. I loved the person I thought she was, but that wasn't who she really was at that time."

Patrick nodded. "Mama told us how selfish and snobbish she was before she accepted Christ into her life. She credits Aunt Leah with leading her to the Lord."

"I didn't really do anything," Mama said. "I just answered her questions and helped her pray the prayer of salvation."

"According to Mama, how you lived your life served as the greatest testimony to her."

Papa seemed to notice Mama felt uncomfortable with Patrick's compliment, as Rachel had. He helped change the subject. "You know Granny had two husbands, like Ivy. Granny said that loving one didn't mean you couldn't love another. She said a good love only increases your ability to love again. According to her, you didn't have to give up your first love, but the heart just grew to accommodate the second one."

"Well, she should know," Patrick said. "I remember Hawk and Granny Em together. They had something special. I'll never forget Hawk, either."

"Neither will I," Mama said. "He and I had some sort of special connection that was uncanny. It scared me at first, but I grew to appreciate it. I missed him and Granny Em so much when they died. I still do."

Patrick looked at Rachel when Mama started talking about a special connection. Did she and Patrick have one too? She felt like she had known and cared for him all her life. But, although she had known him the first two years of her life, he had become a stranger since he'd moved to Stanly County. He didn't feel like a stranger, though.

"Well, we better get back in the saddle," Patrick said.

Rachel noticed some people stared at them, but no one said anything. She knew two women riding astride must appear odd.

Several miles out of Albemarle, they began to climb. They slowed and let the horses take the incline at their own pace. After a while they came to Dr. Kron's house.

Rachel and Mama stayed mounted, while Patrick and Papa went to the door. Dr. Kron gave them permission to ride around the mountain and invited them in for a visit, but they declined.

"Well, at least go around the back and give the horses a drink," the doctor said. "You can fill up your canteens too."

They did but soon continued on. Rachel looked up and the sun appeared to be directly overhead. It would soon be time to eat.

The views were beautiful as they rode. The mountain wasn't as high or as rugged as the ones in Watauga County, but it was heavily wooded with outcroppings of rock, and it gave a panoramic view of the valley below.

They stopped at a small green meadow to have their picnic. A deer quickly loped back into the forest as they dismounted.

They spread their quilt and got the food from the saddle bags. Everyone had grown so hungry, Papa asked the blessing, and they ate in silence for a while.

"It feels cooler up here," Mama observed. "The weather has certainly cooperated today, though. It's so sunny and bright."

"These fried apple pies are delicious," Patrick said. "To whom should I say my thanks?"

"Rachel made everything," Mama told him.

"You're a very good cook, Rachel," Patrick said. "I appreciate your talent."

"Thank you." Rachel bowed her head at the direct praise. It made her even more uncomfortable in the company of her parents.

"Does today's trip make you homesick for the mountains?" Patrick's gaze never left her while he waited for her answer.

"No, I love the mountains, but I'm ready for some new experiences." Did Patrick let out a sigh of relief, or was that just Rachel's imagination?

"Well, I'm ready to get back," Papa said, "but we dread leaving Rachel. It's going to be hard."

"I can imagine, but you know we'll take good care of her." Patrick's expression almost gave the words added meaning.

"We do," Mama said, "but she and I have never been separated. This is going to take some getting used to."

"For me too," Rachel added. She had no doubt she would miss her parents fiercely.

"Shall we pack up and go exploring?" Patrick asked.

The time on the mountain passed way too quickly for Rachel. The views were lovely, and she liked being there with her parents and Patrick. It almost felt as if they'd become sequestered in their own Eden, away from the rest of the world. Too soon, however, they started back down Morrow Mountain to be sure they'd return before dark.

Patrick and Rachel stopped only once to quickly water the horses on the way back. They returned just as the sun had begun to dip below the horizon and a faint image of the moon hung to the side, as if waiting its turn.

"Well, what did you think?" Uncle Sam asked as he came out to help with the horses.

They all told him what a great day they'd had. Patrick went to help Uncle Sam with the horses, and the Moretzes went inside to wash up for supper.

Papa did the devotion, and tears formed in Rachel's eyes just listening to him. He and Mama would leave after breakfast in the morning.

She looked up to see Patrick watching her with a look of understanding in his eyes. She gave him a weak smile. He smiled back and gave a slight nod of encouragement.

Papa gave her some spending money to hide among her things. She thought it was too much, and she promised herself to take as much back home with her as she could next year.

Rachel thought she would have a hard time sleeping. She expected her parents' early departure would keep her up, but she'd been wrong. The day had been enjoyable but tiring, and she quickly fell asleep. When she awoke the next morning, she heard Mama in the kitchen making breakfast. She hurried to join her.

Rachel let Hope wash the dishes by herself this time. She wanted to spend as much time with Mama and Papa as she could before they left, but that time came way too quickly. Soon, they stood beside the packed wagon hating to move. Her parents had already said their good-byes and thank-yous to the others.

"It's how you act when you're on your own that shows your real character," Papa said. "I know you'll conduct yourself well."

Rachel hugged Papa first and felt the tears run down her face. He held her tightly for a long time.

"I love you, baby," he said, and when they pulled apart, Rachel could tell he had to work hard to hold back his tears.

Mama didn't try to hold hers back. She and Rachel held each other and sobbed until they wet each others' shoulder. "You write us often, now, you hear," Mama told her. "I love you so much, Rachel, and I'll miss you until you come home."

Rachel just nodded. She didn't think she could find her voice. Papa helped Mama onto the wagon seat. Mama reached down and took one of Rachel's hands, and Papa took the other. They squeezed at almost the same time. Papa got into the wagon, and they started off. They looked back and waved. Rachel waved back as long as Mama looked, but soon they were gone.

When she turned, everyone had gone back into the house, except Patrick. He stood to one side, just off the porch.

Rachel thought she would go up to her bedroom and finish her cry, but Patrick reached for her hand. "Walk with me."

They walked slowly past the barn, around fields, and into the edge of the woods. The dappled shade made it a little cooler. Rachel heard the new leaves whisper in the breeze, and birds called to each other. Patrick didn't say anything, but he still held her hand, and that comforted her.

They came out of the woods to a creek. Patrick sat her down on a log facing the water and sat down beside her. The brook's song soothed her, and a peace descended.

"Are you sorry you stayed?" Patrick finally asked.

"No, but the parting was hard."

"I know. What can I do to help?"

"You're doing it. You seem to always know what to do or say to make me feel better. I'll miss them, but the hurt is easing."

He put his arm around her shoulders, gave her a gentle squeeze, and then released her.

"Are there fish in there?" she asked, looking at the water.

"Some minnows, but I've never seen anything big enough to eat. It's usually too shallow. Are you ready to go back? I didn't tell anyone where we were going."

"Yes, I'm ready now."

———————————

"I hope we're doing the right thing," Leah said, "because leaving Rachel with Ivy was hard."

Leah looked at Luke as he drove the wagon. Even now her husband was the most handsome man she'd ever met.

"We prayed about it, Leah. This seemed to be the direction God has been leading us, so I think it's what's best for Rachel. Leaving her there may have been difficult, but not as hard as having to leave you for the war."

"You're correct there. At least we made it through and back to each other."

"I shouldn't have worried about how things would be with us when I got back. Our relationship is stronger than ever, and still it grows. Every day I tell myself I don't see how it could be any deeper, but each day it expands. It's an amazing wonder. Come here." He indicated for her to slip closer, and when she did, he put his arm around her.

Leah placed her head on Luke's chest, and he kissed the top of her hair. She stayed like that for several minutes, then straightened up. "I'm glad we gave the land to Moses and Patsy." Remaining close, she took his hand in hers. "I understand them wanting to have a place of their own, so they can hand it down to their children, and I never want to go back to Gold Leaf. I wish we could've done more to help Bertha, but at least we were there for her funeral. I wasn't for Jasper's."

"Those two sure did think the world of you. I'd have never thought slaves would have felt that way about one of their master's family."

"I loved them too, and I never saw them as slaves. Bertha and Jasper were as much a part of my family as anyone else."

Luke's eyes took on that mischievous glint she loved. "How would you like to get a room in Albemarle and spend the night there with just the two of us before we go on to visit Father in Salisbury? It's been a long time since we've been able to do that."

She broke into a grin. "I'd like that very much. I hope you know how much I love you, Luke. I thank God every day for you."

He let the horses continue on their own and gave her a long kiss. By the time they got to Albemarle, they were both ready to stop. Leah hoped Luke's kiss hadn't left her too weak kneed to walk to a hotel room. He still had that effect on her even after all these years.

---

Rachel started fixing dinner as soon as Patrick and she got back to the house. Aunt Ivy offered to help, but Rachel told her she wanted to stay busy and preferred to do it herself.

She heard Uncle Sam and Aunt Ivy talking to Patrick on the porch. They didn't know she could hear.

"I don't think you should take Rachel off alone like that," Uncle Sam said.

"I didn't plan to," Patrick told him, "but I could see her pain, and she needed to get away from the house for a little while. I just wanted to help. You do trust me, don't you? You know I'd never do anything to hurt Rachel."

"We know that, son," Aunt Ivy said, "but you don't want anything to tarnish Rachel's reputation, and it could, if the wrong person got wind of it."

"You're right, Mama. I can just imagine what Blanche would do with such information. I'll be more cautious."

Rachel felt tears slipping down her cheeks again. She wiped them away with her sleeve. She still hurt from her parents' departure, she told herself.

Things changed with Patrick after that. He still watched Rachel in the same way, but he stayed quieter, more reserved. He didn't speak to her directly as much. She noticed the difference at dinner. He ate quickly and then went back outside to work.

The situation didn't improve at supper. Uncle Sam lead the family devotion afterwards, and Patrick made no comments during the discussion. Rachel had never seen him not participate.

Saturday, Patrick came in for meals, but left the house to work outside as soon as he could and said little. He didn't laugh or smile, and neither did Rachel. She felt more like crying than anything else. She missed Mama and Papa, she told herself. That night, after she said her usual silent prayer, she included the situation with Patrick.

*Dear Father, please help Patrick to be happy again. Don't let him withdraw or feel uncomfortable around me. Please help us to be the way we were with each other. With Mama and Papa gone, I need his friendship even more than before. Restore that friendship to me, I pray, in Jesus's name. Amen.*

Rachel couldn't tell any change in Patrick at breakfast Sunday morning. He still sat quietly and seemed withdrawn. He didn't even talk to his parents, unless they asked him something. In the wagon, he sat up front with his parents, leaving Hope, Sammy, and Rachel to ride in the back seat.

At church, Patrick stayed outside with Uncle Sam, while the others went inside to take a seat. Blanche hadn't arrived yet. Aunt Ivy had Rachel move down the bench to give Uncle Sam and Patrick room beside the center aisle. Remembering last Sunday, she wished she could've saved room for Patrick on the end of the bench next to her, when a young man sat down on the bench in front of them and turned around to talk. Then, she decided she was glad there hadn't been room for the stranger to sit beside her. He acted too forward in Rachel's opinion.

"Well, who do we have here?" He looked at Rachel. "How have I missed seeing you around?"

She didn't know how to respond. They hadn't been introduced, so should she ignore him?

"I don't believe I've met you before, so why are you talking to my niece?" Aunt Ivy saved her from having to respond.

"I beg your pardon, ma'am. I was carried away by your niece's beauty and forgot my manners. I hope both of you will accept my apology. My friend, Chance Daniels, had something he needed to discuss with a couple of the men outside. He's from Union County, and I'm visiting there. My name is Axel Jones."

"Mr. Jones, I'm Ivy Whitley, and this is my daughter, Hope, and niece, Rachel Moretz. My husband and older son are also outside."

"Pleased to meet you. I hope it's okay if we join you for church today."

"The church congregation is always happy to welcome visitors, Mr. Jones."

"Do you live with your aunt and uncle, then, Rachel?"

"I'm here for an extended visit."

He should have called her Miss Moretz, but Rachel liked the friendliness of the man. She needed a friend right now.

"Just like me, then. Where is your home?"

"In Watauga County, in the mountains. And yours?

"I was born in Missouri, but I'm living in Tennessee now."

"What brought you to North Carolina?"

"I have friends living here, and another friend and I came to visit."

"How long will you be staying, Mr. Jones?" Aunt Ivy asked.

"Several months, maybe longer. I could even be persuaded to stay permanently." Again he looked directly at Rachel.

Rachel liked Axel's looks. He had medium brown hair, hazel eyes, and a neatly trimmed moustache. She sensed something daring and untamed about the way he carried himself and looked at her, but he intrigued her. She guessed by the glint in his eyes he might also be somewhat a challenge, and she told herself to be cautious.

The bell rang and the men who had remained outside came in. Patrick stopped and stared at Rachel and Axel before taking his seat beside his father. He looked even more unhappy.

"I see Chance sitting down near the back, so I guess I'd better join him," Axel said. "It was a pleasure to meet you, Rachel. I hope to see you again soon."

"Who was that?" Uncle Sam asked.

"Just some young man who seemed interested in Rachel," Aunt Ivy said, "but I don't think we have to worry about him. He's just visiting someone in Union County, so he shouldn't be around much. I thought him too bold."

Blanche made her usual entrance. She looked at Rachel and gave a smile that never reached her eyes. Rachel smiled back.

The pastor spoke on doing what was right, even when others wronged you. After the service, Blanche latched onto Rachel's arm. Patrick and Uncle Sam followed along behind the women, but Patrick did nothing to help Rachel.

"Come," Blanche said. "I just met someone, and I think you would be perfect for his friend. I want you to meet them."

She led Rachel out the front and over to one side. There stood Axel and another man.

"Rachel, this is my friend, Chance Daniels, and his friend, Axel Jones. Gentlemen, this is Rachel Moretz. Don't you think Chance is an unusual name? I just love it, don't you?"

"Rachel and I have already met inside." Axel's eyes were laughing. "I would certainly like to see more of her, however."

Blanche beamed. "Well now, we'll see what we can arrange. Perhaps you would like to come to dinner one night. The three of you can be my guests."

"I'm not sure we'll be able to make it back to Stanly County this week," Chance said.

"What about next Sunday for dinner after church?" Blanche insisted.

"That sounds fine," Chance said. "We'd be happy to accept."

"I'll be looking forward to it," Axel said, looking at Rachel.

"I'm not sure I can make it," Rachel told them. "I'll have to ask my aunt and uncle."

"Pshaw," Blanche uttered. "Leave that to me."

"Well, until next week, ladies," Axel said. Both of the young men tipped their hats and turned to leave.

"Aren't they ever so exciting?" Blanche whispered. She walked with Rachel to where the others were waiting for her. "I want to invite Rachel to dine at my house after church next week," she said. "I just know we are going to be good friends and it will give us a chance to talk. We'll bring her back home."

"I guess that will be fine if it's okay with Rachel," Uncle Sam said.

"Will it be okay with your parents?" Rachel asked Blanche.

"Oh, sure. They're happy with me having anyone I want over. So, it's all set then. See you Sunday." With that, she turned and left.

"What Blanche didn't tell you is that Axel Jones and his friend are also invited," Rachel said.

"How do you feel about that?" Aunt Ivy asked. "We can always send your regrets."

"I think it'll be all right. I found Mr. Jones to be rather interesting, and this will be a chance for me to socialize in a safe environment, since Blanche's parents will be there."

"Well, I don't like it that Blanche didn't mention the other guests," Uncle Sam said. "That's pretty deceptive of her."

"Do you feel comfortable going to Blanche's home?" Those were the first words Patrick had spoken directly to her since Friday morning.

"I'm not exactly comfortable, but I think it'll be okay. I think some ancient Chinese general said, 'Keep your friends close, and your enemies closer.'"

"Where did you learn that?" Uncle Sam asked.

"I've read a lot, since I couldn't attend a school. Grandfather and my parents kept me stocked with plenty of reading material."

"I guess she takes after her father," Aunt Ivy said. "Luke is a walking encyclopaedia, and Leah's almost as bad."

CHAPTER FIVE

# School

AFTER DINNER, RACHEL WENT TO her room, planning to have time to read her Bible, pray, and meditate, but Hope was getting ready to take a nap. Therefore, Rachel took her Bible and went outside.

She ended up beside the creek on the same log on which she and Patrick had sat on Friday. The memory felt bittersweet. She read in Psalms. The book always seemed to encourage her. "Delight thyself also in the Lord," she quoted from memory, "and He shall give thee the desires of thine heart."

"Dear Lord," she whispered, "the desire of my heart right now is to have Patrick comfortable with me, happy, and willing to talk again. Please restore our friendship. I know he probably thinks he's protecting me after what his parents said to him, but help him see this isn't the way. Soften his heart and give us both wisdom, I pray. I do love and delight in Thee, Father. I stand on Thy promises and thank Thee for them. Amen."

Rachel sat there staring at the bubbling water, but not really seeing anything. She cleared her mind, as best she could, and stilled herself to let God speak to her. She didn't feel an answer, but she did feel calmer.

She had decided to head back to the house when she heard footsteps.

"Can I throw rocks in the creek?" Sammy asked.

"Sure, I'll just sit and watch you."

Sammy and Patrick. Her heart started racing. She looked over just as he started toward the log, but he stopped when he saw her.

"Please come and join me," she said. "I need to talk with you."

"I don't think that would be a good idea."

"I heard what your parents told you when we got back Friday. We need to talk. Sammy is here now, so we're not alone."

Patrick seemed reluctant but came up to her. "What do you want to talk about? If you heard what my parents said, you know what we need to do."

She patted the log, and he sat down far on the other end. He angled his body so he could see her well, however.

"Patrick, I need our friendship to be the way it was. I'm having a hard time with my parents gone and you treating me so coldly. I feel all alone."

"I saw what happened at church. You have Blanche and those guys."

"You know that's not the same. I barely know them."

"That should change after Sunday."

"If you'd been with me at church like the other Sunday, I probably wouldn't even be going. You would've kept Blanche from grabbing me and pulling me away. I couldn't think of a way to escape, other than making her angry, and I'm trying not to do that."

Patrick seemed to think about what she had said. She let him have some time.

Finally, he spoke. "After Mama said I could ruin your reputation, I've been trying to keep my distance. I thought it would be best for you. I'm sorry if I've hurt you."

"You're the best friend I've ever had. No matter what else happens, I need you, and I think you might need me some too. You certainly haven't looked happy over the last couple of days."

"You're right about that. What would you suggest we do now? I still shouldn't be alone with you in an isolated place."

"I'd like to go back to the way things were before. If we're going to be off from other people, we'll just invite Hope or Sammy to go along. Won't that work?"

"I'll see what my parents say, but that should be fine. I'm sorry about the way I've handled this. I should've talked with you about it when my parents confronted me. I didn't think it would make such a difference to you."

"Well, it does. You once told me we'd be friends always and forever. I had begun to think you'd lied."

He looked shocked, then the beginnings of a smile played around his lips. "I'm glad to learn our friendship means this much to you."

"Come skip rocks with me, Patrick," Sammy called.

Rachel walked up to the creek with Patrick. She picked up a flat stone on the bank, and threw it diagonally across the water, so it would have more room to skip.

"Five skips," she called. "Who can beat it?"

"Wow!" Sammy exclaimed. "A girl who can skip rocks. You're sure different than Hope."

"I'd say she's different than anyone." Patrick grinned.

Rachel smiled to herself as they walked back to the house. Talk about answered prayer! She had spent time with the Lord, and Patrick appeared.

*Thank Thee so much, Father!*

"You are going to school with me tomorrow, right?" Hope asked Rachel at the supper table.

"Will I be in your class?"

"Yes. I'm in the upper class now. They divide us according to the number of students in each age group."

Rachel looked up from her plate. "How many classes are there?"

"Four right now. That could change next year if the numbers change drastically."

"Okay, then. I'll go with you tomorrow and see how it is. Who's your teacher?"

Hope smiled. "Miss Thomas. I think you'll like her. She's easier than some."

"Easy is not always better," Uncle Sam said.

Hope raised her chin. "It is for me."

"I'll drive you to school tomorrow, if that's agreeable with everyone," Patrick said.

Rachel went to bed happy. Things did seem back to normal as far as Patrick and she were concerned. His face had relaxed and he laughed and smiled again. She still didn't sleep very well, however. She kept dreading both school the next day and dinner at Blanche's on Sunday. She kept telling herself she didn't have to go back to school if she didn't want to, and the same would be true about seeing Blanche or Axel again. Regardless, it took forever for her to get to sleep, and then she slept fitfully.

She got up early and had breakfast ready when Patrick came in from the barn with the milk. They could hear the others stirring about upstairs.

"You look nice this morning," he said. "Are you excited about school?"

"I guess, but I'm not sure my going to school is for the best."

"Probably not." He grinned. "It's back to eating Mama's cooking for dinner for Papa and me. Sincerely though, it won't hurt to give it a try, and you don't have to keep going back. Personally, I feel you're probably more qualified to teach the class than Miss Thomas, but you can see what you think."

"My, but you're spoiling me, Rachel." Aunt Ivy walked into the kitchen. "I appreciate not having to do all the cooking."

"She's spoiling us too," Uncle Sam said with a grin.

Rachel gathered her paper and pencils, and left the dishes for Ivy to wash. When they got to school, Sammy joined the other students playing outside, but Hope and Rachel walked inside. Hope told her the classrooms for the younger students were downstairs and the two classes of older students met upstairs.

Miss Thomas, a thin, wiry woman in her thirties, wore her mousey hair pulled straight back in a severe bun. She squinted, as if she might need glasses, but she smiled at Rachel. "Do we have a new student today?" Her voice almost squeaked.

"Yes, Miss Thomas," Hope answered. "This is my cousin, Rachel Moretz, from Watauga County. She's staying with my family for a while."

"I see. How old are you Miss Moretz?"

"I turned sixteen in February."

The teacher squinted to see Rachel better. "And how much schooling have you had?"

"I've never been to a formal school, because there wasn't one close enough to where I live, but my parents taught me at home. I should be able to keep up with your higher group."

"We'll see." She sounded doubtful. "What is the last book you read?"

"*Les Misérables*, but I read the English translation instead of the French."

"Okay." Miss Thomas appeared surprised or perhaps skeptical. "Why don't you have a seat over here by the window for the time being? You and Hope will probably be in separate groups. I have three. And, please fill out this information sheet."

Rachel had a seat where the teacher indicated and began completing the form. Soon the other students came in making a lot of noise. Rachel counted ten girls and eight boys. They seemed to range in ages from about thirteen up.

"Quiet, students," Miss Thomas said. "Take your seats and get quiet now."

The students noisily took their seats, but many kept talking. Only a few were even looking at Miss Thomas.

"We have a new student today. Let me introduce her. Would you please stand, Miss Moretz."

Rachel stood and handed Miss Thomas her completed form. At least, she'd been listening. The moment Rachel stood, all eyes turned to her, and the room became quiet.

"Now, that's better." Miss Thomas smiled. "This is Rachel Moretz from Watauga County. She is Hope Whitley's cousin and is staying with the Whitley family. Let's see."—The teacher looked at the information sheet. "She's sixteen years old and has three younger brothers. She'll begin working in the advanced group, and we'll see how that goes. Those in the advanced group, please get out your Shakespeare books, finish reading, and be able to discuss *Macbeth* in about thirty minutes. Here's you a book, Rachel. I know you've missed most of it, and you won't be required to make it up."

"That's fine, Miss Thomas. I've read the play several times, and I think I remember it well enough."

"Wonderful, now the middle group, get out your books and read the next chapter. And my younger group, bring your reading books to the front bench."

The morning dragged by. Rachel first looked back over *Macbeth*, but she remembered the play, so she pulled out some paper and began a letter to her parents. She told them she'd been invited to Blanche's house for dinner Sunday, along with two young men, but she didn't mention what Aunt Ivy and Uncle Sam had said to Patrick or what difficulty it had caused. That problem seemed to be resolved, so there was no need to worry them. She told them she had started school with Hope, but she was beginning to think she might be wasting her time. She ended by telling them how much she loved and missed them. She had just finished the letter and folded it away when Miss Thomas came over to discuss their reading.

Rachel answered every question Miss Thomas asked her, but she didn't volunteer any information. She could have answered all the questions, even the ones the others missed. She would have enjoyed having a free discussion of the play, but Miss Thomas didn't encourage one.

Miss Thomas assigned her group of five students to do some pages in their mathematics book next. Papa had taught her high computation skills, and Rachel finished the page quickly, even though she had to copy the problems onto her own paper and then work them out. When Miss Thomas saw her sitting and not working, she came over, looked at her paper. She nodded and moved on to look at what the others were doing.

"Rachel, would you please show Mr. Hinson step by step how to work some of the problems."

"Yes, Miss Thomas."

"Charles," the boy whispered to Rachel as she moved to stand beside his desk. He was a tall boy with reddish brown hair and pale blue eyes. He looked to be one of the older boys. He appeared to be getting lost in the middle of a problem, so Rachel had him take it one step at a time and corrected him when he missed a step. By the fourth problem, he seemed to understand.

"Miss Thomas." A hand of another boy shot up.

"What do you need, Mr. Drye?"

"I need help with my problems too."

Miss Thomas looked bothered. "Mr. Drye, you are just about my best student in mathematics. I can't believe you need help."

"But, I do."

"Well, I'll come help you in just a minute."

"Oh, never you mind. I've just figured it out."

The other students snickered. Apparently Mr. Drye only needed Rachel's help.

"Do you think you can do the rest on your own?" Rachel asked Charles.

"I think so. Thank you for your help. You'd make a good teacher."

Rachel smiled. "Well, call me if you get stuck on a problem."

Recess came next. Hope came up to Rachel, and they walked outside together. Not all the classes came out at the same time, so she didn't see Sammy.

Mr. Drye came up to Rachel immediately. "I'm George Drye," he said. "I'm glad to have you in my class."

"Thank you," Rachel said.

"Where do you go to church?" he asked.

"Hope and I go to Mt. Olive Baptist."

He glanced over at Hope. "Oh hello, Hope." He looked back at Rachel. "Maybe I'll see you there Sunday."

"Come on." Hope led her over to the side. "I need to go to the little girl's room."

Hope led her around to the back of the school. Rachel saw two outhouses, one with a sign that said Girls, and the other said Boys.

"Wait for me," Hope said. "It's always better not to come here alone. Some of the students try to pull pranks when they can."

As she waited for Hope outside the door, one of the younger girls came up. "You're very pretty," she shyly said.

"Thank you. What's your name?"

"I'm Nancy Clark. I'm thirteen years old."

Hope came out and Nancy went in.

When they went back, most of the girls jumped rope, and some of the boys were playing roller bat because they didn't have enough players or time for a regular game. Hope and Rachel sat down on a bench, and Charles came up.

"How'd you get so good in mathematics?" he asked Rachel.

"My parents taught me."

"You seem real smart in most everything. I like school, but I don't guess I'll get to come back next year. I'm sixteen now, and Pa said I needed to start working like the man I am."

"I'm not sure how much I'm going to come, either. This is the first time I've ever gone to a school away from my home."

He looked around. "Seems to me you know just as much as Miss Thomas now, but don't tell her I said so." He smiled.

"It's almost time to go in, so let's get a head start." Hope frowned. "I just love how everyone starts talking to you and totally ignores me."

"I'm sorry, Hope."

"Oh, it's not your fault, except that you're so pretty. I saw how you tried to include me with George Drye, but he never noticed me just the same."

They had a spelling bee when they went inside. Rachel won easily.

Miss Thomas read from Walt Whitman's *Leaves of Grass* before dinner. Thankfully, the long morning had ended.

They went outside for dinner. Hope and Rachel sat under a tree to eat the food Rachel had packed for them. George and Charles came up and asked to join the girls, to which they replied, "Sure."

Rachel looked in her dinner pail to see a folded, torn piece of paper inside. She'd placed her dinner on the shelf above the coat rack, and someone had dropped a note inside. She left it in the bag, since she didn't want everyone to know about the note.

"Could I fetch you a cup of water, Miss Rachel?" Charles asked.

"Yes, thank you." She handed him her tin cup.

"I might as well get yours when I get mine then," George said to Hope, and Rachel tried hard not to laugh.

"Here you go." Charles handed Rachel her filled cup. "I pumped it until the warm water left, so it should be cool."

"You're very thoughtful. Thank you."

He seemed sweet too, but Rachel knew better than to tell him. She liked Charles, but George appeared way too cocky.

When they went inside, there was another note on her desk. Someone had folded it and written her name on the outside. She put it in her lap and unfolded it. *I think you are divine. George.* How immature. Did George really write it, or was someone playing a prank? She hadn't looked at the other note yet, but had left it in her dinner bucket. She'd just have to read it later.

Miss Thomas said they would have a history lesson next and then science. The whole class studied them together. Rachel didn't learn anything new. This felt like the longest day ever. She decided it had been much better to have her parents teach her.

"I'm really impressed with your abilities, Miss Moretz," Miss Thomas told her. "I don't know when I've had a student with so much potential. I would like to use you to help some of the younger students, if you don't mind."

"I don't mind helping others, but I'd like to learn some things, too, Miss Thomas."

She seemed flustered, as if she didn't know what to say. "Of course you do," she finally said.


Patrick sat in the wagon waiting for them when school let out. "How was it?" he asked.

"I think you were right," Rachel said. "I don't think I learned anything today, and I'm not sure the school has anything to offer me."

"I'm sorry." He didn't look surprised.

"She created quite a stir, though," Sammy said. "Even the students in my class kept talking about how pretty she is. I became special, because I'm her cousin."

Hope didn't look as excited as Sammy. "Everybody seemed interested in her in our class, too, but that didn't help me any."

"I don't know," Rachel told her. "George did get your water for you when we ate our dinner."

"Only because Charles Hinson got yours first."

Patrick looked at Rachel and raised his eyebrows but didn't say anything. They were almost home before he spoke. "We missed you at home, Rachel," Patrick told her. "Dinner was very stale and dry without you."

Rachel smiled. "Are you using a pun, Mr. Whitley?"

"Who, me?" he laughed.

"Are you going back tomorrow?" Hope asked.

"I don't think so. I think I'll be better off to stay home and help on the farm."

"But, I wanted you to help me with my homework."

"I can still do that, Hope."

When they got home, Rachel remembered the note in her dinner pail. She took it out and read it. *Rachel, I think I love you.* It wasn't signed. If the first note had really been from George, then Charles likely wrote this one. Yes, she'd better stay home from now on. She didn't want to hurt Charles's feelings, but Rachel just wasn't interested in him romantically.

Rachel wrote a letter to Miss Thomas. She felt the woman deserved an explanation, since she didn't plan to go back. *I'm needed to help around the farm,* she wrote, and she thanked her for the day at school.

"Do you think it's close enough to the truth?" Leah asked Patrick. "I don't want to imply she's inadequate. It's hard to teach so many different levels."

"It is the truth," Patrick told her. "We do need you here."

When Patrick left to take Hope and Sammy to school Tuesday, Rachel gave him her letter to her parents to mail. He would go right by the store with the post office.

She spent the day cooking, gathering eggs, helping Ivy with the washing, and weeding the flowers planted around the house. She even baked oatmeal cookies for when Hope and Sammy came from school. They could have some with milk.

"M-m-m-m, it smells good in here," Patrick said as he came in to wash up and change clothes. He had been wrestling a young heifer back into the pasture, and he smelled like it.

"I baked cookies for after school. I'll get you some with milk, if you'd like."

"That sounds great. I'm glad you decided not to return to school. I like having you here. Is that too selfish?" He didn't look all that contrite.

"I don't think so, since I like being here too."

Patrick went upstairs and quickly cleaned up. He barely had time to down some cookies and milk before leaving to pick up Sammy and Hope.

"You're sure a hard worker," Aunt Ivy said as she joined them at the table. "You're like your mother there. Leah could always work rings around me."

It didn't take Patrick long to pick up the two students. Hope handed Rachel two notes before she sat down for cookies. "They're from George and Charles." Hope scowled. "Neither one of them paid me any attention today, other than to ask where you were."

George asked her to come back to school, so he could continue to see her. If she couldn't do that, he asked permission to call on her. Rachel knew how she would answer him.

Charles's was going to be more difficult, and, by the writing, she felt the unsigned note yesterday had been from him. He'd written:

Dear Rachel,

I missed you today at school. I didn't have anyone to help me with my math, and there was no one I wanted to eat dinner with. Please come back, but, if not, then would you allow me to come to your house after school, so you could help me with my mathematics problems? I usually do okay in my other subjects, but math is harder for me.

Yours truly,

Charles

Rachel went to her room and replied to George right away. She wrote:

George,

I won't be able to return to school, since I'm needed to help with the work on the farm. I'm honored you would like to call on me, but I don't think that would be best. There is someone else who has already expressed interest, and I will be having dinner with him Sunday.

May God bless you,

Rachel

When Rachel went downstairs with the notes, Patrick had gone to the barn. She went to meet him. Since they were standing within sight of the house, she felt it would be okay for them to have a private conversation.

"Hope brought me two notes from boys at school. I would like for you to read them and give me some advice."

She handed him the notes. He read them and looked up with a questioning look on his face.

"I had no problem answering George's." She handed him the reply she had written, and he read it.

"I think you let him down as easily as you could and still be firm." He handed the letter back.

"I'm having trouble replying to Charles's letter," she told him. "I think George is just infatuated with a new face, but Charles seems more serious. He's so nice, I don't want to hurt him, and I would like to help him with his studies, but I don't want to encourage him. Even if I tell him this, I think he'll probably become more involved if I tutor him. What should I do?"

"You're not interested in either of these two courting you?"

"No. Definitely not."

He smiled. "I tell you what. I'm pretty good in math, so tell Charles you will be busy preparing supper, but I can tutor him on Mondays and Thursdays after school."

"Can you take time away from the farm?"

"I can spare thirty minutes or so. I usually take a break and help eat the after school snacks you prepare about then, anyway." He looked amused.

"Thank you, Patrick. I can always count on you to help me, but please let me help you with some of the planting. Mama and I often helped Papa."

"I think you're doing too much around here already, but we'll see."

She went back to the house and wrote Charles. She wanted to give Hope the replies to take tomorrow. She wrote:

Dear Charles,

I won't be able to help you with your mathematics, since I'll be busy with such tasks as preparing supper. I do most of the cooking here. However, Patrick, my older cousin, said he would be glad to help you on Mondays and Thursdays. If you can come, we'll see you Thursday after school.

May God bless and keep you,

Rachel

CHAPTER SIX

# Sunday Dinner

THURSDAY CHARLES CAME FROM SCHOOL with Hope and Sammy. Rachel was curious and wanted to see how the tutoring session went, so after setting out muffins, jam, and butter with the pitcher of milk, she busied herself in the kitchen.

When Hope and Sammy went upstairs, Patrick and Charles sat at the end of the table and worked. Charles seemed to watch Rachel at first, but then he concentrated on his studies.

Rachel could tell Patrick had strong mathematical skills, and he was very good at explaining difficult concepts. It didn't take long for them to finish, and Charles seemed to understand how to do the problems on his own.

Charles thanked Patrick over and over. He'd planned on walking home, but Patrick insisted on taking him.

Sunday came all too soon. Rachel had plenty of misgivings about going to Blanche's for dinner. She thought about finding some excuse, but she didn't feel comfortable with lying and hated to cancel at the last minute. She didn't want to anger Blanche, either, if she could help it. Blanche seemed to be the vindictive type.

"God, please hold me close to You today, and help this to go well," she whispered.

She dressed for church with trepidation. She considered wearing her emerald dress again, but decided to wear a golden brown one instead. It had a gold or olive sheen among the brown, depending on movement and the light.

Patrick stood waiting for her at the bottom of the stairs. He smiled warmly. "You look lovely."

"I'll save you a seat beside me at church," Rachel said. "I'm afraid Axel may plan to sit with me, and I don't want that."

"It'll be my pleasure. Do you think I could inveigle a last-minute invitation out of Blanche?" His eyes twinkled in laughter.

"I wish, but I think she invited Chance for her."

Axel met them as they stopped the team. "I realized I hadn't met you, sir," he said to Uncle Sam, "and I wanted to rectify that. I'm Axel Jones." He put out his hand.

Uncle Sam shook his hand. "I'm Sam Whitley, Rachel's uncle. I'm glad to meet you, and this is my older son, Patrick. Why don't you stay out here and talk with Patrick and me?"

Axel shook hands with Patrick and looked at Rachel as if he'd rather go inside with her, but he stayed with the men. Uncle Sam appeared to be asking some questions, when Rachel glanced back from the church entrance.

Patrick took his place beside Rachel at the far end of the bench as the service began. He quickly patted her hand and smiled. "So far, so good."

"I'll be praying for you," Patrick whispered after the service.

"Thank you," Rachel whispered back.

Blanche collected her, introduced her to Mr. and Mrs. Furr, and escorted her to their coach. Rachel wondered how they would arrange the seating, since there would be two separate conveyances.

"When might we expect Rachel home?" Uncle Sam asked the Furrs. "She usually prepares supper on Sunday."

"I'll have her back by around three thirty, then," Mr. Furr said. Blanche didn't looked pleased.

Rachel and Axel ended up riding with Mr. Furr, and Mrs. Furr rode with Chance and Blanche in his wagon. Again, Blanche looked unhappy. She had wanted her parents to drive and let the young people ride together, but Rachel breathed a sigh of relief.

Axel still sat much too close to her, and he had his arm around the back of her seat. She looked up to see Patrick staring at them. He looked about like she felt.

The Furrs' home didn't look huge, but it had been decorated in a very lavish style. The furnishings had to be expensive, but Rachel preferred a simpler style. The meal took forever with multiple courses served by two servants.

Blanche seemed to expect Rachel to be at a loss at the formal dinner, but Rachel performed without a mistake. Mama had taught her well, and some of the dinner parties at Grandfather's had given her practice. Axel and Chance seemed more ill at ease than she.

Conversation at the dinner table stayed general, but Blanche wanted them to walk in the flower garden behind the house after they ate. Mr. and Mrs. Furr sat on the back porch, where they could see the couples but stayed out of earshot. All the taller shrubs were around three perimeters with the side toward the house open.

Rachel liked the garden, which looked larger than Grandfather's but similar. Blanche led Chance toward one end, and Axel took Rachel to the other.

"You're so beautiful," he told her. "I like how your dress almost changes color when you walk, but you'd be lovely in anything . . . or nothing." He gave her a wicked grin.

Rachel felt like slapping that grin off his face, but she took a deep breath to calm down. "Mr. Jones, I am not accustomed to men being fresh with me, and I'm offended by it."

"My apology, but please call me Axel. I guess I've forgotten most of the social graces I've been taught, but I don't want to insult you."

"What do you do for a living?"

He hesitated. "I'm involved in several different business enterprises. What do your parents do?" Apparently, he preferred not to talk about himself.

"They farm, like my uncle, but their farm is in the mountains of Watauga County."

He gave her a warm smile, which transformed his face and made him quite handsome. "Yes, I remember you're a mountain girl. I'm pretty much a country boy at heart, although I've spent some time around Nashville recently. Didn't I hear Blanche say you have connections to Salisbury?"

"Yes, my grandfather lives there."

"What does your grandfather do?"

"He's a doctor, but he's semiretired now. He treats a handful of his former patients, but he's not taking any new ones."

"That explains how you can fit into Blanche's world." His tone of voice indicated he didn't like Blanche's world.

"I thought you fit in fine."

"I can get by occasionally, but I wouldn't want to do it often. I wouldn't mind to have all this, but I would hate to live so proper and be so snobbish."

"Even the furnishings here are too pretentious for my taste," Rachel agreed.

"See, I knew we had a lot in common. Come walk behind the row of hedges with me. We won't stay there long—just long enough for me to steal a kiss."

"No. I hardly know you."

"Come on, and we'll get better acquainted. How many men or boys have you kissed?"

"None, except for family."

He chuckled. "You are an innocent, aren't you? But I like that about you. You're not like Blanche."

They heard Blanche arguing with her parents and went to see what the problem was. Axel put her hand in his arm as they walked toward the house.

"But we won't be alone," Blanche was saying. "There will be four of us."

"After you drop Rachel off, there will just be you and two men," Mr. Furr said. "I won't have you riding around without a chaperone. Besides, I told Rachel's uncle I would bring her home around three thirty, and I plan to do just that."

Rachel hoped her expression told Mr. Furr she appreciated him taking her home. She had no doubt Axel would demand a kiss if he had the chance, and who knew what else he'd want to do. There was something about him Rachel didn't trust.

"You still have time to go in the house and play a game or something before time for Rachel to go," Mrs. Furr said.

Blanche wanted to play cards, but the men only knew how to play poker, so they ended up playing checkers. Chance beat Blanche, and Rachel beat Axel, so Chance and Rachel ended up in a final game. Rachel won easily.

"You're supposed to let the man win," Blanche whispered to Rachel.

"Papa and Mama taught me to always do my best at everything," Rachel told her.

Mr. Furr drove Rachel home, and Axel rode with them. Chance stayed at the Furrs'.

"I've enjoyed being with you today," Axel told her. "I'd like to come calling on you."

"I had a good time today too," she told him, "but I'm not ready for a serious relationship, and I stay busy at the farm."

"We'll just have fun together, then, and you can't work all the time. You need to relax some."

She wouldn't describe being with Axel Jones as "relaxing." She felt she had to be on her guard with him all the time.

"I'm honored by your interest," she said, "but I feel I must decline. I wish you well, Axel, and hope you meet the woman for you soon."

He seemed to fume for a while, but he told her good-bye and thanked her for her company. He helped her from the coach, and she breathed a huge sigh of relief as they drove off.

When Rachel arrived, Patrick sat waiting on the porch. "How did it go?"

"It went well, thanks to Mr. Furr." She told him everything, and his frown deepened. She reached over and patted his hand. Just his presence soothed her. "I don't plan to see him again. I feel fortunate not to have to fight off his advances this time, and I don't want to be put in such a position again."

Patrick squeezed her hand and smiled. "I'm glad you are so responsible and look at everything in such a mature way. You act wiser than your sixteen years, and I'm happy you confide in me."

"I guess the fact that I'm the oldest child and my few friends have all been adults influenced me, but I don't know what I'd do here without you, Patrick. I came here to be a companion to Hope and help her through those hard early teen years, but I find I can't talk with her nearly as well as I can you. I don't really understand it myself, but I'm very thankful." She paused. "Now, I'd better go see what Aunt Ivy wants for supper."

Patrick lightly brushed the back of her hand with his lips before he released it, and an exciting tingle ran up her arm, like the sparks from a firecracker. It seemed an odd gesture for a cousin, but he'd also become her dear friend. If not for Patrick's friendship, she'd more than likely go back to the mountains early.

On Tuesday, they had a surprise. A servant of the Furrs rode up with a note to Rachel from Blanche, and an invitation from her family for all the Whitleys to have dinner with them the following Sunday.

"My husband is out in the fields now," Ivy told the servant. "Tell Mrs. Furr I will let her know something tomorrow."

"Yes'm." He tipped his hat and left. Blanche's note read:

Dear Rachel,

Axel said you refused to see him again. What are you thinking? We need to talk.

I realize you probably wouldn't come to visit if I invited only you, so your whole family will be invited. Mother likes your aunt, and Father respects your uncle, so please come. It will be a chance for us to get better acquainted, since you and I couldn't spend any time alone last Sunday.

I'll look forward to seeing you. Please don't disappoint me.

Your friend,

Blanche

Rachel handed the note to Patrick and waited until he finished reading it. "Blanche isn't going to let me off her hook, is she?"

"We could just not go."

"I would do that if I thought Blanche would let things drop, but I'm sure she won't give up that easily. She'll be determined to get her way. At least I'll have you with me this time."

Sam took the acceptance note Ivy had written to the Furrs Wednesday when he went to pick up some flour and sugar from the store. Blanche knew how to manipulate things to get her way. The woman would make a dangerous enemy.

Although they knew each other, none of the family had visited the Furrs' home before, so Rachel told the family what to expect, and they weren't surprised by the formal dinner. Aunt Ivy had been even more thoroughly instructed in the social graces than Mama. She'd attended all the social functions that went with living on a large plantation before the war. Mama had never liked that way of life, but Aunt Ivy had. The Furrs seemed pleasantly surprised.

"I'll have to have you over for tea sometime," Mrs. Furr told Aunt Ivy. "I think Frank and I need to increase our circle of friends. We've become too stagnant."

"I haven't had much time to socialize in the past," Aunt Ivy told her, "but with Rachel here, I do have more free time now."

"Do you have servants?"

"I had one, but she became sick, and I haven't been able to replace her."

"Good help does get harder to find all the time."

Conversation continued as the meal progressed. Everything went well, until Blanche pulled Rachel off to the side right after they'd finished eating. "So tell me why you won't see Axel?"

"He's too forceful for me. I don't want to constantly be fighting him off."

"Oh, don't be such a good little girl. You'll never have any fun."

"I have more fun than when I'm with a wild crowd. That's just not me, and it's not who I want to be. I'd like to be your friend, but please don't try to coerce me into things I don't think are right for me."

Blanche huffed, and Rachel almost expected her to stomp her foot. "Fine, then. I'll find someone else for Axel."

"What are you two whispering about?" Patrick came to her rescue again.

"Just girl talk." Blanche batted her lashes at him. "You know how it is."

Patrick laughed. "I'm afraid I don't."

"Well, maybe you should be around me more, Patrick. I'm sure you could learn a thing or two."

Was Blanche flirting with Patrick? Rachel thought she wanted to see Chance.

"But would it be anything I cared to learn?" Patrick asked pleasantly. The words would have been cutting otherwise.

"Why don't you try it and find out," Blanche said.

"I think I'd better pass. Your bite is probably worse than your bark."

"Oh Patrick, you do have the sharpest wit."

"Shall we join the others in the parlor?" He put his hand on Rachel's back and guided her to where the others were sitting. He dropped his hand before they arrived.

Rachel sat and answered Mrs. Furr's questions about her grandfather, his home in Salisbury, and his activities in the community.

Hope and Sammy didn't say much, but they sat and listened. Rachel was proud of Sammy. He could be well behaved.

Aunt Ivy told Mrs. Furr about growing up at Gold Leaf in Anson County before the war and all the social events and balls. Mrs. Furr seemed quite enthralled. Uncle Sam and Mr. Furr talked about local politics.

"I read an account in the *Charlotte Democrat* several weeks ago where revenue officials here in Stanly County have been trying to break up a moonshine ring," Mr. Furr said. "The officers were met by about two hundred armed men and had to retreat."

"Are that many men involved in moonshining?" Uncle Sam asked.

"More than that are probably supporting it, if you know what I mean. The paper said the officers are girding up for an all-out war, so we all need to be vigilant. I'm trying to keep an eye out for my two women. Anything could break loose."

"Oh Father, you know the papers tend to exaggerate. I don't think things are that dangerous, and if it were, men like Chance and Axel would be good men to have around." Blanche gave Rachel a pointed look.

"Would you like to go for a short horse ride before supper, Sammy?" Patrick asked when they got home.

Sammy nodded. "Yeah, sure."

"Would anyone else care to join us?" Patrick's eyes told Rachel he wanted her to come too.

"Let me change to my riding skirt," she said, "and I'll come."

"Sammy and I'll need to change too. We'll meet you downstairs in a few minutes."

Patrick and Sammy had led up the three horses when Rachel went out. Patrick helped her and Sammy into their saddles, and they started off. Sammy took the lead.

"I overheard part of your and Blanche's private conversation after dinner," Patrick told her. "I didn't think you would mind, since you've kept me informed of everything. Do you think you've heard the last of Axel?"

"I hope so. Blanche said she would find another woman for him. I hope she does, and I hope he'll accept that."

"Do you think he might still try to see you?"

"I wish I knew, but to be honest, I'm not sure what Axel might try. He was nice enough most of the time, but I sensed an unpredictable wild streak. I have a feeling I was seeing the best side of him too."

"Well, I think you've handled the situation well, considering everything, and I'm proud of you, Rachel. I just hate I left you to handle the lions alone that Sunday Blanche cornered you."

"I'm glad you've helped me the rest of the time. I think without your help, I would've just packed up and gone home."

"The way you describe Axel, he may have followed you there."

"I think he's been living in Tennessee, so you may be right, but Papa and Aaron would handle him, and he'd have no opportunity to see me anywhere else."

"You be sure to let me know if you suspect something, or if anything doesn't feel right to you. I don't want there to be a chance you might be placed in an awkward or dangerous situation."

---

Patrick looked at Rachel riding easily beside him. She looked as comfortable in the saddle as he did. She looked beautiful.

He marveled at how comfortable she was with him. He felt sure she would tell him anything and wouldn't hesitate to share her thoughts and secrets. If only she didn't view him as a beloved family member or just a friend.

He almost wished he could see her as a sister or cousin, but he loved her as a man loves a woman. He feared his heart would be broken into thousands of pieces before this ended.

*Why, God? Why do I feel this way?* He'd tried to curb his feelings and squelch his love, but it was like trying to hold back a waterfall with his bare hands.

Even if Rachel did ever come to have similar feelings for him, they would still have insurmountable problems with their family. Rachel was only his half cousin, but she was still his cousin. Mama and Aunt Ivy had grown up thinking they were full sisters, and that's how they considered each other.

Patrick had done some reading and he knew it was legal in North Carolina and most states for even full cousins to marry. People used to do that more often before the war, but now research said birth defects could come from related people marrying, and society had begun to frown on such unions more. The remote areas would probably change slowly, however.

He would just have to be patient and put it all in God's hands. Patrick had discovered he had more patience than he thought. He decided he would never say anything to Rachel about how he felt, unless she indicated she loved him in the same way. He would just keep praying and depend on God. That was the best thing to do, anyway.

"Is there a good place to go fishing around here?" Rachel asked. "I'd like to go sometime."

"Sammy and I go to the Rocky River," Patrick said. "He and I both like to fish. We'll go Saturday or Sunday afternoon, when he's out of school." He turned to his brother. "Sammy, Rachel wants to go fishing with us!"

Sammy grinned. "That's great! I bet she even baits her own hook."

"You're right," Rachel said, laughing.

Patrick shot her a glance. "You're changing one ten-year-old's opinion about girls."

"And what about his older brother? I notice you don't court anyone."

Was Rachel flirting with him? He'd like to think so, but he doubted it. "That's not because I wouldn't like to. I'm just waiting for the right woman to come along and notice me."

"Maybe you'll need to make her notice you."

This conversation had just gotten very interesting. "And how would I do that?"

Rachel gave a nervous-sounding laugh. "I don't know. I have no experience in this field. Perhaps you'd need to be a very good friend first."

"You think so?" Patrick suddenly felt a glimmer of hope.

"Yes. I know I'd never want to marry anyone I couldn't respect and admire, and I'd want him to be my very best friend. Mama and Papa have the strongest, deepest love of anyone I know, and they're also the best of friends. They tell each other everything. Papa even told Mama about the time he was in Andersonville Prison, but it was so horrid he won't talk of it to anyone else."

"I'll remember to be a good friend to any woman I want to impress. I guess that's as good a place to start as any."

She gave him such a warm smile that his heart did a flip.

# CHAPTER SEVEN

# Hope's Birthday

AXEL AND CHANCE WERE AT church on Sunday, along with two of their friends. Axel came up to the Whitleys as soon as they got down from the wagon, and introduced J. T. Jackson and Merriman Little. Mr. Little looked about fifty, and Mr. Jackson appeared to be in his early forties. Uncle Sam invited them to come over and talk to some of the men, but they told him they were waiting for some other of the men.

"Axel wanted us to meet Rachel," Mr. Jackson said. "She made quite an impression on him, and I can see why."

"Are you married, Mr. Jackson?" Uncle Sam asked.

"I am. I married my cousin and we've been very happy. Zee and I've been married for about five years now."

"Where do you folks live?"

"Chance and I live in Union County now," Mr. Little said, "but J. T. and Axel are visiting from Tennessee. J. T. and I fought for the Confederacy together in the war, so we're old friends."

"I'll take the women in and get us seats," Patrick told Uncle Sam. "It's nice to meet you both." He nodded to Mr. Jackson and Mr. Little.

Patrick took a seat on the end of the bench. With Hope on Rachel's other side, there would be no place for anyone else to sit beside her. Axel had followed them in, but he took a seat on the bench in front of them and turned around. Rachel looked at Patrick for support, and he lay his hand over hers on the bench.

"I've missed seeing you, Rachel," Axel said.

"How can you miss someone you've seen only twice?" she asked.

"With some people, it's love at first sight." He said it softly, but she knew Patrick and Hope heard, because Hope's eyes got big, and Patrick's hand tightened over hers.

"And some people know immediately they are all wrong for each other," she replied.

"You're more hardhearted than I thought you were. Where's your kindness and Christian spirit?"

She sucked in a long breath. He was going to make this as hard as possible. "I wish you the best, Axel, but I also have that independent mountain spirit you hinted at once. I know my own mind, and it's useless to force something that's not there. Don't waste your time trying to pursue me. Find someone else who'll appreciate your raw appeal. I would never consider marrying anyone who doesn't have a strong Christian faith."

"Do you have feelings for this guy?" He nodded at Patrick. "Patrick, is it?"

"Patrick's my cousin and good friend. That's all."

"J. T. married his cousin. It's done, you know."

"I'm not interested in marrying anyone right now, and I plan on waiting until I find the man who's right for me."

"I guess this is good-bye, then."

"Farewell, Axel." He got up and went toward the back.

Patrick squeezed her hand. "You did great. I don't think you need me around at all."

"If you only knew how untrue that is and how much I depend on you."

Patrick raised his eyebrows. "Just like when you were two?"

"I guess, because I don't remember much from then, but I do know how it is now."

"How do you feel about me, Rachel?"

The preacher started the service, and she turned her attention toward him to keep from answering. *How do I feel about Patrick?* She didn't know. She felt closer to him than anyone else here, and he'd quickly become the best friend she'd ever had. She would miss him terribly when she went back home. This realization disturbed her. How would she ever make it without Patrick to confide in, encourage her, and protect her? She didn't want to find out.

She didn't like the direction her thoughts had taken, so she concentrated on the message. She would take her questions to God in a time of solitude later. He would help her work through things.

Sunday afternoon, Patrick took Sammy and Rachel fishing. They took the farm wagon, drove for a while, then walked down to the water. She liked the pretty spot, which seemed quiet and peaceful, with plenty of shade.

Rachel baited her hook and dropped the line. She sat down on a huge flat rock, and Patrick joined her. Sammy would see a fish jump and move toward it, until he ended up several yards away.

"You never did answer my last question from church," Patrick said.

"I know. I'm a little confused about that. You're the best friend I've ever had, but I'm not sure I know exactly how I feel. I just realized today how much I'll miss you when I go home." She cautiously watched his reaction.

He looked at her, and his eyes softened. They held hers for several seconds, before he spoke with his voice as gentle as his eyes. "Just please tell me when you figure it out. No matter how you feel about me, you can let me know. You can tell me anything."

"Yes, I can, and it gives me a freedom and security that's hard to define. By the way, how do you feel about me?"

"I think I feel much the same as you. I'll miss you beyond imagination if you leave, but that's months away yet, and I plan to enjoy the time we have together. It would be foolish to let what might happen later destroy our happiness now. It's so rare to find a friendship like this." They sat quietly, and Rachel let the peace soothe her. The frogs croaked, the birds sang, and the water gurgled. When the moment felt right, she spoke up. "I think I finally got rid of Axel for good. Don't you think he'll move on now?"

"Do you mean out of the area or to find someone else to court?"

"To find someone else."

Rachel felt a nibble on her line. She waited for another pull and she jerked her pole up. She'd caught a huge fish.

Sammy came running. "Look at that! Do you see her fish, Patrick? I didn't know they grew that large here!"

"I see it." Patrick laughed and turned to Rachel. "You want me to take it off the hook for you?"

"Please," she said politely. "I always have trouble holding the fish with one hand and getting the hook out. I think my hands are too small. I'll help you clean them."

"That's a deal."

"I can't believe Rachel caught more than either of us," Sammy grumbled on the way home.

"I'm glad she did," Patrick told him. "I'm looking forward to Rachel frying them up for us. Can't you just imagine how good they'll taste when she cooks them?"

The middle of May came and the weather grew warmer. Aunt Ivy made plans for Hope's birthday. Hope wanted to invite all eighteen students in her school class and several of the young people from church, so Uncle Sam decided to pit cook a small hog, and Rachel would make some potato salad using Mama's recipe for mayonnaise. It would be easier to make for a crowd than chopping the cabbage for slaw. They also would have fresh garden peas to cook, and Rachel planned to cook them in a white sauce, like she sometimes did the potatoes. She would bake several pans of bread the day before and would also make the cakes, only one of which would be decorated. She could also set out some pickles.

"Don't you think we should get some extra help to come in and help Rachel with all the cooking and preparations for the party?" Patrick asked his parents.

"If I had someone to help with the preparations, like peeling potatoes, and the clean-up, that would be a big help," Rachel told them. "I'll do the cooking. There'll be a lot of dishes to wash, but if it's too expensive to hire someone, I can manage. I'm sure Aunt Ivy will help."

"We can hire someone for the day for very little," Aunt Ivy said, and Uncle Sam nodded.

Patrick took Rachel shopping for presents. Rachel bought Hope a leather diary, and helped Patrick pick out a nice silver pen and ink set. They knew Aunt Ivy planned to give Hope two dress lengths of fabric with thread and lace, and Uncle Sam had bought her a silver vanity set with brush, hand mirror, and comb. Hope would love the attention she'd get.

The day before the celebration buzzed with activity. Rachel spent much of the day baking the bread, but she still went back and forth to watch Uncle Sam and Patrick construct the pit, while she gave the dough time to rise. Rachel hadn't seen pit cooking before, but she wondered if Mama remembered it from her plantation days.

First the men dug a large hole. Then, they cut some green brush and small branches, leaving all the leaves on them. The more leaves, the better they said. They also gathered enough fairly large rocks to line the bottom of the pit, and they put a group of rocks to the side to stack on top later.

When they went to kill the hog, Rachel returned to the house to finish her baking. She'd seen hogs butchered plenty of times, although it was always when the weather turned cool. This one would be fine, however, since they were going to cook it all right away.

Before supper, the men went out and built a fire to heat the rocks. When only red hot embers glowed inside the pit, they put in a rectangle of tin and lay the whole butchered hog on it. They covered everything with the twigs and leaves, until the pit was filled. Then they put boards over the pit and covered it all with dirt.

"The hog will cook all night, and the inside of the pit will stay hot, because it's so well insulated," Patrick told her. "It should be pull-off-the-bone tender when we take it out tomorrow."

Rachel baked the cakes first thing after breakfast and left them cooling while she made the frosting. Aunt Ivy had borrowed some extra pots, pans, plates, and silverware for the occasion.

Her helper came at eight thirty. Annie was a pretty colored girl of eighteen who had been married for two years. Annie stayed quiet around Rachel at first, but Rachel liked her. She worked hard and did each task quickly and well.

She began by washing up the dirty dishes from breakfast and baking. Then, she started peeling potatoes. By this time, she realized Rachel would treat her well, and she began chatting away while she worked. Rachel didn't mind. It made the time pass faster and the chores go easier.

Uncle Sam and Patrick set up the tables outside. They covered one of the tables with a clean tarp for the roasted pork. Aunt Ivy put white sheets and then tablecloths to accent them on the others.

Annie shelled the peas while Rachel made the potato salad. They had everything ready to set out at eleven thirty. The invitations said noon, but of course, some started arriving early.

Uncle Sam and Patrick stood behind the roasted hog to serve it. Rachel would be behind the table with the other food and help, but the guests would serve themselves. Annie put on a white apron and would be at the beverage table to pour the drinks—apple cider, milk, water, or coffee.

Aunt Ivy and Hope planned to greet the guests and start them through the line. Birthday presents would be piled on the ground to be opened later.

Twelve of the students from Hope's class came, including Charles and George.

Blanche also came, and she brought Axel and Chance. "I knew you wouldn't mind," she said. "Chance has come calling on me several times, and Axel comes when I find him a partner."

Rachel didn't say anything, but she wanted to tell Blanche how much she minded. She hated how Axel watched her so closely. She hoped he would behave.

When everyone had gone through the food lines once, the servers left the tables to eat themselves. Everyone could serve themselves on seconds.

Patrick picked up one of the extra quilts Aunt Ivy had brought out for those who might forget to bring theirs. He led Rachel over to a spot between two trees in the shade, and they ate.

The pork was succulent and delicious, just as Uncle Sam had hoped. Rachel liked the faint smoky taste and the sauce too.

"Patrick, I want to thank you for your help with mathematics," Charles said as he stood before them with his food. "I almost hate to see school end."

"You're very welcome," Patrick told him. "Come join us."

"Your food is wonderful, Rachel," Patrick said as Charles sat down. "I've never eaten peas in a white sauce like this, and how did you make this potato dish?"

"I'm glad you like everything. The potato salad is a German dish, and it's easy to make, all except the mayonnaise dressing. It's often hard to get the right consistency and still have it taste as it should. This time, it did as it was supposed to, though."

"I'll say."

"I believe this is the best food I've ever had," Charles said. "Did you learn to cook from your mother?"

"Yes, and she and I like to try new recipes too."

"Well, here I find you with your cousin again." Axel stood before them.

Rachel frowned at the interruption. "My cousin treats me better than anyone else."

"I see you're getting more like Blanche and have a following." Axel looked at Patrick and Charles.

"These are just two of my friends."

"Well, I'm enjoying this, and I think the birthday girl is too." Axel looked over at Hope.

After everyone had their fill, Aunt Ivy presented the special cake to Hope. Then Annie came back out, and she and Aunt Ivy served the cake.

Charles got up to get some first. "Can I bring you a piece, Miss Rachel?" he asked.

"No thank you, Charles. I've eaten too much already. I'll pass this time."

"Well, I'm going to try some." Patrick jumped up and walked to the serving table with Charles.

Blanche must have been waiting to get Rachel alone. "I'm going to tell Chance good-bye tonight," she whispered. "Axel let it slip that Chance is already married. Can you believe the cad?"

"I'm surprised you're here with him, then."

"Oh, he's a good escort, and I never go to a party alone. Besides, Hope said there would be dancing, and Chance and Axel are excellent dancers."

"Maybe you could start seeing Axel, or is he married too?"

"Oh no, Axel's not married, but I've already been courted by him. I never go back to an old beau. There's too many fish in the sea."

Patrick and Charles came back, and Blanche moved off.

"What did Blanche want?" Patrick asked.

"She was sharing some of her courting details with me, but I can't understand why. I'm surprised she feels she can confide in me."

Patrick looked thoughtful. "Perhaps she thinks you'll eventually come around and do what she wants."

"Everyone thinks Blanche is so pretty, but I think you are much prettier, Miss Rachel. And nicer too," Charles said quietly.

Patrick nodded. "I agree with you there."

Hope began to open her pile of gifts. Rachel stayed seated, glad for the chance to be off her feet before the dancing began. She'd been standing most of the day.

Rachel didn't pay attention to what most people had given Hope, but Blanche brought the nicest gift—a beautiful gold locket on a delicate gold chain. Axel gave her a bottle of perfume.

After all the presents were opened, several people helped the family take the leftover food into the kitchen. Most of what Rachel had cooked had been eaten, but there was still some pork left.

Annie already had all the pots and most of the plates washed, and she started consolidating the food and washing the empty serving pieces. She'd been a tremendous help, and Rachel wondered how she'd have even gotten all the work done without her.

When the tables had been put away, the musicians started tuning up for the dancing. Rachel had been to only a few events in Salisbury where there'd been dancing, but Mama and Papa had taught her the dances they knew.

Rachel hadn't realized how much she'd missed Papa's fiddle playing until the group started playing. The music sent her spirit dancing, even before her first partner.

"Save the waltzes for me unless you're willing for your partner to hold you too close," Patrick whispered in her ear.

She smiled and nodded.

The first dance was a country reel, and Rachel wasn't familiar with it, but when Charles rushed up and asked her to dance, she agreed. She found it wasn't hard. Patrick sat and watched.

George danced with her next, and Patrick danced with Hope. Because of the type of dance, she and Patrick were partnered for some of the moves. He smiled at her and moved expertly around her.

The next dance sounded like a waltz, and Axel asked her to dance. She told him she had already promised the dance, and Patrick appeared at her side. She found it easy to follow his lead. She knew the waltz best, so she just relaxed in Patrick's arms and flowed with the music wherever he led. The dance ended way too soon. She could have continued that dance forever.

Axel asked for the next dance, and since it was a reel, she went. Patrick danced with Aunt Ivy, then moved to Rachel through parts of the dance.

The lead musician called "ladies' choice" for the next dance. Rachel had never heard of this. She moved toward Patrick, but Blanche beat her to him. Rachel asked Uncle Sam to dance.

Blanche tried to move very close to Patrick in the waltz, but he would step back each time. Finally, he held her firmly away from him, and they finished the dance.

Patrick frowned. "I should have told Blanche no, but she took me by surprise, and I didn't know it would be a waltz. If there's another ladies' choice, I'll be promised to dance with you, unless it's Mother or Hope that asks."

Rachel looked around. "I'm ready to sit this one out. I need a break."

"I'll get us some cider." Patrick hurried to the beverage table. "You dance well," he told her as they sat on the quilt and sipped their cider.

"I haven't had much practice, but I enjoy it, especially with a good partner like you."

"We do move together in harmony, don't we? We dance like we talk, easily and in accord." He winked at her, and she couldn't help but smile.

Rachel accepted dances for the reels from whomever asked her, but she only danced the waltzes with Patrick. She wished there'd been more than the five of them.

The party ended and everyone left. By the comments given, it had been a huge success.

Annie had washed all the dishes, and the kitchen sparkled. Uncle Sam would take her home and pay her. Rachel slipped her five extra dollars and hugged her. The huge tip might be more than she'd made working, but the girl had been worth her weight in gold.

"Are you tired, Rachel?" Patrick asked as they sat in the parlor to await Uncle Sam's return, so they could hold their family devotion.

"Yes, but it's a happy tired. Everything went so well, and I had a good time."


Mrs. Furr invited Aunt Ivy and Rachel to tea Sunday afternoon at three. Blanche greeted them at the door, but if Mr. Furr was around, he stayed hidden.

"I've heard nothing but rave reviews about Hope's birthday party," Mrs. Furr said. "Who did your cooking? I heard how exceptional the food tasted."

Aunt Ivy looked at Rachel. "Rachel did all the cooking, except for the roast. She's much better than anyone we could hire, although I don't know how she accomplished all she did."

"You did hire Annie to help," Rachel added.

"How many people did you have there?" Mrs. Furr asked.

Aunt Ivy thought a moment. "I think Sam said about thirty-four, not counting the musicians or help."

"I thought it was the most fun of anything that's been held around here in a long time," Blanche said. "We really must hold an event here, Mother. I think a ball would be fun."

"We'll see, dear. Maybe we can do something in the winter. It's soon going to be too hot to do much dressing up and dancing."

Blanche pouted. "It's never too hot for dancing."

Mrs. Furr served tea, tiny pieces of bread and ham, and cookies. Blanche poured and served the tea. Rachel thought the bread and ham could have used some of her mayonnaise dressing to keep it from tasting so dry.

On the last tutoring session, Charles brought Rachel and Patrick gifts. They were beautiful detailed wood carvings. He gave Patrick a raccoon and Rachel a rabbit.

"Did you carve these?" Rachel asked in awe.

"Yes, I made them for you to show my appreciation."

"You're very talented," Patrick said, "but you didn't need to give me anything. I enjoyed helping you. You learned quickly and were easy to teach."

"I didn't do anything," Rachel said.

Charles shyly looked down. "You were kind, found me a tutor, and it made me happy just to see you."

"You're a very special person," Rachel told him. "You wait and the right girl for you will come along." He looked away but nodded.

# CHAPTER EIGHT

# Gatherings

"DID YOU HEAR THE NEWS?" Uncle Sam asked after church one Sunday. "Deputy Marshall Fenton of Wadesboro arrested a W. G. Kennedy for manufacturing counterfeit silver money from pewter. His nephew was arrested for passing the bogus money. Some men from Stanly County testified they'd received counterfeit money from Kennedy."

"Between the moonshining, bootlegging, and counterfeiting, what is this area coming to?" Aunt Ivy said.

Uncle Sam frowned. "Not much good, that's for sure. It's hard to know who to trust nowadays."

In June it felt hotter than anything Rachel remembered, and she knew July and August could be worse. They set out tubs of water in the sun so they could take a warm bath after supper, and sometimes the water became almost too hot.

Uncle Sam enclosed an area to one side of the back porch, and they used it to take a bath in the summer. He said he planned to put a little stove in it sometime, but he hadn't got around to it yet.

Rachel wanted to go to the creek to bathe and cool off, but she couldn't get Hope to go with her. Hope didn't like the outside, and neither did Aunt Ivy, but they'd told her to not venture out alone.

She did manage to talk Patrick and Sammy into going wading in the creek after supper. "That was refreshing," Rachel said as she walked up to Patrick and Sammy. "I feel better." She'd stayed in her own section of creek, so there would be no question of impropriety when she held her hem up.

———————————

Patrick looked up at Rachel from his seat on a log. The bottom of her dress had gotten wet and clung to her, as if it wanted to hold her tightly too. Her hair had come loose, and tendrils swayed when she moved or a breeze picked them up.

Did she have no idea how alluring she was? He knew she didn't. He looked away. He had no business staring at her like that.

"I appreciate you two coming to the creek with me," she said. "I wanted to come earlier, but Aunt Ivy said I shouldn't come alone."

"I'm glad you waited for me. You shouldn't come alone, especially with all this talk about criminal activity and so many strangers around." Would she know the stranger meant men like Axel?

After Patrick and Sammy walked Rachel to the house, they turned and went back to the creek for a bath. Sammy had a good time playing in the water and splashing Patrick. Rachel had been right. It was refreshing. Strange how his thoughts seemed to always double back to Rachel.

"You like Rachel, don't you, Patrick?" Sammy asked him.

"Certainly I like Rachel. She's our cousin. Don't you like her?"

"Yeah, but I mean you re-al-ly like her, don't you?"

"Yes, I really like her." Patrick laughed. "What makes you ask?"

"I've seen how you look at her and how you act with her. I think she likes you too."

Patrick got out, dried off, and got dressed. He'd had more than enough of Sammy's inquisition. Apparently, Patrick hadn't done a good job of disguising his feelings if Sammy had picked up on them so easily. Did the others suspect how deep his feelings went for Rachel? No, his parents would have had a talk with him if they suspected. Hope would have blabbed it out.

It had been hard for him not to say something to Rachel himself. Their relationship was so open and honest, he had to watch himself. His natural tendency would be to tell her everything. He hated to keep any secret from her, but this one had to stay hidden unless, by some miracle, she told him she loved him first. That would not likely happen. He wanted to keep their special friendship, even if he couldn't have anything more. He would try his best to do nothing to jeopardize that.

He'd bombarded God with prayers for the situation. He didn't ask God to give him Rachel. He asked for God's will to be done in the matter, and for God to help him live with whatever He had planned. He could wait patiently, because he had Rachel's friendship. Whatever happened, he wanted her to be happy.

So far, she wasn't interested in anyone else. He'd really need God's strength and help if that ever happened. He wasn't sure what he'd do if she married someone else. He'd face that nightmare when it came.

He tried not to imagine what it would be like to be married to her. She remained so far beyond his grasp right now, it didn't seem possible. First, he would need to feel God's blessing. He would never go against his heavenly Father. Next, Rachel would have to fall in love with him, because he knew that was the only way she would ever marry anyone. Then, they would have to get their parents' approval. Rachel would never defy her mother and father. She loved and respected them too much. The only necessary element already in place was his love for her.

He wished he could hope, but he dared not. He wished he could see a joyous future, but he couldn't. Well, worrying himself into a hole deep enough to bury him standing up wouldn't help anything. Instead, he planned to take each moment with Rachel as a gift. He would be happy in the present. He'd follow Jesus's teachings and let tomorrow take care of itself. He could do little else.

"Look," Sammy called out, "I'm getting all wrinkly."

"Well, I'd say it's time to come out. Let's go see if there's any of Rachel's blackberry pie left. I'm beginning to get hungry again."

---

Uncle Sam had stopped by the post office on his way to pick up supplies. He brought Rachel a letter from her parents. She suddenly realized she wasn't missing them as much as she did at first. Still, she eagerly opened the letter.

Dear Rachel,

It was so good to get your letter. We're sorry school didn't work out for you, but it is good to know we taught you well. I wish your brothers took to their studies as seriously as you did. Only Mark seems really interested.

Things are going well here at the farm. Aaron planted an extra field of corn this year. They almost ran out of cornmeal last year.

When we left there, your father and I spent the night in Albemarle. We were so emotionally shaken by leaving you, neither of us felt like traveling on. It helped to spend some time with just the two of us. Luke has always known what to say and do to make me feel better, and I hope I do the same for him.

We spent only three days in Salisbury. Luke needed to get home, so we could finish the planting. Your grandfather and

Clara are well. Both of them are moving more slowly than they used to, but they're still the same caring people.

I hope when you marry, Rachel, you can find a love like mine and Luke's. I know it's what you said you are looking for. It's what I pray for too. Besides our deep love, he and I are so much more together than we are as individuals.

It would be quite amazing, when you think about it. Granny had two strong loves in her life, Edgar and Hawk. Your grandfather loved Luke's mother, Sarah, that completely, and then came Luke's and mine. If you can do as well, that would make four generations for us. What blessings!

We miss you terribly. If there wasn't so much to do on the farm when we got back, we may have turned around and come back for you. You were almost my constant companion, as we did our work. You also carried part of my workload, and I have twice as much to do without you. I feel I've left a piece of me in Stanly County, and I have. Yet, I am so proud of the woman you've become. Not only are you attractive, but you have a deep faith, you're kind and caring, mature and responsible, and you have plenty of intelligence and talents. If I could order a daughter from God, she would be just like you.

Although personally I hate the idea, I know you'll probably leave us to live the life God has for you. Above my own selfishness, I want your happiness. I want you to find great love, marry, and have a family of your own. I want you to have a life as blessed with love as mine has been.

Know we'll always love and cherish you. Your papa sends his hugs, kisses, and love. Write and tell me what's happening in your life. Be the open and honest daughter, you've always been, even if we can't be there in person.

Love you forever,

Mama and Papa

Rachel had tears in her eyes when she finished reading the letter. Her mother and father were so special, not just as parents, but also as people—God's people. She felt blessed to have such parents, where she'd grow up in a household filled with love and knew of Jesus from her earliest memory. She heard Patrick come in, and she hurried down to share her letter with him.

Rachel wrote her parents back as soon as she had the time. She decided to tell them about Blanche and Axel.

Dear Mama and Papa,

I was so happy to get your letter. I've missed you too. I don't think I told you that I was so devastated just after you left that Patrick took me for a walk to keep me from feeling too sorry for myself.

Patrick has been wonderful. I think he's picked up taking care of me and protecting me, just as he did when he was there and we were children. He's like my big brother and best friend, all rolled into one.

One of the young women, Blanche Furr, has been both a friend and an adversary to me. She's been cordial, but she has her own agenda and is determined to have her way. Patrick has helped me to deal with her, and things haven't gotten out of hand.

She did set me up to see a friend of hers, Axel Jones, at her house with her parents there. Blanche was seeing Axel's friend at the time. It was not a successful meeting. Axel wanted to be too forward in his speech, and he expected me to let him take me home alone. I told him his forwardness offended me, and thankfully, Mr. Furr insisted on taking me home. Axel rode with us, but I'll not see him again. I sense a wild side to him that I don't trust. I don't really trust Blanche, either.

Please know you've taught me well, and I will handle myself responsibly. Uncle Sam, Aunt Ivy, and Patrick are taking good care of me. I wish Hope and I had a closer relationship, but perhaps that will come in time. At least she's not unfriendly.

Hope had a birthday celebration, and about thirty-four guests came. Uncle Sam and Patrick roasted a small hog in a pit they dug. I'd never seen this done before. Have you, Mama? Perhaps you remember it from growing up on the plantation.

I cooked the rest of the food for the affair, but Uncle Sam hired a girl to help me with the preparations and clean-up. She was a great help too. Everyone seemed to enjoy the food and kept complimenting me on it. You've also done a good job of teaching me to cook, Mama.

After the meal and after Hope opened her many presents, we had a dance. The musicians made me realize how much I've missed hearing Papa play his fiddle. I danced almost every dance with different people. It was fun.

Tell the boys, I send them my love, and tell the Carters "Hello" for me. I miss all of you, but I'm glad I came.

Mama and Papa, I love you so much. No girl could ask for better parents. Although we've lived pretty isolated there, you've given me all the skills I've needed to fit in here. Keep writing me. I love to get your letters.

Deep love and hugs,

Rachel

The Furrs invited them to a Fourth of July Celebration on Friday. It would be a large formal dinner with Blanche doing a piano recital afterwards. Ivy and Hope wanted to go, but none of the others did.

"Why don't you and Hope go?" Uncle Sam asked his wife. "You can either take the wagon or ride horses, whichever you'd prefer."

"We'll take a wagon, since we'll have to dress up, but I'd really like for you to go too, Sam."

"I'll go for you, if you really want me to. Patrick, Sammy, and Rachel can go fishing or something."

"I guess just Hope and I can go, but what will I tell them?"

"Tell them we had other plans, or tell them we had things to do around the farm. Either is true."

Friday, Rachel packed the four of them a picnic dinner, and they went south to fish on the Rocky River.

"Rachel can really fish," Sammy told his father. "She caught more fish than anyone when we went fishing before. She even baits her own hook."

Uncle Sam laughed. "I'm glad. I'd like to come home with a lot of fish to eat."

"Me too," Sammy said.

They got to the river, unpacked their things, and began to fish. Uncle Sam and Sammy stayed upstream, and Rachel and Patrick went down a little ways, dropped their lines, and sat down.

"I'm glad you didn't want to go to the Furrs'," Patrick told her.

"Would you have gone with me if I had?"

"Yes. I would have gone to protect you from Blanche's new scheme, whatever that might be."

Rachel smiled. Patrick seemed to always be trying to make things easier for her. "That's the main reason I didn't go. I didn't appreciate Blanche trying to match me up with a man like Axel. Besides, a formal dinner and piano recital sounded rather dull. I'd much prefer to be fishing."

"I like that about you, and I like the fact you don't try to impress others. You're just you—honest, kind, smart, responsible, and hardworking."

"Well, you have many admirable qualities too. I can't figure out why you aren't already married."

"I've told you. I'm waiting for the right one, the one God has for me."

"I think all of us want that."

Uncle Sam and Sammy still hadn't caught anything, but Rachel and Patrick had caught three each. The two Sams decided they needed to move downstream.

They washed their hands and stopped to eat dinner. They'd worked up an appetite, and the food quickly disappeared.

Uncle Sam looked at her. "Sometimes I feel as if we're working you too hard, Rachel, but we sure enjoy your cooking."

"Not at all. I'm used to working at home, and I'm glad you like the food. I like to cook."

"That reminds me of something I've been meaning to ask you, Papa," Patrick said. "Do you think we could get Annie to come over and help on wash days? That would save Mama and Rachel a lot of backbreaking work."

"That's a wonderful idea. I don't know why I didn't think of it. I'll go ask Annie tomorrow."

Patrick looked at Rachel and smiled. Sometimes he seemed like her guardian angel.

They each caught one fish after the picnic, but then the fish seemed to quit biting.

Uncle Sam got up and began packing up their things. "Let's go see if Ivy and Hope are home yet. We can clean these fish, and Rachel can fix them for supper."

"What are you going to have with them?" Sammy asked.

"Maybe slaw, fried potatoes, cornbread, and blackberry cobbler."

"M-m-m-m, that sounds good."

That Sunday, Blanche was all excited. "A new place has just opened again south of here. Rocky River Springs has healing mineral waters. Axel, Chance, and J. T. went. If Chance hadn't turned out to be such a cheat, I would have gone with them, even if I had to sneak off. Axel said it was a good place to relax and socialize, and he declares the water made him feel better. I just have to try it. Will you go with me, Rachel?"

"I don't know. Do people bathe in the waters? Are there separate facilities for men and women?"

"No, silly. You drink the water. Let's take our families and go. The resort is supposed to be really nice, and they have special events scheduled too."

"I'm not sure I'm interested. I don't think any water can be better or healthier than our mountain springs at home."

"I'd like to go," Hope stated. She'd overheard the conversation.

The families talked, and Aunt Ivy and Hope decided to go with the Furrs. Uncle Sam, Patrick, and Rachel weren't interested and planned to stay home. Mr. Furr agreed to drive the women.

When Aunt Ivy and Hope returned, they had mixed feelings about the day. They had enjoyed the resort, but the water didn't impress them.

"It was just regular water, as far as I could tell," Aunt Ivy said.

"Give it a chance, Mama." Hope told her, "The healing may not happen immediately, and maybe it takes more than one glassful."

Aunt Ivy looked disgusted. "Well, that's not likely to happen. I have no intention of going back soon."

Rachel wondered what her mother would think of the water, since it was supposed to promote healing. Her mother knew a lot about healing. Rachel was happy she'd decided not to go, however. The springs did not sound worth Blanche's company to her.

"Why did you break up with Axel?" Hope asked Rachel in bed that night.

Rachel and Patrick's friendship had grown deep and strong, but Hope still remained distant most of the time. Rarely did she want to talk like girls usually did.

"I didn't really break up with him, because we weren't courting. I went to dinner at Blanche's, and he was there. He became too forward and improper. There's an untamed quality about him that makes him too unpredictable. I couldn't see any kind of future with him, unless it was one of misery. Why do you ask?"

"I danced with him a couple of times at my birthday celebration, and he seemed nice."

"'Nice' is not a term I would use to describe Axel Jones. I'm afraid he'd expect any woman he courted to act in a brazen, wanton way."

Hope changed the subject. "Do you know who is courting Blanche now?"

"I don't know of anyone special. I think she still has plenty of admirers around her, but I don't think any one man's courting her."

"She's been nicer to me than usual, and some of her former beaus have been more attentive too. I like it."

"You should take your time, Hope. Don't rush things."

"I'm fifteen now. That's old enough, don't you think?"

Rachel simply answered, "Good night."

# CHAPTER NINE

# Rendezvous

HOPE GOT UP BEFORE RACHEL the next morning. When Rachel went to make the bed, a note fell from underneath Hope's pillow. Rachel first started to put it back. She didn't pry into another's personal things, but something told her to read the note.

Dear Hope,

Axel wants to see you. He is quite taken with you. Why, I think the poor man is besotted, because I've never seen him so excited over a woman. He's sure you'll be more willing to let him court you than Rachel. We're both stunned by how cold she turned out to be to him, but I'm sure you'll be different.

He wants you to meet him Sunday night where the road to your farm meets Big Lick Road. He'll be there as soon as it turns dark, so sneak out as soon as everyone is asleep. He'll have you back before daylight.

You can tell me your answer when we go to Rocky River Springs Saturday. I'm so proud of your maturity. You have become quite the young woman. I think you may even rival me in a few months. Take care now.

Your friend,
Blanche

Rachel put the letter back and ran to find Patrick. Surely Hope had more sense than to do this, but they needed to make certain. Hope came in from outside and passed Rachel on the stairs.

Aunt Ivy had the coffee ready. "I thought we'd just have bread and jam this morning. It's almost too hot to cook, even this early. We're all running a little later than usual this morning too. At least you did some baking yesterday."

Rachel picked up the basket. "I'll go gather the eggs, then." She hoped she'd catch Patrick coming from his morning chores.

When she was almost to the chicken coop, she saw him come from the barn with two buckets of milk. He smiled as he drew closer.

"I need to talk with you," she said.

"Okay." His face grew serious as he set the buckets down. "What's wrong?" He stood before her.

She told him about finding the note and what it said. She saw disbelief then anger in his eyes.

"I'll need to tell Papa about this."

Rachel nodded. "We don't know if Hope plans to do it. I'm praying she said no."

"I do too, but Papa and I will watch to make sure. Let's pray about this now."

He took her hand. "Dear Lord, please be with Hope, give her wisdom, guide her, and keep her safe. If she is planning to do this foolish thing, show the family what to do to stop her and how to help her. We pray this in Jesus's name. Amen."

Patrick put a hand on her arm. "I'm so glad you found out about this and came to me. Papa's still in the barn. I'll go talk to him now."

They rode to church more subdued than usual. Rachel hadn't had a chance to talk with Patrick privately again, but she knew he'd talked with Uncle Sam, and one of them must have told Aunt

Ivy. Their long faces indicated they knew. Hope seemed lost in her own thoughts.

Sam stayed outside, but Patrick went into the church with the women. Rachel didn't see Axel.

"Hello, Patrick. How are you doing?" A handsome, well-dressed young man approached them. He had medium brown hair and hazel eyes.

"Julius, when did you get back?"

"Two weeks ago. It took longer than I expected to pack up and get everything taken care of."

"Rachel, this is Julius Clark. He's just home from college, and I guess he'll be our new lawyer in the area. Julius, this is Rachel Moretz from Watauga County. She's the daughter of Mama's half sister and is staying with us for several months."

"It's a pleasure, Miss Moretz." He seemed to assess her carefully, and the twinkle in his eyes said he liked what he saw.

"It's nice to meet you, Mr. Clark. Will you begin your practice soon?"

"I think I'll take a little time to relax and look at my options. I hope to open my practice in the fall, hopefully in September. How long do you plan to stay here?"

"We haven't decided exactly, but I'll be here through the winter, anyway."

"Good. That should give me time to get to know you better. I'll look forward to seeing you again." He nodded and went to take his seat beside a lady and gentleman, whom Rachel assumed were his parents.

Patrick seated her, Uncle Sam and the other men came in, and the service began. The message centered on giving God total control of your life. Rachel wanted God to be in control of hers, for she'd trusted and depended on Him for a long time. It was how Mama and Papa had taught her to live. She wished He would take over and make all her choices for her, but it didn't work that way. He always required she make the choices, and that could be difficult.

"Let's go for a walk," Patrick said after the dinner dishes were done.

The day had turned into a hot one. The summer made it hard for Rachel. She wasn't used to all this heat and humidity.

"Could we go in the creek?" Sammy asked.

"Not today," Patrick told him, and Sammy ran ahead.

"I can go back early, and you and he can go in the water," Rachel offered.

"No, I want to talk with you about Hope."

"What did your father say?"

"He wants to wait and catch Hope in the act, so we'll know for sure what she's planning. He also wants to scare Axel."

"He told your mother, didn't he?"

"Yes, he did, and she wanted to confront Hope right away. I think they had an argument. Did you hear them?"

Rachel shook her head. "No, I didn't. I hope this can be handled so that Hope doesn't know I read her note."

"It will if Papa has his way, which seems to be the way things are going." Patrick gave a slight smile.

"Do your parents argue often?" Rachel wanted to know. "I never remember Mama and Papa yelling at each other. If they have a disagreement, they talked it out calmly."

"My parents can be volatile, but it doesn't happen often. Mama usually begins the shouting. Papa is more pointed, which infuriates Mama at times. The disagreement explodes, they stay mad at each other for about two hours, and then they make up. I think they like the making up, because they always seem closer after that."

"I think an explosive relationship would bother me. I like my parents' way better. They stay close all the time, so they don't need anything to make them closer." Rachel looked at Patrick to try to determine how he felt.

"Their arguments use to bother me a lot when I was younger. Before they were married, Mama broke off their engagement, because she got this silly notion it would be better for Papa to marry his cousin than her. This happened just after the war. They worked things out, but it made me insecure. I was afraid they would break up again when they argued. I eventually came to realize they loved each other very much, and they always got over the arguments."

"So . . . you and Uncle Sam are going to watch Hope." Rachel wanted to make sure she knew the situation.

"Yes, actually Papa wants to go up to where Axel is and wait for Hope to come. We'll take our guns and confront him."

"I don't like it, Patrick. There's something about Axel that's dangerous. I'd feel better if you stopped Hope before she got to Axel and just left him sitting there all night waiting for her."

"I'll suggest that to Papa, but it's really up to him. Don't worry, we'll be fine either way." He must have noticed the look on her face. "We'll be careful, and we'll trust in God to protect us. Nothing bad will happen to us."

How could Patrick know that? Rachel still didn't like it, but she could do nothing more at this point. Patrick said he would suggest they meet Hope before she got to Axel. Like Patrick said, it would be up to his father.

"I'll be praying for you until you are home safely," she told him.

"That's bound to help." He gave her a reassuring smile.

They walked in silence for a while. They were comfortable enough with each other that they didn't need to say anything.

"Julius seemed interested in you today," Patrick finally said.

"I thought he might be. Tell me about him and his family."

"Julius did very well in school, although he was energetic and stayed in his share of trouble. His family seems to be very well off. I don't know them well, but I'd say their way of living is similar to Blanche's family. They live in the Big Lick area, but on the Albemarle side. Are you interested in him?"

"I don't know."

"The man who wins your heart will be very blessed, Rachel. Just be very careful who you give it to. Make sure he's worthy of you and will treasure you." Patrick's voice had a strange quality to it.

"Don't worry. As my best friend, you'll have a hand in helping me decide. I won't be hasty or irresponsible. It didn't take me long at all to know Axel wasn't for me."

"You did come to that conclusion right away, and I thank God for it." He gave her a big smile.

"Don't you trust me to do what's best?"

He sighed. "That's what I'm counting on."

They called to Sammy and turned to go back to the house The time passed much too fast when she was with Patrick. She just hoped tonight would go as quickly, but she had the feeling it would be a long night.

Rachel intentionally slowed her breathing as she lay in bed pretending to be asleep. She'd been praying off and on since she'd come to bed.

Hope lay beside her, but Rachel could tell she wasn't asleep. Rachel hoped Hope had told Blanche she wouldn't meet Axel. That would make everything so much simpler.

She knew Patrick and Uncle Sam would be waiting outside. She didn't know if they'd be hidden close to Axel or closer to the house. She hoped the latter, but Patrick hadn't had a chance to let her know.

She felt Hope slowly move to a sitting position beside her. The moonlight was bright as it glowed through the window and illuminated the room, but Rachel didn't look. She heard her cousin quietly getting dressed. Rachel's heart beat hard.

Hope eased open the door and moved out. Rachel heard her taking the stairs as lightly as possible, but there were still a few creaks. When she heard the front door close softly, Rachel got up and dressed too. Then, she knelt beside the bed and prayed.

She didn't know how long it had been before she heard the front door open and close and noise below followed by Hope crying. She went to see what had happened and if everyone was okay. She heard Aunt Ivy behind her.

"Sit." Uncle Sam's stern voice sounded angry.

As far as she could see, Patrick looked fine but worried. His eyes found hers, and she longed to run to him but held herself back.

"What happened?" Aunt Ivy asked.

"We intercepted her halfway to the main road. She hurried toward Axel. I haven't questioned her yet. I brought her back here first, so you could hear too."

"What in the world were you thinking, Hope?" Aunt Ivy asked. "I can't believe you would do such a stupid thing."

"You did something similar before you were married." Hope's voice shook, but somehow she still managed to sound defiant.

"What I did was stupid too, but I thought Sam and I would be married right away. Were you trying to elope?"

"No, I was just wanting to be with Axel."

"And what did you think you would do?" Uncle Sam asked.

"Ride somewhere, talk, get to know him better."

"You'd certainly get to know him better," Aunt Ivy said. "You'd have ended up being intimate enough to get with child."

"Let's all take a seat." Patrick motioned Rachel to the sofa and sat down beside her.

Aunt Ivy sat down also. Uncle Sam and Hope had already taken a seat.

"How did you find me out?" Hope asked.

"That's not the question here," Uncle Sam said. "The question is what we're going do about you. Who set this up for you? I know you've not had that much contact with Axel."

"No one."

"You're lying, Hope," Aunt Ivy said. "I can see it in your eyes. Now who helped you? Was it Blanche?"

Hope nodded.

"How did she tell you about this?" Uncle Sam asked.

"She wrote me a note."

"Go get the note," Uncle Sam said.

"I don't have it."

"Hope." Aunt Ivy's tone said she knew Hope wasn't being truthful.

"It's in my room."

"Go get it," Uncle Sam repeated. When Hope had left, he asked his wife, "What are we going to do with her?"

Rachel looked at the clock. It was one o'clock.

Aunt Ivy rubbed her face. "I'm going to have a long talk with her in the morning, but I'll go along with whatever punishment you decide."

"Here." Hope came back and handed the note to her father. "What's going to happen to Axel?"

"To start with, he's going to sit out there for the most of the night wondering when you're coming and then figuring out you're not. I liked the idea when Patrick suggested it. I wanted to meet him with guns, but this will be better because it'll prolong his discomfort, and none of us will be in danger."

Hope wiped her tear-stained eyes.

"Your mom and I are going to have to consider what your punishment will be. You go on to bed and get some sleep, but I want you to know how disappointed I am in you right now. We've brought you up better than this. You've sneaked out at night to meet a man, lied, and been immature and irresponsible. You're lucky we did catch you, because only God knows what would have happened to you if you'd succeeded. I know you'd have had a miserable, horrible night."

"I don't think I can sleep now." Hope started crying again.

"Then I suggest you lay there and think about what you've done and the possible consequences. Go on now."

Hope did as she was told. Aunt Ivy followed her.

"I'm glad no one was hurt," Rachel said.

"Thank you, Rachel," Uncle Sam whispered. "Thank you for everything. Without you, all this would have ended very differently."

Rachel looked at Patrick. "When do you think Axel will give up and leave?"

"I don't know." Patrick looked half amused. "Maybe in a couple of hours. Maybe at first light."

"Well, I'm going to bed," Uncle Sam said. "Are you two coming?"

"In just a minute," Patrick said.

He watched his father climb the steps, then looked at Rachel. He looked tired.

"That was a good idea you had to meet Hope halfway down the road and leave Axel waiting. Papa liked it too."

"I'm glad. I didn't want a violent confrontation. I don't think Axel would scare easily, and, even if he did, he'd likely try to get revenge."

"You don't have a very high opinion of the man, do you? You knew he wasn't to be trusted the first time you spent any time with him. To have grown up as isolated as you have, you have a remarkable ability to judge a person's true character."

"I'm not sure I should take the credit. I think it might be God directing me, and He'll do it for any of His children, if we'll just stop to listen."

Patrick gave her a melting look, as if he wanted to take her in his arms, and she would have liked that. A hug would feel good right now. She must be more tired than she thought.

"I guess we'd better try to get a little sleep," Patrick finally said. "Are you ready to go up?"

"I think I'll give Hope a little more time to get to sleep first. You go ahead."

"Good night, Rachel."

"Good night, Patrick. Sleep well."

When the house grew quiet, Rachel lay down on the sofa. She didn't want to take the chance of having to answer any of Hope's questions tonight. It wouldn't be long before time to get up anyway.

The next morning after everyone had finished eating, Uncle Sam told Hope, "For now, you are not to go anywhere alone. For example, at a store or in church, you are to stay right beside one of us. You're not to even talk with anyone without family with you."

"I'm going into town this morning," he continued. "I have some business to take care of, and I'll see if Annie will come to help out on laundry day. Hope, I want you to do more around the house too. Rachel has ended up doing too much, because you gladly let her and your mother take care of most of the chores. I want to see the work divided equally three ways. I want you to wash the dishes now. Then, you will help hoe the garden, gather the vegetables, pick blackberries, or whatever is being done. If you think you're old enough to be courted, you are old enough to pull your weight around here. Do you understand?"

"Yes, sir."

"We'll talk more later."

Uncle Sam was gone all morning. He came in just as Rachel finished putting dinner on the table. "Annie said she can't come on Mondays, but if you can make Tuesdays washday, she'll be here. She said she'd also be glad to help with anything else you needed, if she finished the laundry early."

They ate dinner and the two men went out to mend some fences. Hope helped more than usual, but she stayed quiet and sullen. The day moved at a snail's pace.

On Tuesday, Patrick helped carry the first tubs of water, and Annie washed clothes until noon. Rachel insisted Annie eat dinner with them, which seemed to surprise her. She remained quiet through most of the meal, but she ate plenty.

"Dis be really good, Miss Rachel," Annie said. "Ya sho' is a good cook. Now, I'll jus' wash des dishes fo' y'all."

Due to Annie's efficiency, Rachel found she wasn't as tired at the end of the day as usual, although she still found the heat oppressive and draining. She walked outside to sit on the porch and see if she could enjoy an evening breeze. The crickets serenaded and the stars beckoned. This place had begun to feel more like home.

The rest of the week was filled with work. The women canned vegetables from the garden and made blackberry jam, besides tending to other daily tasks. Hope did her share of the work. By Sunday, they were all ready for a day of rest.

Julius Clark came up to her and Patrick as they walked into the church.

He smiled warmly. "I am glad to see you again. How was your week?"

"Busy," Rachel said. "We've been canning all week."

"Then how about doing something different and coming home with me for dinner? My parents said they'd love to have you."

"I appreciate the invitation, Mr. Clark, but I'd prefer not to go, unless another family member comes with me."

"That would be fine." He looked puzzled. "Bring anyone you'd like."

"Let's make it another time, please. I've already planned for dinner today."

"Shall we say next Sunday then?"

"Very well, if Patrick would accompany me, and my aunt and uncle approves, that will be fine."

"Sure, I'll come if you want me to," Patrick said.

Julius looked surprised. "Let's go ask your aunt now, and I'll introduce you to my parents."

Aunt Ivy gave her permission. Mr. and Mrs. Clark were cordial, but for some reason, Rachel wasn't excited about going to their house for dinner. After this week, she felt drained emotionally and physically. No social engagement sounded particularly inviting.

"Are you sure you want me tagging along with you next Sunday?" Patrick asked when they sat down.

"I'm sure. I don't want to end up in another situation like I did at Blanche's. Do you mind going?"

"No, I don't mind."

After the service, Blanche tried her best to get Hope alone to talk with her. Aunt Ivy and Uncle Sam made sure that didn't happen.

"I talked with Blanche's father Monday," Uncle Sam said at the dinner table. "I showed him the note Blanche had written Hope. He was understandably upset. I don't know how he plans to handle it, but I have a feeling he's been too lenient on his daughter. That's probably part of her problem."

"Papa, did you have to tell on her?" Hope asked.

"Yes, I did. What she did was very wrong. I also heard some startling rumors at church today. Some of the men say J. T. Jackson is really the outlaw Jesse James. They say Merriman Little and Chance Daniels used to be part of the outlaw's gang, and they may still be on occasion. Axel Jones came here to visit Merriman with Jesse, so they figure he's riding with Jesse now."

"What would Jesse James be doing in Stanly County?" Aunt Ivy asked.

"Besides visiting his old friend, some think he may be either involved in the moonshining and counterfeiting rings or is thinking about getting involved."

"What do you think, Rachel?" Aunt Ivy asked. "You probably know Axel better than any of us. Do you think he could be mixed up with a gang of outlaws?"

"I'd hate to think so, but he might. I did sense a wild side to him. Of course, I don't really know."

Aunt Ivy gave Hope a pointed look. "See what kind of man you were about to sneak out with, Hope."

Hope didn't say anything, but she looked rather pale. Rachel sure hoped Hope was beginning to see the seriousness of what she'd almost done.

# CHAPTER TEN

# Julius

SUNDAY, PATRICK AND RACHEL DROVE to the Clark home instead of riding with the Clarks. This would enable them to leave at their convenience, rather than someone else's.

When they got there, they saw Julius help Blanche out of his family's coach. Patrick and Rachel looked at each other.

"What do you think she's up to now?" Rachel asked.

"I don't know, but I'm guessing Julius is trying to even up the couples. That would mean Blanche has been invited for me. Why do I feel like I'm being fed to the lions?"

Patrick gave a resigned smile, but Rachel didn't feel like smiling. She didn't appreciate the idea at all and wondered why it bothered her so much. She just didn't like being manipulated like this, she decided.

The dinner went better than Rachel had feared. Mr. and Mrs. Clark were gracious hosts, and Blanche tried to be on her best behavior. Rachel didn't see her flirt with either Patrick or Julius.

The Clark home was lovely. Although larger than Blanche's, it wasn't as ostentatious. Everything spoke of wealth, class, and good taste.

The food tasted better too. It was served by colored servants, and Rachel guessed they had a full-time cook.

Julius turned on the charm. He gave Rachel almost his full attention and talked with her more than anyone else.

"Let's stroll in the garden before we sit down," Julius suggested after they'd eaten.

The garden turned out to be a true English garden, larger than the Furrs'. Tall hedges bordered it on four sides, and each side had an entranceway.

Rachel hesitated, because they couldn't be seen from the house, but then she remembered Patrick would be close by. Julius and Axel were two different people, she reminded herself.

Julius crooked his arm for her to take hold of. "I'm so glad you agreed to come. Since the day we met, I haven't been able to get you off my mind. This is such a small place, there's not many chances for the unmarried people to get together, except at homes. Otherwise, church is about it."

"Are you planning to practice law in Big Lick?"

He shook his head. "Probably not. I've been considering Albemarle, but I'm open to a new place too."

"Are you enjoying being home?"

"I am, although at first I was at loose ends by not having to study. I've recently been reading for pleasure, however."

"I like to read too. My parents taught me at home. They encouraged me to read, and we'd discuss the books. Of course, we did most of this in the winters, when we had more free time on the farm."

"I imagine the winters can be quite rough in the mountains."

"Yes, we had blizzards and were pretty snowed in sometimes."

"You'll not find it that severe here." He patted her hand.

"What are you reading now?" Rachel would like to have someone to discuss books with. She wondered if Patrick read much, maybe during the winter, when he didn't have to work so hard.

"I'm reading *Tom Sawyer* by Mark Twain right now. It's light reading and different from the law books I've had to read."

"I've read *Tom Sawyer*. I found it to be an interesting story." Rachel heard the excitement her voice held. She did love books.

"Oh, good. Perhaps you'll discuss it with me when I finish."

She smiled up at him. "I'd like that."

"Ah, I've finally got a smile out of you. You know, I have another novel you might enjoy. It's *Alice Lorraine* by Blackmore. It's set in Sussex and Spain during the Napoleonic Wars. It tells of Alice, along with her brother, trying to save her family from ruin. I started it, but didn't much care for the book. I think a woman might find it more enjoyable. Would you like to borrow it?"

"I would, but I may not have time to read it for a while. We're awfully busy at the farm now."

"You can keep it as long as you like."

"Have you read any books by Christian Reid?"

Julius thought for a moment and then shook his head. "No, what's he written?"

"It's a 'she.' Her real name is Frances Fisher, and she's from Salisbury. I learned of her through my grandfather, who's a doctor there. She's probably more read by women, but you might like *A Daughter of Bohemia.* I think it's her best. I'm sorry, my copy is in Watauga County, so I can't offer for you to borrow it."

"That's okay, I'll get a copy, and we'll discuss it too. I don't know of another person around Big Lick with whom I might be able to discuss books, unless it's Patrick, and I'd much rather discuss them with you."

Rachel heard Patrick and Blanche laughing together somewhere in the garden. They sounded as if they were having a good time, and she wondered what they were saying. Rachel liked the visit too. Julius had been the perfect gentleman, and she looked forward to discussing the books with him.

"Would you permit me to call upon you sometime?" Julius asked. "If you are agreeable, I'll ask your uncle Sunday at church."

"Yes, I'm agreeable."

After the garden, they went inside and played chess. Blanche appeared lost in the game, and Patrick won easily. The two of them then watched Rachel and Julius play.

Julius turned out to be a good player, but not as good as her mama or papa. Rachel won.

"Wow, you're really good, Rachel," Julius said. "I've never been beaten so handily before."

"I can thank my mother and father for any chess skills I might have. They're both excellent players and pretty evenly matched. I rarely beat one of them."

"Rachel and Patrick should play now," Blanche said.

"I don't think there's time for that," Julius said. "I imagine a match between them would go on for a long time."

The afternoon went faster than Rachel had expected.

When she and Patrick got ready to leave, Blanche put her hand on Patrick's arm. "I hope you had as good a time as I did today," she said softly. "I would enjoy seeing more of you. I don't think we've really had a chance to get to know each other well. I fear we both may have gotten the wrong impression."

"I did enjoy the visit, and I'll see you at church Sunday," Patrick told her.

Disappointment showed on Blanche's face, but she quickly hid it with a smile. "I'll look forward to Sunday, then."

"This went very differently than when I went to Blanche's house," Rachel told Patrick on their way home.

"You liked Julius, didn't you?"

"Yes, I did. He likes to read, and we discussed some books and made plans to discuss more."

"I like to read too, but I usually don't have time for it until the harvest is all in."

"Yes, I think Julius mentioned you liked to read. However, I think you had a good time too." She looked at him. "I heard you and Blanche laughing together in the garden."

"Blanche acted the most pleasant today I've ever seen her. I'm still not sure I trust her, though. We both know how she can be. After all, she had a part in that fiasco with Hope."

"People can change." Now, why did she say that? She certainly didn't think Blanche and Patrick were right for each other, although she did notice what a striking couple they made. However, looking attractive didn't mean a couple would be well matched.

The following week became just as busy as the last one had been. They all worked hard as the heat bore down, especially when they cooked or canned.

Thunderstorms often rolled through in the evenings. Rachel found the sound of the ones here to be much different than those in the mountains. They came more frequently here too. The best thing during the week came in the form of a letter from her parents. She opened it eagerly.

> Our dear Rachel,
>
> We were sorry to hear about your problems with Blanche and Axel, but it does sound as if you handled yourself well with no harm done. I'm glad Patrick has supported you so well. He's always been like that with you. I guess he's one of the Lord's many blessings.
>
> I'm happy everyone had fun at Hope's birthday celebration, but it sounds as if you had a lot of work to do. I'm glad you still felt like joining in on the fun. I do remember some of the plantations held pig roasts, but I don't remember that we did. Ivy may remember better than I do. She was always more caught up with the social events.

Our crops are looking good this year, and your father is pleased. He and Aaron are working hard now to get in enough wood for the winter. The twins are helping them.

Your grandfather and Clara wrote and asked me to tell you to come see them if you get a chance. They'd love it if you and any friends or family want to visit for a while. I think they miss having children around or company.

I imagine you are pretty busy with the farm and household activities, but please write us again soon. We wait with great anticipation for your letters. Know we love and miss you very much.

Love and kisses,
Mama and Papa

Soon, Sunday was there. Rachel knew Julius would probably ask Uncle Sam if he could come calling on Rachel. This would be the first time she'd ever been courted, although she knew Axel had been interested in doing so.

When they got to church, Julius stood waiting in the front yard with the men. He gave Rachel a huge smile.

After Patrick and she were seated, Julius came up to them, looking pleased. "Your uncle gave me permission to call on you this afternoon, if that's agreeable with you, say about two."

"Yes, I'll look forward it."

"As will I. Two o'clock can't get here fast enough for me."

Julius left to sit with his parents, and Rachel turned to Patrick. He looked unhappy.

"What's wrong, Patrick? Don't you approve of Julius?"

"He's okay, I guess. I just hoped you and I could get together, like we often do on Sunday afternoons. I enjoy our conversations, and we're too busy through the week now."

Her excitement fell. "I'm sorry, Patrick. I enjoy our time together too. Shall I tell Julius we need to make it another time?"

"No, that wouldn't be right, since you've already told him to come."

"I'll tell him I have other plans for next Sunday. Maybe I can invite him over to supper one night this week instead. I'll ask Aunt Ivy about it today before he comes."

"Great. Once he tastes your cooking, we'll never get rid of him." Patrick's tone sounded teasing, but his eyes looked serious.

"I thought the food at his house was just as good."

"I didn't. I don't think anyone can beat your cooking."

The service started and Rachel turned her attention to the pastor. She had to admit, she looked forward to seeing Julius again.

Rachel could tell Julius impressed Aunt Ivy and Uncle Sam too. Patrick excused himself to his room not long after Julius arrived. Maybe he wanted to take a nap.

Rachel and Julius walked around the farm but stayed within sight of the house. Julius often put his hand on her back as they walked, in much the same way Patrick sometimes did. Then, they came back and sat on the front porch.

"Do you like it better here or in the mountains?" Julius asked.

"That's a difficult question. I like the scenery and the landscape in the mountains better, but I like being here where I get to see more people."

"How isolated is your farm in Watauga County?"

"It's about a two-hour ride to Boone, and the only close neighbors are the Carters. Aaron helps Papa farm, and he married Papa's younger half sister, Maggie. Papa and he were in a Confederate prison together at Andersonville. They've been good friends ever since."

"Your father fought on the side of the Yankees, then?"

"Yes, he did. He was captured at Gettysburg."

"All my family and just about everybody around here supported the South."

"My parents never believed in slavery, so he didn't like the thought of fighting to sustain it. He went to Tennessee and volunteered when he thought he was about to be conscripted by the Confederate army."

"My family lost a lot in the war. We had a small fortune tied up in our slaves. I had several uncles and aunts who owned vast plantations. Father had been wise enough to have some gold and silver hidden away, so he's been able to come back after the war. Personally, I don't see what was wrong with slavery. Seems to me the slaves were better off then. Have you seen how the colored live around here now?"

"No, I haven't, but from what Mama's told me of plantation life, I don't think anything could be much worse than the slave cabins, if you could even call them cabins. And, the abuse could be awful too. Moses, a former slave who stayed with us during the war, had his tongue cut out for speaking up. I just can't understand such cruelty. Moses was a good man."

"Well, I can see we're not going to agree here, and it really doesn't matter anymore, since slavery is illegal now."

"We have a colored girl who comes to help on wash days and special occasions. I really like her. She's friendly, efficient, and a hard worker."

"You're new to this area, Rachel. Let me warn you not to get too friendly with the colored. It could cause trouble for you."

"What do you mean?"

"Just that people might get the wrong idea about you and treat you and your family differently, but I don't want us to disagree. Let's change the subject. I've finished *Tom Sawyer*."

They discussed the book for a while. She liked reading Mark Twain, but Julius seemed to think his writings were a little too frivolous. Rachel wondered if he saw the undying themes in Twain's stories.

She had to admit, Julius knew how to carry on an interesting conversation. She imagined he would be good in a courtroom.

Then she turned to him. "I thought I would ask you to supper Saturday night. Aunt Ivy said it would be okay."

"I'd love to come. What time?"

"Let's make it seven. Uncle Sam and Patrick like to work late on the farm, now that it doesn't get dark so early. They'll want to clean up before supper too."

"Seven o'clock is perfect. Should I come earlier, so we'll have a chance to visit longer?"

"No, make it seven. I'll be cooking earlier."

Rachel read Julius's surprised expression. He probably thought they had a cook and kitchen help like his family did. "Would you like to play another game of chess or checkers?" she asked.

"I do like to play chess, but I'm not sure I want to be beaten again." He laughed. "Oh, I brought you *Alice Lorraine* to read. Let me get it from my buggy before we go inside."

They played chess in the parlor, and Rachel won again. Rachel had remembered Blanche saying women were supposed to let the man win, and she briefly considered doing that, but it seemed deceitful. She refused to pretend to be different than she was. If losing to a woman bothered Julius, then that was his problem, not hers.

He left about four thirty, Rachel moved to the kitchen to fix supper, and everyone began to reappear.

"Julius seems like a nice young man," Aunt Ivy said at supper.

"It's not fair Rachel has a beau, and I don't," Hope grumbled.

"Rachel is older than you," Uncle Sam said, "and the way you've acted, I haven't seen enough mature or responsible behavior to warrant the privilege of a beau. You do your chores, find a young man I'll approve of, and we'll see."

"How would I find a young man with one of you always with me?"

"The same way Rachel did. You don't need to be by yourself to have someone interested in you."

# CHAPTER ELEVEN

# The Picnic

PATRICK LOOKED ACROSS THE SUPPER table at Rachel. She looked radiant. *Lord, what am I going to do?* This was what he'd been dreading. Julius had started courting Rachel, and she seemed very interested. Why had Patrick introduced them? Well, he didn't have much choice, and they would have found each other anyway in such a small church.

He had no doubt Julius would fall in love with Rachel. What man wouldn't? She was amazing . . . and wonderful. Julius would surely ask her to marry him soon. Would Rachel accept? Would she fall in love with Julius? Patrick's stomach knotted, and he suddenly lost his appetite.

"You aren't eating much," Mama told him. "Aren't you feeling well?"

"My stomach feels a little queasy. I think I'll just go up and lie down for a bit. Please excuse me."

Rachel looked concerned as he left the table. He sure wished she'd see him as more than just a friend, but he knew that wouldn't likely happen, especially now with Julius in the picture.

Patrick had to admit Julius and Rachel made a striking couple. They both had attractive good looks with their darker coloring. Julius was not a bad fellow, either. He might be a little conceited, but Patrick had liked him well enough when they were in school together. He seemed used to having his own way, but he wasn't obnoxious about it.

Patrick opened his Bible to where it fell and looked at Proverbs. He hoped the verses would comfort him. He read for a few minutes, but when he came to Proverbs 18:22, he stopped. It said, "Whoso findeth a wife findeth a good thing, and obtaineth favour of the Lord." That was not a comforting message at all, right now.

*Dear Lord, what is Thy will in all this? Why have I fallen in love with Rachel if she's not the one for me? Is there a lesson I need to learn? I've been patient and waited for her to recognize I'm the man who'd bring her love and happiness, but she still doesn't see that. Is Julius the man Thou hast chosen for Rachel? If he is, give me the ability to let her go and to find peace in Thy service without her. Lord, I'm hurting. Please help me, I pray. Amen.*

Patrick let his Bible open again. This time it opened to Romans 5. "But we glory in tribulations also: knowing that tribulation worketh patience; and patience, experience; and experience, hope. (vs. 3a-4)"

Could he dare to keep hoping? Could he go on as if nothing had happened? He guessed he had little choice, but his hope in a future with Rachel felt damaged and weak.

*My hope is in the Lord.* Patrick didn't know where that thought had come from, but he recognized its truth. His hope *was* in the Lord. He would try to stay focused on that, and let God be his strength. God would see him through.

When Patrick started toward the barn to do the evening milking, Rachel followed him. He wasn't sure he wanted to talk with her right now. He feared she might guess some of the things he felt, but he smiled at her anyway.

"Are you feeling better?" she asked with concern on her face.

"Some. Did you have a nice afternoon?"

"Yes." She didn't sound very convinced. "How do you feel about slavery?"

Where did that question come from? Did she follow him out here just to ask him about slavery? Instead of voicing his thoughts, Patrick answered, "I've never thought people should be owned. Why?"

"I just wondered. Julius said his family supported the Confederacy in the war."

"Most of the people around here did. Mama and Papa did too. At least, Papa fought for the Confederacy after they conscripted him. I don't think he believed in slavery, though."

"Yes, but I think Julius liked the idea of owning slaves."

"Really? That surprises me. He's always seemed more fair-minded than that to me." Did this mean Rachel and Julius were already having differences?

"Have you read *Tom Sawyer*?" She changed the subject again.

"Yes, I have."

"What did you think of the book?"

"I liked it. As well as being a good story, it brought up some interesting questions about how we as a society treat each other, especially those from different social classes."

"Exactly." Rachel sounded enthusiastic now. "Twain pointed out some of society's hypocrisy. What did you think of Tom? Because of his youth, did you see him as petty or shallow?"

"No. I liked the way Tom put others first. He even took Becky's punishment for her, and he testified at Injun Joe's trial. Tom certainly matured as the book progressed. Did you and Julius also disagree about the novel?"

"Some . . . I guess." She looked away, as if she hated to admit it.

"Are you seeing Julius again?"

"Yes, I invited him to supper Saturday, and I don't plan to see him Sunday."

She must be trying to leave Sunday free, so they could spend time together. That brought a smile to his face.

"I'll let you get to your milking, then. I need to finish up in the kitchen anyway."

She smiled her good-bye.

--------

If possible, August seemed even hotter than July to Rachel. She finally took time to write her parents. She wanted to tell them about Julius.

> Dear Mama and Papa,
>
> I have some news. I have met a young man. Uncle Sam has approved of him and allowed him to court me. His name is Julius Clark, and he's just finished law school. He's a little younger than Patrick. Patrick actually introduced Julius to me at church. They went to school here together.
>
> After the problem I had with Axel, I appreciate what a gentleman Julius is. I'm seeing him about once a week, since we've been so busy with canning and the other chores around the farm. I think you'd like him.
>
> I can't say that I love him, yet, but am very fond of him and enjoy his company. The biggest disagreement we've had has been over slavery. Julius seems to have supported it, but he says our different ideas don't matter, because there's no longer any slavery.
>
> Please pray God will show me His will and will direct my path. I'm taking things slowly and giving myself time to determine how I feel.
>
> Everything else is going well. Since we're so busy, I won't write as much now, but I'll try to write more later. By that time, perhaps I'll know better how I feel about Julius.

I love and miss you as always. Do you think you could come and spend Thanksgiving and Christmas with us? Bring the boys too. I can't imagine the holidays apart from you.

Love always,
Rachel

She saw Julius once a week. He wanted to get together more, but she told him she had too much work to do right now. When the harvest was in, she would have more time.

He also wanted to take her someplace, like Rocky River Springs, and he said she could invite someone like Blanche or Hope to go with them, but she declined.

"Let's go on a picnic, then," Julius had suggested. "We can ask Patrick and Blanche to go with us."

Rachel didn't like the idea of having Blanche matched with Patrick again. She knew Patrick wasn't fond of Blanche, or she didn't think he was, but Blanche apparently wanted him to court her. A picnic might be fun, however, but they did need to invite someone else, so there'd be a chaperone.

Rachel had an idea how she might help Hope and be able to go on a picnic with Julius too. It was worth a try.

"If you were to come on a picnic with someone whom your father would approve, who would you choose?" Rachel asked Hope.

"I don't know."

"Would you go with George or Charles?"

"George seemed interested in Melinda Hall before school was out. Charles seems nice, but he's awfully shy."

"If I could arrange for Charles to accompany you, would you go on a picnic with Julius and me?"

"Yeah, anything would be better than sitting around here on Sunday afternoon. If Papa will give his permission, I'll go."

"Do you know how we can get in contact with Charles?"

"Not really. Papa might know."

Rachel caught Uncle Sam when he was coming in from working in the field.

"If you'll make sure Hope stays right with you, I guess it will be fine if she goes," Uncle Sam said when she asked him about her plans. "Hope has been doing chores lately, and Charles seems like a responsible young man."

"Do you know how to contact Charles? I don't think he comes to our church, does he?"

"No, his family lives on a small farm off Big Lick Road west of here a few miles. Why don't you ask Julius to get in touch with Charles? I don't think it would look right for me to do it, since I'm Hope's father."

"That's a good idea. If Julius wants to go somewhere with me as much as he indicates, he'll be glad to invite Charles."

Julius did like the idea. "Sure, I know where Charles lives, and I'll go ask him tomorrow. We'll plan it for Sunday afternoon, if that's okay with you."

Rachel found she liked leaving Sunday afternoons free when possible. Patrick, Sammy, and she had become a regular threesome after Sunday dinner. They went fishing, took walks, rode the horses, and even waded in the creek a few times.

Still, they could hardly ask Charles to come on a workday. She knew how busy he must be on the farm.

Patrick and Uncle Sam used any spare time they had to cut wood. Cooking and canning had taken a lot. Of course, with the mild winters down here, they would probably be able to cut more on some of the better days through the winter months too.

Julius got everything worked out and came by to tell her. He would go by and pick up Charles Sunday morning to go to church with him. Charles's family went to church farther away.

Rachel planned to pack their dinner Sunday morning, and Julius would transfer it to his coach. He promised to park it in the shade and cover it with a quilt.

Hope couldn't contain her excitement Sunday morning. She changed dresses three times before she felt satisfied, and she had Rachel put her hair up to make her look older.

Rachel planned to wear her most comfortable church dress, a lightweight silk in a burnished gold color. Its simple style suited her, and it fit her well.

"Oh, you look beautiful," Hope said. "That style and color really suits you. Do you think I'm filling out more?"

Rachel looked at her cousin. She had developed some subtle curves. "Yes, you are. You're looking quite the young lady."

"You've made Hope very happy," Patrick whispered as he helped Rachel into the surrey.

Rachel looked at him as he climbed in beside her. He didn't look too happy. Something had been bothering him lately. Rachel wished she could stay home today, so she could learn what was wrong. She felt sure he'd confide in her, if they ever had time for a private conversation. Her conscience gave her a pang. She felt she was deserting her friend when he might need her. She'd make sure she had no plans next Sunday.

Julius drove them to a pretty spot near a pond. They spread the quilt under a huge oak tree, and Hope helped her set out the food.

She'd fixed fried chicken, field peas, corn, yeast rolls, and apple cobbler. They had apple cider to drink.

"This is delicious," Julius said. "I bet you didn't know you were in for such a treat today, did you Charles?"

"I'm not surprised," Charles said. "I saw how well Rachel could cook when she used to give me some of her cookies after school."

Julius eyebrows shot up. "Oh, were you there to see Hope?"

"No, Patrick tutored me in math the last weeks of school."

After they'd finished eating, Julius patted a place on the quilt beside him and looked at Rachel. "Come here, sweetheart."

He'd never done anything like this before, and she wondered if he hoped to stake his claim in front of Charles.

Charles had been watching her ever since they'd sat down, but he sat right across from her, so it would be hard for him not to.

Rachel scooted over as Julius indicated, and he put his arm around her back.

"Let's walk down to the pond." Charles put out his hand to help Hope up. "We'll stay within sight," he told Rachel and Julius.

"This is nice," Julius said when he and Rachel were alone. He eased back against the broad tree trunk and pulled her back with him.

A gentle breeze stirred the leaves and broke the repressive heat. Rachel relaxed.

"I've wanted to have you in my arms for a long time. I guess one arm is a start." He looked pleased.

"I think it's good to take things slowly and get to know each other well," she told him.

"Oh Rachel, if you only knew how hard that is."

"But you're too much of a gentleman to do otherwise."

"I'm glad you regard me so highly. I'll certainly try to live up to your expectations. I would never do anything to hurt you. I'm too fond of you for that."

"Then please slow down. Give me more time, Julius."

Rachel stiffened at the thought he might be about to declare his love and ask for her hand. She definitely wasn't ready for that. But he didn't say anything else, and she relaxed again.

Rachel woke up with her head resting on Julius's shoulder. She must have dozed off. She sat up straighter and found him looking at her. "I'm sorry. I didn't mean to go to sleep on you." She immediately realized how that sounded. "I mean on your shoulder." She'd never felt so embarrassed.

He laughed. "Would I be a rogue if I said you can go to sleep on me anytime you want?"

"Yes, you would. Please don't embarrass me even more."

He looked at her lips, as if he wanted to kiss her, so she stood up. She saw Charles and Hope sitting beside the pond, talking. She looked back at Julius. "Let's go down to the water before we go home."

Julius jumped up and took her hand. At least she felt safe with him, not like with Axel. Julius would never do something she asked him not to.

Patrick stayed in his room when Rachel got home. She sent Sammy up to get him when she had supper ready, but Patrick sent down word he didn't feel like eating. Worry creased her brow, and she could tell Aunt Ivy felt it too.

She followed him, when he came down to milk, but he walked so fast, she had to run to catch up. If she didn't know better, she'd think she had done something to upset him. When she caught up with him, she took his arm to slow him down. "What's the matter, Patrick? You act as if something's bothering you."

"Nothing I can talk about out here like this," he said. "Don't worry, Rachel. God will help me work things out."

"I want to help too," she pleaded. She should have stayed home today. "I'm here for you Patrick. We're best friends forever, aren't we?"

"Yes, best friends forever." He gave her a weak smile and started for the barn again.

That night, Rachel couldn't sleep for thinking about Patrick. She'd never seen him this distraught before, and she didn't like it one bit. Patrick had always been the strong one. He'd always been there for her, and he'd protected her countless times. She couldn't imagine what could be wrong.

*Dear Lord, please be with Patrick. Please comfort him, surround him in Thy love and make things right for him again. He's such a special friend. I hurt when he hurts, and I'm suffering for him now. He loves Thee, like I do, Lord. Bless and help him, I pray. Amen.*

Patrick came to breakfast the next morning, and he looked and acted some better, but he still didn't eat as much as usual. He rolled the food on his plate like a cat might play with a mouse. Very little made it to his mouth. Had he been working himself to exhaustion?

"Sam, I think you're working Patrick too hard," Aunt Ivy said, as if she'd read Rachel's mind.

"Don't blame me." Sam looked at Patrick. "I've tried to get him to slow down, but he won't. He's working hard enough for three men. You see if you can get him to slow down."

"I'm fine," Patrick said. "I want to stay busy." He got up and left to resume his work.

"I'll see if I can get him to listen to me." Rachel ran after him. "Patrick, please slow down."

He stopped, and she laughed. He had misunderstood what she meant.

"No, I mean please don't wear yourself down by working so hard."

"I need to work hard. It helps me sleep better at night."

She looked at him carefully. "You don't look like you're sleeping very well now. Look, Patrick, I need you. Please don't get sick on me. I'm worried about you."

He frowned and shook his head. "Do you really need me, Rachel? You have Julius now."

"Julius could never replace you. I can tell you anything and confide my deepest secrets. I can't do that with Julius. Just yesterday, I said something without thinking and embarrassed myself in front of Julius. I've never been embarrassed with you. You know me so well, if I said something wrong, you would know what I really meant."

Patrick took a deep breath. "Thank you, Rachel. I'm glad you feel that close to me. Regardless of any other problems, you can always come to me."

"I thought you felt that close to me, too, but you've let something get you down without talking to me about it. I don't understand. If something was bothering me, I'd come to you first. I've prayed for you, Patrick."

"My problem doesn't seem so big right now. Talking with you has helped, and you're right. I should have come to you earlier. I'm sorry I shut you out."

"I want to help you any way I can. You've always done that for me. What else can I do to help?" She tried to let him hear her sincerity.

"I think I need a hug right now. Would that be possible?"

She spread her arms in answer. He moved toward her and wrapped his arms around her, as hers encircled him. She felt wonderful in his arms. He might need the hug, but it was doing things for her too. She felt safe and protected, but she also felt her blood rushing and her heart start pounding worse than a heavy sledge hammer.

What was this all about? Her head felt so light, she could barely think as she pulled back. His eyes were soft and misty, but she felt he looked into her very soul.

"Thank you." He sounded as if he had to push the words out. He cleared his throat. "I'll take it easier today, if that would please you."

She smiled at him, patted his shoulder, and went back to the kitchen. She hoped he felt better. He still hadn't told her what had been bothering him, but if he'd come through it, that would be enough.

"Well now, we know who has the most influence on Patrick around here." Uncle Sam laughed at dinner. "He seems to be his old self this morning. He accomplished plenty, but didn't work like he was fighting a fire."

"Rachel just knows how to ask," Patrick told his father.

"Oh, is that it?" Uncle Sam's eyes sparkled as if he understood something Patrick didn't.

Rachel got a reply to her letter that week. Eager to see what her parents said about Julius, she tore into it.

Dearest Rachel,

We were delighted to get your letter and glad you told us about Julius. He does sound like someone we'd like, except on the slavery issue. You know how strongly your father and I feel about that. Although it's true slavery has ended, I'm afraid mistreatment and abuse has not. Do you think Julius will treat all others the way you think he should? It could be very disappointing to you, if he doesn't.

We're glad you're taking things slowly. You know the problems your father and I had, because he didn't with Ivy. People suffered over his and Ivy's haste—the two of them and me most of all. Your father wanted me to tell you to be very sure before you agree to marry. He says you will know beyond a doubt when the right one comes into your life. I agree, because he and I knew.

Your grandfather also experienced a similar situation, when he married the wrong person. He was so deeply in love with Luke's mother, he was devastated when she died. He remarried too quickly, and he had to live with Frances for a long time. Thankfully, he and Clara are much happier.

Please know we are praying for you with every prayer we make. We trust you to listen to God's guidance, because you always have. We know He has the best for you, if you will wait on Him.

We're not sure about the holidays right now. You know it's often hard for us to travel from here in the winter, because of the unpredictable, harsh weather. Bringing all the boys and the Christmas presents might also present a problem. We'll consider the possibility, however.

Take care, darling daughter. We love you and support you. May God be with you and guide you.

Lots of love,
Mama and Papa

Her parents had given her some good advice. She'd take it to heart and depend on God.

Patrick began to act like himself again, and Rachel praised God for it. Her prayers had been answered.

Rachel refused to see Julius Sunday afternoon, but she invited him to supper Monday night. He seemed okay with that.

After Sunday dinner, Patrick, Sammy and she rode out around the fields. The crops were looking good. They would began harvesting in September and hire extra hands to help.

Patrick looked at her and smiled as they rode side by side at a leisurely pace. "I like it that you have a split skirt, so you can ride better."

"I'm glad you approve. It does make riding easier and less tiring. Mama was smart to think up the design. We've since heard that some women out west have done the same thing."

He nodded. "There's a wooded area past the last field. Let's go sit in the shade for a while."

Patrick helped her down and then Sammy. They tied their horses, and Sammy went exploring. Patrick led her to a fallen log.

"Stay within sight," Patrick reminded his brother.

"It is cooler here," Rachel said as she sat down.

"So how did the picnic go last Sunday?" Patrick sat down beside her.

"It went well. I got lots of compliments on the food. I think Hope and Charles had a good time too."

"Did you and Julius have any more discussions on books or slavery?"

"No." She laughed. "Maybe it's better we stay away from those topics. Actually we didn't talk that much. I embarrassed myself by falling asleep on his shoulder." She saw the stunned look on his face. "I didn't have my head on his shoulder until I woke up," she told him. "Julius is not like Axel. He's always a perfect gentleman in his actions."

"Are you getting serious about him, Rachel?"

"I don't think so. Not yet. I've told him to take things slowly and give me plenty of time to get to know him well."

"I think that's wise, and I'm glad you save some Sunday afternoons for me."

"I am too. I enjoy the time we spend together even more than I do the time I spend with Julius. I miss you when we go too long without being able to talk together like this."

The smile he gave her made her heart skip a beat. My, how she loved making him happy!

CHAPTER TWELVE

# The Box Social

THE CHURCH DECIDED TO HOLD a box social. Rachel had never heard of one before. It was being held to raise money for the building fund. When they got enough money, the church hoped to do some remodeling.

All the single women were supposed to cook a supper for two, secretly box it up, take it to the church, and the single men would bid on them. The man with the winning bid would then eat his meal with the cook. Hope seemed excited and had already asked Rachel to help her with her food.

"Maybe you'd better help me too," Aunt Ivy said, "or Sam and Sammy will be disappointed. The married women are supposed to cook for their husbands and younger children, and the husband could give a donation."

The social would begin Saturday at five. Rachel began cooking after the dinner dishes were done. She helped Ivy prepare her box first, and then Hope. She cooked hers last. Each one had a different menu, so they took a while to prepare.

Rachel wrapped her box in a scrap of pale green silk and tied it up with a dark green bow. Ivy wrapped her box in white with a sky blue bow, and Hope used yellow calico with a white bow.

"Leave them on the table and we'll have the men load and unload them. That way no one will know exactly who goes with each one."

The young men stood around and watched the boxes come out of the wagon. This is how they planned to determine the one they wanted to bid on. There were even several there who didn't usually come to this church.

It surprised Rachel to see Axel there. She hadn't heard anything of him since the incident with Hope and had hoped he'd gone back to Tennessee.

Blanche came up. "Axel and J. T. are going to be leaving soon," she whispered between Rachel and Hope. "He wanted one more chance to see the two of you."

Uncle Sam noticed him too. "He's not going to get a chance to eat with one of my girls. I'll bid whatever I have to prevent that if need be."

Blanche carried her own box up to table. The box, wrapped in gold paper and tied with a red ribbon, looked more lavish than any of the others.

"Time for the bidding to commence," the auctioneer called. "Guys, get your wallets out and bid generously. This is going to a good cause, and you know our womenfolk can cook. It'll be worth every penny, especially when you have the privilege of such charming company. This is your chance to be in the company of that lady you've always wanted to get to know better."

Axel looked across the way and winked. Rachel looked away. She couldn't tell if he was winking at her, Hope, or both. The cad!

"Yellow . . . green?" Julius came up behind her and whispered.

She started not to tell him, but then she remembered Axel. Anything to prevent him from getting her box.

"Green," she whispered back, and he smiled somewhat smugly.

The first few boxes went for ten cents to a quarter. One went for fifty cents. Then the auctioneer picked up Rachel's box. "I can tell this is mouthwatering from just smelling the aroma," he said. "The box is lovely, as I'm sure is the young woman who comes with it. What will you start me with? Who'll give me twenty-five cents?"

Charles raised his hand. Hope looked stricken.

"He's probably not sure which is mine and which is yours," Rachel told her.

"Who'll give me fifty?"

George raised his hand.

"A dollar?"

Charles's hand went up again, and George shook his head.

"Let's not waste our time, boys. Two dollars?"

Axel raised his hand, and Rachel tensed. *Please God, don't let Axel win this bid.*

"Three," Patrick called, then raised his hand.

"Four," Axel responded.

"Five," Julius said.

"Six," Axel replied.

"Seven," Patrick said before Julius had a chance.

"Eight," Axel countered.

"Nine," Julius said.

"Ten," Axel said, a little more hesitantly this time.

By now the crowd had grown deathly quiet. They were probably as stunned as Rachel. No meal was worth this fortune.

"Eleven," Julius bid.

"Twelve," Patrick said.

"Thirteen."

"Fourteen."

"Fifteen."

"Patrick." Uncle Sam put his hand on his son's shoulder. "Axel is out of the bidding now. You don't need to bid any longer. Don't be foolish."

"Fifteen dollars, going once, going twice, sold to Julius Clark for fifteen dollars. Thank you, Mr. Clark. Come collect your box and your lady."

Rachel stepped out to stand with Julius, who now held her box. Patrick looked as if he didn't know what to do next. He probably didn't know what box to bid on now, and she felt sorry for him. She wished he'd won her box.

"Let's wait and see who gets Hope's box," she told Julius, and he nodded.

The auctioneer held up Hope's calico box. "What am I bid for this lovely box? Who'll start this one at a dollar?" Patrick held up his hand. Rachel smiled. Patrick knew she had cooked it.

"He'd better not dare," Hope whispered through clenched teeth.

"Two," Axel said. Hope looked as if she didn't know whether to smile or cry.

"Three," Patrick said.

"Don't do this," Aunt Ivy whispered to Patrick. "Hope wants to eat with Charles."

Poor Patrick. His parents weren't going to let him win either of the family's boxes.

"Four," Axel said.

"I'll back you for any amount you need to win," Uncle Sam quietly told Charles.

"Ten," Charles said, and Axel shook his head at the auctioneer.

Blanche's box went next. Some of her usual admirers started the bidding, but Axel bid three dollars. Patrick bid five, and won the bid. Patrick collected the box and led Blanche off to her quilt. Rachel could tell Blanche didn't like it that her box sold for much less than Rachel's or Hope's.

Rachel took Julius's arm and let him lead her to a quilt. She didn't see Axel after that. He must have left.

"Well, that is the most exciting box social we've ever had around here," Julius said. "And I'm sure it raised the most money ever too."

"You spent way too much money on my box, Julius."

"Nonsense, dear. Don't you know how much you mean to me? I'm sure I could outbid anyone here, and I would have paid whatever it took. I was determined to have your box."

Rachel couldn't help glancing over at Patrick and Blanche eating on her blanket. Blanche said something, and Patrick laughed. *Oh Patrick, Blanche isn't good enough for you. She'll only break your heart.*

"I know you want to take things slowly, but it hasn't taken long for me to know I love you and want you for my wife," Julius said. He held up his hand when she started to protest. "I know you're going to need time to come to a decision, but I wanted to make my intentions clear, so there's no misunderstanding. When you're ready, I'll ask your uncle for your hand. We'll be married anywhere you want—here, in Watauga County, in Salisbury. I'll be patient, because I want you to be sure, but please don't take too long to decide. I want you desperately, and I dream of you every night. I can't help it."

He sounded very confident she'd say yes, but at least two things were good about this secret proposal. He wasn't expecting an answer right away, and he'd asked her in a place where he couldn't expect to kiss her.

"I'll think about it and give you an answer as soon as I can."

He nodded. "You know, as an only child, I'll be able to provide for you and give you anything you'll ever want."

"All I'll ever ask from a husband is his love and faithfulness, deep faith in God, integrity, and a close relationship."

"Yes, well, pretty things never hurt either. You deserve to have the best of everything, and it'll be my privilege to give them to you."

"Where would we live?"

"I'd like to stay close to here, because of my parents, but I'd go anywhere you wanted, as long as it's a town or city that would support my law practice. You could do only the things you liked and hire servants for all the rest. We'd be living the good life, Rachel, what most people only dream about. I'd treasure and cherish you for the rest of my life, and I'd be the envy of every man who ever meets you." He reached over and put his hand over hers.

"I'll consider all you've said."

"Can I see you tomorrow?"

"I've got plans with the family tomorrow. Why don't you come to supper on Tuesday?"

"Okay, at seven?"

"That will be fine."

"Will you start sitting with me at church?"

"Not yet. If we become engaged, I'll begin sitting with you then."

The clouds hung dark and low Sunday as they drove to church. At least the day felt cooler than normal, although the humidity must be high.

When they got home, the rain started, and Rachel's hopes fell. She'd wanted to go somewhere and talk to Patrick about Julius's proposal. She needed his perspective, because she felt so confused.

She liked Julius; she liked him a lot, but did she love him enough to marry him? She just didn't know. If Patrick didn't tell her what he thought she should do, he'd at least give her a clearer way to look at the dilemma.

She'd roasted a chicken for dinner, and everyone ate their fill. By two o'clock, everyone except Patrick and she had gone upstairs for a nap.

"Would you like to beat me in chess?" He laughed. "At least my mind feels fairly clear today, and I might be up to the challenge. I've seen how well you play, but we've never had the time for a game yet."

"I'd rather talk first, if you don't mind."

"Sure. What do you want to talk about?"

"First, let's talk about the box social."

"I'm sorry that I got carried away bidding on your box. I realize you probably wanted Julius to win, and I almost spoiled it for you."

"That's not it at all. I would have been happy if you'd won my box, although I don't think Julius planned to let that happen. He said he would have bid whatever it took."

"If I'd known, we could've raised enough money to renovate the church right now." His eyes twinkled.

"Did you enjoy eating with Blanche?"

"She wasn't my first or even my second choice, but it wasn't so bad. She has started acting more ladylike around me."

"Do you think it's just that—an act?"

"Probably. She's probably doing what she thinks will reel me in. She likes conquering, and I'm a challenge. Don't worry, Rachel, I'm not interested in Blanche."

"I just don't want to see you hurt." Surely he didn't think Rachel had grown jealous.

"Give me credit for having some sense. I know what Blanche can be like."

"I do. You're the only man I've ever met who may be as intelligent as my father, and I assure you that's a great compliment. In fact, I want to get your perspective on something. Julius proposed to me at the box social. He said he'll wait for me to make a decision before he talks to Uncle Sam, but I'm all confused. I don't know how I feel about him."

"That may be your answer, Rachel. You should be very sure about the man you marry."

"You're right. That's what my parents have written too. I know I like him, but I don't think a deep love has developed yet. Do you think it will with more time?"

"I don't know." He seemed ill at ease. "Only you can answer that question. Do you think he has a deep love for you?"

"I think so. He says he does."

His eyes searched hers. "Have you talked about the important questions? Does he have a deep faith like you?"

"I'm not sure. I know he attends church regularly."

"But, you don't know if he's accepted Christ as his Savior or if he has a personal relationship with the Lord?"

"No, I don't. I'll try to find out."

"Does he want children and do you?"

"I certainly do." She looked away from Patrick's intensity. "But I don't know how he feels."

"Where will you live?"

"He says anywhere I want, as long as it is where he can open his law practice."

"So, that means a town or city. I know you love the country. Would you be happy living somewhere like Salisbury?"

"That's a good question, but wouldn't I be happy anywhere if I loved him enough? I guess that's what I need to decide, but how do I do that?"

"Ask yourself if he's your best friend. Remember when you told me the person you married should be your very best friend. Ask yourself how you'd feel if you knew you'd never see him again. Would you be devastated, lost without him, feel like dying? You've told me how deep your parents' love is. Do you love Julius as much as your mother loves your father?"

"I knew you'd put things in proper perspective for me." She felt better all of a sudden. "Are you ready to play some chess now?" "If it's okay with you, I'd rather just sit here with you for a while." "Oh, that's fine with me."

Rachel lay in bed that night, thinking about what Patrick had said. If she answered those questions, she didn't think she'd fallen in love with Julius yet, but would a strong love develop with time? Should she wait and see or let Julius know what she thought? After praying about it, she decided, to be fair to Julius, she needed to tell him exactly how she felt, no matter how hard it might be.

Wednesday they ate supper, and Rachel invited Julius to go on a short walk with her. There was still enough light, and she planned to stay in view of the house.

"I've been doing much thinking about your proposal," she began. "I'm very fond of you, and I like you a lot, but I don't think I love you right now enough to marry you. I don't know if such a love will develop in time or not. I thought it only fair to tell you what I'm thinking. I don't want to give you false hopes and hurt you more."

"I'm not happy to hear this, but I appreciate your honesty. However, you're not going to get rid of me that easily. I'll take my chances. I'll treat you so special that you'll have to fall in love with me. As long as there's any hope, I'll court you. At least it's not a definite no." He put his hand on her back and led her to the porch. They sat down, and just sat for a while. "Come to dinner at my house again Sunday."

"Could we make it Saturday instead? Sunday is usually our family day, and I hate to miss it. We all work so much during the week, we only have time together at meals and our family devotion."

"Sure, Saturday will be just as good. I'll pick you up at eleven thirty. Are you comfortable enough with me now to go without a chaperone?"

"I think I am, but we'll need to ask my uncle. Since it's in the daytime, and your parents will be there, it should be fine."

Uncle Sam gave his permission, and Julius said good night. She walked him to his buggy, and he took her chin in his hand and looked into her eyes. "I love you, Rachel." He kissed her lightly on the forehead.

"Have you told Julius you're part Cherokee?" Patrick asked as they started to their bedrooms.

"No, I haven't thought about it. Like you said, it doesn't seem to be an issue here."

"It shouldn't be, but I remembered you thought he might be prejudiced, so it might be smart if you make sure it doesn't matter to Julius."

"You're right. I'll do so Saturday when I go for dinner."

When Julius picked her up Saturday, he seemed in high spirits. She guessed he liked the idea of finally getting her alone.

"Do you want to have children?" she asked him as he drove.

"I'd like to have one or two eventually, but I'd rather wait for a few years first. If we have a boy first, that would be enough for me. If it's a girl, I'd want to try for a boy. I'd like to have a male heir."

That wasn't the best answer, but Rachel could live with it. She wondered if he had five girls, would he still want to keep trying for a boy. Well, all that would likely be in God's hands, anyway. At least he wasn't opposed to children.

The meal was delicious again, and it seemed more intimate with just Julius and his parents. Of course, she knew Julius much better this time too.

"I've arranged for us to go horseback riding," he announced. "I understand you ride well."

"I like to ride, but I didn't bring my split skirt, and I don't ride sidesaddle."

"Are you saying you ride astride?" He seemed appalled.

"Yes, but the skirt I use is designed especially for it. It almost looks like a normal skirt. I assure you it looks quite proper."

"Not if you're astride a horse."

"It's the way my mother rides too. In fact, my mother designed our skirts, and I think women are wearing something similar for riding in the West."

Julius gave her a hard look. "I must say, I'm shocked. I'll not have you riding around like that. People will think it's indecent."

"What if I didn't ride in public at all? What if I rode only with you?"

"Well, I might could compromise to that. The groom would have to know, though, and my parents may eventually find out, but I can handle them."

"So, I guess we'll need to wait for another time to go riding. I'd like to walk in the garden again with you anyway. I have two things I'd like to talk with you about."

"Certainly, the garden will be better if you want to talk." Julius seemed joyous, and she wondered if he expected her to accept his proposal.

They strolled through the lovely paths for a while. Even in the August heat, the garden looked wonderful. They sat down on a bench that faced a fountain.

Rachel took a deep breath. "It is beautiful and so peaceful here."

"I'm glad you like it. Marry me and it'll be yours."

"How strong is your faith, Julius? Have you accepted Christ as your Savior and been baptized? Do you have a personal relationship with the Lord?"

He looked disappointed. "Well, let's see now. So many questions. I believe in God, but I have never been baptized. How does one have a personal relationship with God? That doesn't even sound possible to me. I'll attend church with you regularly, and we'll take our children too. I'll never stand in the way of your faith, but I won't appreciate it if you try to make me think just like you."

"I see." She paused. "There's also one thing I need to tell you. I had forgotten about it. My paternal grandmother was half Irish and half Cherokee. That would make me one-eighth Cherokee."

"Indian?"

"Yes, Cherokee Indian."

"I didn't know. Why didn't you tell me at the start?"

"Like I said, I didn't think of it. Is it important?"

"Well, of course it's important. Our children might have dark skin. You've given me an even bigger shock than wanting to ride astride. I'll need to think about this."

"Don't bother, Julius. I can tell you're not the man for me. Please take me home."

"Now don't be hasty. I didn't say I didn't want to marry you. I just need to think through things and look at the possible ramifications."

"Just take me home."

"Yes, I suppose that might be best under the circumstances."

They rode back in silence. Rachel guessed Julius needed to do some thinking of his own, and she saw no need in talking. She couldn't imagine a future for her with such a man. She felt empty, hollow. How could she not see what he was like from the beginning? She guessed they'd not held the right conversations, and she'd ignored the differences she did see. She'd been trying too hard to make this work. She shouldn't have. She should have worked harder to see the potential problems. At least she had never fallen in love with him. She might be hurt, but she would soon be over it.

"Can I see you next Saturday or Sunday?" he asked as he helped her from the buggy. "That will give us enough time to collect our thoughts."

"Mine are quite collected, organized, and labeled, and I find no reason to see you again. I don't know what you love, Julius, but it's not me. If you really loved me, it would make no difference that I'm part Indian. It's never made any difference to Mama that Papa's one-fourth Cherokee. I want a husband who cares about God and the character of a person, not their blood lines. Marriage would never work for either of us. We just think too differently. Can't you see that?"

"Perhaps you're right. How about a good-bye kiss?"

"No, I'm saving those for my husband, but good-bye, Julius. I enjoyed our time together, and I wish you the very best."

"You too, Rachel, you too." He took her hand and kissed the back of it. "So long."

CHAPTER THIRTEEN

# Aftermath

PATRICK AND UNCLE SAM WERE out cutting wood when Rachel got home. She wanted to run to Patrick and tell him what had happened. It would be wonderful if he put his arms around her for comfort and held her close in a hug.

She had to start supper instead. Tomorrow they could have a good, long talk after church and dinner. She could wait until then.

*I thank Thee, Lord, for answering my prayers, and showing me Julius wasn't the man for me. If there is a man for me, please show me soon. I could use some comfort and reassurance right now, and I don't want to be let down again. The disappointment over Axel wasn't as severe, since I'd known him for such a short time, but he was not what I'm looking for. I realize now, I wanted Julius to be the one, and I'm somewhat disillusioned. I never understood before how Papa could have thought he was in love with Aunt Ivy at one time but have been so wrong. Now I understand better, and I see how it's imperative I don't make a hasty decision. I thank Thee for Thy guidance, Father. Be with me and show me Thy will, I pray, in Jesus's name. Amen.*

Patrick watched Rachel carefully from across the table during supper. Did he sense something had happened?

"Is everything all right?" he asked after the family devotion.

"I'll tell you about it tomorrow."

He looked like he wanted to refuse to wait, but finally nodded. "I'm here if you need me," he whispered.

Julius didn't come to church Sunday. Rachel hoped she hadn't kept him out of church. She didn't think seeing him again would be too painful for her now. She'd had time to think and pray, and she now viewed him more realistically. Before, she had focused too much on his good traits and what she'd wanted to see, instead of the entire portrait.

---

The church service seemed days long to Patrick this morning. He knew something had changed when he first saw Rachel's face yesterday afternoon. Since Julius wasn't in church this morning, he assumed it involved him.

She had been hurt. He could feel it, as if it were his own pain. But she didn't appear to be terribly distraught or overtly that upset, so maybe it was something minor.

He'd know what the problem was, if this morning would ever pass. Why did the joyous times sprint by at breakneck speed and the miserable moments go at a snail's pace?

Finally, with dinner over, he gathered Sammy and Rachel and they set off for the creek. The running water seemed to soothe Rachel and make her feel better.

Sammy ran about chasing minnows and tadpoles, and Patrick and Rachel sat under a shade tree and watched. He waited until she seemed ready to talk, although he wanted to ask questions right away. She spoke first.

"Julius and I had a lengthy conversation yesterday, or maybe I should say 'disagreement.' First, he objected to the idea of me wearing my special skirt and riding astride, although he finally compromised to say I could do so privately with just him. Then, he doesn't seem to like children very much, but he does want a male heir. He would prefer a son to start with, but if daughters came, he would want more children, until he had his son."

Patrick watched as tears formed in her eyes and began trailing down her cheeks. He reached over and took her hand for support. She gave him a weak smile through her tears, as she tried to wipe them away with her other hand.

"I don't know why I'm crying now," she said. "These are the first tears I've shed."

He softly kissed the back of her hand to tell her it was okay and to offer what comfort he could. A part of him wanted Julius to be wrong for her, but he didn't want her hurting like this.

"Julius doesn't have much faith, either. He believes in God, but has never accepted Christ into his life or been baptized. He doesn't think a personal relationship with God is possible."

Patrick held her hand more firmly. He knew how serious this problem was, and he knew Rachel would see it that way too.

"I might have tolerated his views on the first two issues, but I wouldn't compromise on the question of faith. And there's more. He didn't like the idea of my Cherokee blood. He feared one of our children might turn out too dark. I told him good-bye." She sniffed and the tears came more steadily.

He pulled her into his arms, and she sobbed on his shoulder. He didn't know what to say, so he tried to let his arms comfort her.

Sammy came up and asked, "What's wrong with Rachel?"

"She and Julius have had some problems, and he won't be coming to see her again. I think she'll be okay once she cries it out. You go on and play, and I'll help Rachel."

Sammy nodded and left, as if he didn't have any idea how to help a crying woman. Patrick wasn't sure he did either, but Rachel pulled out of his arms, and he handed her his handkerchief.

"Did you figure out you loved him, Rachel?" He asked it gently, because he knew Rachel needed his tenderness, and she was too distraught to see his love.

"No." She shook her head. "I think I had been hoping he was the one for me. Next to Axel, Julius looked promising. I guess I'm disappointed, but I'm glad I found out sooner instead of later."

Patrick wanted to tell her she could quit looking, because he was the one for her. He bit his tongue to keep from declaring his love, but he knew this wasn't the time. Even if she didn't love Julius, she did like him, and she needed time to get over him and her feelings of rejection. Patrick didn't want her coming to him, because she needed to fill the void left by Julius. He wanted her to choose *him* as the love of her life.

"I wish we had more freedom to be alone together," she told him. "It's hard for me to wait until Sundays to talk with you."

He picked up her hand. "It's been hard for me too. I knew something was wrong the moment I saw you."

But, if they were alone more, Patrick would have a lot harder time being patient. *Please help Rachel, Lord, and give me the right words to comfort her. If it is in Thy will, grant her love for me to grow and prepare a way for us to be together with our parents' blessings. Amen.*

"God has someone for you, Rachel. Be patient. He'll show you His will in His timing, and that will be at the best time. There's a reason you don't know who the man is now. We don't know the why, but God does." *I need to take my own advice, don't I, Lord?*

She gave him a smile. "You're right. I shouldn't be trying to force something to happen."

"That's my girl." *Don't I wish!*

"I'll be fine, Patrick. Thank you for listening. I feel much better already."

She smiled again, and he wanted to kiss her so badly, he had to fight his body from leaning toward her. He needed to let go of her hand too, but he didn't. He'd let her break that contact. It felt so good to touch her in any way, and his thumb rubbed the back of her hand. He'd held her twice now, and it had been ecstasy, but it later made him yearn for her more.

"You're so good to me, Patrick. I don't know what I'd do without you."

Was it possible Rachel loved him as the man for her and didn't recognize it?

How long would it take her to see him like that? What could he say to help things along without doing something too soon?

"You know," Patrick began, "if you'd married Julius, we couldn't have these sessions. You'll need to find a husband you can talk with about anything and everything, like we do. He'll need to always be there for you."

"You're right. I hadn't thought of that. If I married, I'd have to move away, and I'd not get to see you often. Besides, I don't guess a husband would tolerate us together so much. He wouldn't understand. Well, maybe I just won't marry, not for a long time anyway." She smiled up at him.

*Oh Rachel, it's me. Can't you see? I'm the one for you.*

Patrick stood, still holding her hand, and pulled her to her feet.

She gave him a quick hug. "I guess it's already time for me to fix supper, but I could stay here forever with you."

"I could too."

---

Rachel was amazed how much better she felt after talking with Patrick. She still didn't understand why she'd cried. Perhaps she was just feeling sorry for herself, but it had felt wonderful when Patrick had pulled her into his arms. He was always so patient and gentle with her.

"I'll no longer be seeing Julius," she told the others during supper. "We had some irreparable differences, and I knew he wasn't the man God had for me."

"I'm sorry, dear," Aunt Ivy said. "I went through that once, and it can be very painful. Let us know if we can do anything to help."

"I'm already feeling better." She looked at Patrick. "I'll be just fine."

"Good for you," Uncle Sam said.

As soon as Rachel could find the time, she wrote to her parents.

Dear Mama and Papa,

Thank you for your advice, love, and support. I've decided Julius and I had too many differences to consider marriage, so I'm no longer seeing him. The two biggest problems were he has never accepted Christ's forgiveness, and he had trouble with my Cherokee heritage. I feel sure God has guided him out of my life with good reason.

I felt disappointed and hurt, but, since I knew I hadn't fallen in love with him, I'm recovering nicely. I told Patrick all about it, and that helped. He's so easy for me to talk with. I think he may be the best friend I'll ever have.

I feel God does have someone for me, and I'm determined to be patient and wait on Him. In the meantime, I'm happy, so there's no rush.

I do hope you can come down over at least part of the holidays, but I'll understand if you can't. Know that I love you and am glad we can at least talk through our letters.

Love forever,

Rachel

---

Leah stared at the letter in her hands. She and Luke had read it twice already. "Are you thinking what I'm thinking?" she asked her husband.

"That Rachel may already be in love with Patrick?"

"Yes, and she doesn't realize it at all. She certainly talks like he's the most important person in her life right now."

"I agree," Luke said, "but that doesn't have to mean it's a romantic attachment."

"But, knowing Rachel, don't you think it's likely?"

"Probably."

"I'd like to go down there over Thanksgiving, Christmas, or New Year's. I'd like to see Patrick and Rachel together. That'll tell me a lot. Do you think we can work it out to go?"

"We can try. Rachel may come to realize how she feels before then. I did notice Patrick watched her closely when we stayed there the two weeks. I thought he seemed interested then."

"I did too, but I told myself it was because of the way he'd been so close to her when they were young."

"How do you feel about it, if the two of them are in love?" Luke asked.

"I'm for whatever God wants and their happiness. I've always liked Patrick. He was a fine boy and, from what I've seen, he's grown into a godly man. What do you think?"

"I agree with you. You know Patrick better than I do, since I was gone when he lived here, but he impressed me. He's an extremely hard worker, and seemed to be caring and kind. I think he'd take care of Rachel and treat her well, but we may be rushing ahead of things. Neither one may have deep feelings for the other."

"I know, but I think it's good to consider the best course of action, in case it's true. We'll not reveal our suspicions, and we won't try to meddle. We'll just be there to help them if we're needed."

"I'm in agreement with all that. Let me think about when it'll be better for us to go, and we'll talk about the arrangements."

He reached over and pulled her into his arms. "I love you so much, Leah. Do I tell you that too much?"

"I never get tired of hearing it. I love you so much I feel my heart will explode with the love. God certainly blessed us when He put us together."

"Amen to that."

---

Julius didn't come back to church for several weeks. When he did, he didn't speak to Rachel. Instead, she saw him talking with Blanche.

Seeing Julius didn't bother her. She could have talked with him without a problem, because she held no resentment. She was just thankful she had realized he wasn't the one for her before too late.

She looked over at Patrick on the bench beside her. He felt her gaze and turned to smile at her. Why couldn't someone just like Patrick come along for her? The thought struck her with such a force it jolted her to the very core.

Could she be in love with Patrick?

The pastor began the service, and she should pay attention, she told herself. She needed to hear God's word. She'd take out these troubling thoughts and examine them more thoroughly in a quiet moment. She'd take it slowly and not say a word to anyone until she knew.

Rachel thought of little else the following week. She'd even gone through the list of important questions that had indicated the problems with her and Julius. She knew Patrick so well she didn't have to ask him.

He had as strong a faith in the Lord as anyone she knew. He'd accepted Christ into his life at an early age and had a close personal relationship with Him. They had a shared faith.

Patrick didn't mind her Cherokee blood. He thought it was something to be proud of, and he'd told her so.

He also loved children. He was so good with Sammy, and Sammy adored his older brother. Patrick had a high regard for women, and she knew he'd be just as pleased with a daughter as he would a son.

He didn't like slavery, either, and he believed in treating everyone with equal love and respect. In fact, they agreed on almost everything. Patrick could even see the deeper meaning in books, and their discussions were always intriguing.

And where they'd live wouldn't be a problem. They would probably live here, but it would certainly be on a farm, because that's what Patrick liked. Yet, she knew she could live anywhere and be happy as long as he was there.

He was the one person she didn't want to ever give up. She could go without seeing her parents better than she could go without Patrick, and she could certainly talk with him about anything. She'd done that ever since she'd come here.

He had comforted her, protected her, and done anything he could to help her and make her life better. He'd even had Uncle Sam hire Annie to help her.

She loved Patrick with all her heart. She had no doubt about it. Now the question was, did he love her? She'd have to think about that one more, but surely God wouldn't give her this burning desire for such a godly man and not intend for them to be together. Surely Patrick would come to love her, even if he didn't love her now.

She shook her head at herself. She wondered how long she'd been in love with him. Surely for a long time and perhaps close to the beginning of her stay here. She just hadn't admitted it. She'd considered him as family and a dear friend.

That was another problem. What would their families say? Hadn't Aunt Ivy once thought Uncle Sam should marry his cousin, and Patrick was only Rachel's half cousin? What would her parents think? Would Mama and Papa be disappointed in her for falling in love with Patrick? Would they think eight years was too much difference in their ages?

She reminded herself to consider one obstacle at a time. First she needed to figure out if Patrick would ever want to marry her. Then, he and she would handle the other problems together.

*Dear Lord, I need Thy help again. Help us to be together if it be Thy will. Guide me and help me to say, do, and think only things that are pleasing to Thee. I really feel Patrick and I were meant for each other, but if I'm wrong, then show me Thy way. I put Thee above all things in my life. Help me to be the person I should. Amen.*

# CHAPTER FOURTEEN

# The Harvest

"THE HARVEST LOOKS GOOD THIS year," Uncle Sam told them at the supper table. "Patrick and I will begin it sometime next week, and we'll hire helpers to come in the week after that. We'll need to feed them dinner." He looked at Rachel. "We'll have Annie come to help you from Tuesday on."

"Make it simple, especially on Monday," Patrick added. "It's not quite as hot now, so make it stew or something that's easy."

"Hope and I will help you too," Ivy said.

"I bet these will be the best harvest meals those men have ever had," Sammy stated, and they all laughed.

"Why do you think Charles hasn't asked to see me?" Hope asked Rachel as they cleaned up after supper. "I thought he enjoyed our time together at the picnic and the box social."

"Maybe he's waiting until after their harvest is in," Rachel told her. "It could be his father doesn't want him to come until then. Did you enjoy your time with him?"

"I did." Hope paused. "More than I thought I would. He's not quite so shy when it's just him and one other person, and he seems steady and dependable. I'd like to get to know him better."

"I always thought there was something special about Charles, and I think you're seeing that too."

"You didn't want him for your beau?"

"Oh no, it wasn't like that for me, but I'd like to see him happy. I think it'd be easy for him to get his heart broken. You need to tread with caution, until you find out if you really care for him."

Hope sighed. "A man has it so much better. He can go ask a woman or her father if he can come calling, but we women have to just sit back and wait. How do you stand it, Rachel?"

"I try to learn patience and look to God's timing. I just know if he's the one God wants for me, he'll come. I can be patient, when I remember that."

"You really believe that?"

"Indeed, I do. I gave my life to God years ago, and I trust Him to manage it for the best. I just have to stay close to Him, listen for His guidance, and trust Him completely. It's not hard when you realize He wants the very best for His children."

"Maybe I need to work on my faith, while I wait for Charles." She smiled. "But what about Julius? He came, but he wasn't the one."

"I've come to believe Julius came into my life for a purpose. It could have been to show me what's important in a husband for me. After Julius, I know what I'm looking for and will be able to recognize the right man more quickly now. I'll also be better equipped to reject the wrong ones."

"You're always so positive. I like that about you."

"It's not just me. It's that I know Jesus. As David said, 'The Lord is on my side, I will not fear; what can man do unto me?'"

Rachel lay in bed, thinking of Patrick that night. She felt certain he cared for her, but did he love her romantically? Sometimes, when he looked at her, she thought he did, but at other times she wasn't sure. How did one go about telling the difference between love for a family member and friend from that of a lover in someone's expression?

She needed to be patient. At least she could be around the one she loved. She saw him every day, cooked for him, and spent Sunday afternoons with him. Real blessings!

When Rachel got the letter saying her Mama and Papa were coming for Thanksgiving, she couldn't contain her joy. She would confide in them and see what they thought. She didn't want to put something like this into a letter. She just hoped they wouldn't tell her to forget about Patrick, because she knew she'd never be able to do that. He was woven into the very fabric of her being.

Her parents wrote to say they planned to bring the boys and leave them with Grandfather and Clara in Salisbury. They all would love that. Then, her parents would come here alone and bring Christmas presents.

Mama had written to Aunt Ivy too. They would come a few days before Thanksgiving and stay for a little over a week. They would visit in Salisbury on their return and leave for home whenever the weather permitted before Christmas. Rachel hoped the weather would hold for them, but Papa was good at planning and Mama was good at managing. God would take care of them, and they'd be fine.

"I think you're the most excited I've ever seen you, Rachel," Uncle Sam said. "You must really want to see your parents."

"I am excited. It will have been over seven months since I've seen them. I've never been away from Mama before or from Papa, since he came back from the war. It will be good to have them here for part of the holidays."

"You aren't planning to go back with them, are you?" Concern permeated Patrick's voice.

"Oh no, I hadn't even considered that." Was he worried she might leave him? He must have no idea how much she loved him, but the fact that he didn't want her to go warmed her heart.

"If she's as smart as she seems to be, she'll stay here during the winter at least," Aunt Ivy said. "The mountains have never been my favorite place, but the winters there are brutal."

"I don't know why you say that, Mama," Patrick teased. "I don't think you ever stepped a foot outside all winter."

"I did so. I went out to greet Sam when he came home wounded that December."

They all laughed.

Five colored men came to help with the harvest. The large group of cotton pickers had already come and gone. They went from farm to farm and brought their dinners with them.

It wouldn't be any problem to cook for five more people, six counting Annie. Why, she'd cooked for almost forty people for Hope's birthday party.

She did cook a hearty stew on Monday, like Patrick had suggested. She baked biscuits and cornbread to go with it, so they could have their choice, and sweet potato pies for dessert.

Uncle Sam said they could set up a table outside for the men, but Rachel thought that was unnecessary. The dining table would seat eight.

"The women can eat before or after the men, and there'll be enough room," she told him. "Sammy can choose which group he wants to eat with."

"The way these men usually eat," Uncle Sam said, "you'd better eat yours before them. Otherwise, there may not be anything left."

Willie, Annie's husband, came with the workers. He was a rather handsome young man with dark skin and seemed to notice everything. Rachel could tell he liked it that the help was allowed to eat at the family table.

"Dis be mighty fine eats, Miss Rachel," one of the men said, "Ya sho' is a fine cook."

"De sweet tater pie's 'bout de best I ever had," Willie agreed.

"I'm glad you gentlemen are enjoying your meal," Rachel said as she refilled their glasses or cups.

Tuesday, Annie put the clothes in the tubs to soak, and she helped Rachel for a while before she finished the wash. She left them in the rinse water during dinner, then would wring them out and hang them after everyone ate.

"Willie sho' wuz taken with ya, Miss Rachel," Annie told her. "He sez ya even calls dem workers 'gen'lemin,' an' served dem yo'self. Sed ya cooked better dan inny white woman he ever seen too."

"I saw he took in every detail. He seemed very bright."

"He be dat. Don't much git by my Willie."

"Well, I like you and Willie too."

Wednesday, Annie came there to help Rachel with all the meal, so she cooked a beef roast, potatoes in white sauce, sautéed onions, green beans, yeast bread or cornbread, and pecan pies.

"You outdid yourself today, Rachel," Uncle Sam said. "This is a feast. If you keep cooking like this, I won't have to pay the men. They'll work for your meals."

The other men raved about her cooking, and Annie wanted her to repeat the directions for the potatoes. Patrick didn't say much, but he listened, smiled, and gave her a look that said he was proud of her.

Thursday she cooked chicken 'n dumplings and had apple cobbler for dessert. She fixed the dumplings mountain-style, like her family preferred. She made them more like biscuit dough, so they were light and fluffy, instead of being flatter and heavier.

"I's never seen dumplin's like dis," Annie said as she sampled some, "but dey sho' is good."

All the men agreed. Of course, Rachel figured, as hard as they worked and as hungry as they got, just about anything would taste good. They usually ate seconds of everything, and very little was left when they went back to work.

The rest of the week went in much the same way. Uncle Sam seemed pleased with how much work the seven men accomplished. Even Sammy worked with them some, especially in the mornings.

When they finished up Saturday afternoon, everyone looked tired, but Uncle Sam said he felt good about what they'd accomplished. The workers would be back Monday. They should finish up in another week.

The next week went much the same, but Rachel felt tired after Saturday's dinner dishes had been done. She was glad there wasn't another week of it.

"We sure are going to miss you next harvest season, Rachel," Uncle Sam said. "Those men are still talking about your dinners, and they asked to help here again."

"Let's don't talk about Rachel leaving yet," Aunt Ivy said. "She won't leave until April, because winter is still raging in the mountains in March."

"And between now and then, we just need to come up with a way to keep her here," Patrick said.

For the first time, Rachel had reservations about spending Sunday afternoon with Patrick. She feared she'd say something that would let him know how much she loved him, because she wasn't used to hiding anything from him. She didn't even like the idea of hiding anything from him. Well, she'd just go and try to act normal. If she said something inadvertently, then she'd just hope it would be for the best. At least then, she would probably know how Patrick felt about her.

She hoped if he only saw her as a good friend, she'd still be able to stay through the winter as planned. From all the comments he'd made, Patrick didn't want her to leave, either.

"Rachel, what's wrong?" Patrick asked as they strolled over the farm with no particular destination in mind.

Rachel had already determined she would not lie to Patrick, but she hoped she wouldn't have to tell him how she felt about him today, either. She wanted to stall for time until Mama and Papa came and she could talk with them. So she stalled. "Why do you think anything's wrong?"

"You're being quieter than usual today."

"The quiet moments we spend together didn't used to bother you."

"They don't, but something is different today. I sense you have something on your mind."

"If I have something on my mind, it's probably you." She laughed, hoping he'd think she was teasing.

"If I were on your mind, I'd hope you'd have a happier expression than what I'm seeing."

"I'm sorry, Patrick. Am I turning out to be bad company today?"

"You could never be bad company for me, Rachel. I cherish every moment we have together, but if there's something on your mind, I hope you would share it."

"Haven't I always?"

"I don't know. Have you? This is the first time I've ever noticed you answering so many of my questions with another question. What kind of answer is that?"

"I guess I get that from Papa. Mama says it's one of his few bad habits, but he tends to answer a question with a question too."

"I'm surprised they're visiting for Thanksgiving. They must really be missing you, because I had the impression they wouldn't be back until they came for you."

"Is that why you were afraid I might go home with them?"

"I guess I am afraid they'll want you to return with them."

Rachel searched his face. "And . . . you don't want that?"

"You should know I don't. I'd miss you too much. How do *you* feel?"

Rachel was going to have to be careful, or she would say too much. "I want to stay here through the winter, like we originally planned. I don't think my parents want me to return now, or they would've said something. My parents are pretty forthright. They aren't underhanded."

"Neither are you. That's one of the many things I like about you. You are completely honest and open with me."

Rachel bit her tongue. She'd never felt so guilty about anything. *Lord, am I doing the right thing? Am I handling this in the manner I should? Please guide me.* Perhaps she should go on the offensive, like in chess. "You've been wonderful to me while I've been here," she said. "How do you feel about me, Patrick?"

He paused, as if weighing his answer, and this was unusual for him. He usually had ready answers. "I think you're my best friend and my favorite person," he finally said.

"I asked you how you feel about me, but you answered with what you think about me."

"What are you digging for? This is the most unusual conversation I've ever had with you. You're being indirect and vague and not like yourself at all, but then you ask me a question and don't want to accept my answer. Do you already know what answer you want me to give? If so, then tell me and I'll give it back to you."

"You're being rather evasive yourself. What's wrong with us today? I don't like this, either. I don't want to be at odds with you. It makes me feel like crying."

"Oh Rachel, I'm sorry I spoke so sharply with you. Can we start over?"

"Yes, let's."

"I see Sammy up ahead looking at something in the grass. Come here. Let's make things better with a hug while his attention is diverted."

She almost fell into his arms, but perhaps this wasn't such a good idea. With the other two hugs, his arms had felt wonderful, and they had affected her, but nothing like this. She felt something flow between them that almost melted her into a puddle at his feet. Perhaps the fact she now recognized how much she loved him made the difference.

He must have felt it, too, because when he pulled back, he looked shaken. He stood looking into her eyes, as if he were trying to find something of great consequence. Although she became afraid of what he might see, she couldn't move her eyes away from his. Then, he sighed and blinked, and his eyes softened. For a moment she thought she could see intense love, but he moved his head, and it was gone.

No one spoke at first. Patrick took her hand, and they walked toward Sammy. He jumped up and ran after a grasshopper.

"I think God has something great in store for us, Rachel," Patrick finally said, staring straight ahead. "I don't know exactly what His plan is, but I hope we can both walk with Him until it's revealed."

He looked at her, then, and she wanted to ask him what he meant, but after the rugged conversation they'd had earlier, she felt she'd better not. She squeezed his hand instead, and he smiled at her. She felt close to him for the rest of the afternoon.

School would start on Wednesday, and Hope told Rachel she dreaded it. She hadn't heard from Charles, but she didn't think he'd return to school.

"Why must I go back?" Hope asked her father. "Why can't I stay here and help with the household chores like I've been doing?"

"I want you to go at least one more year," Uncle Sam said. "Go until you're at least sixteen. Patrick went until almost eighteen."

"Yes, but he had a better teacher. I'm not going to learn that much more, if I do go another year."

"You don't even know for sure who your teacher is going to be this year. Give it a chance before you make up your mind you don't like it."

"Maybe Charles will be there," Rachel told her. "He does like school."

"I guess I can go and give it a chance," she finally agreed.

Hope came home from school Wednesday in good spirits. Charles hadn't been there, but George thought he might come soon. His family still worked to finish up the harvest.

The school had announced they would hold a fall festival at the end of October to raise money for some extra projects. It would be a time of fun and games for all. There would be special music, hayrides, food booths, bobbing for apples, chess and checker tournaments, horseshoe tournaments, cake walks, fishing for prizes, grab bags, and more.

"You should enter the chess tournament, Rachel," Patrick said.

"Patrick likes chess too," Hope said. "You both should enter."

Patrick shook his head. "I saw how Rachel defeated Julius, and I think she's the better player."

Rachel looked at him. "You could enter with me."

"I don't want to be an adversary," he said. "I'll be there with you, but I'd rather be cheering you on than playing against you."

"What's involved?" Rachel asked.

Hope smiled. "You pay an entry fee, and you keep playing as long as you win. The winner takes home a plaque."

"I'm not sure," Rachel said, "but I'll consider it. The chess tournament sounds like it'll take a long time. I might prefer to do some of the other things."

"The chess might not take as long as you think." Patrick's eyes twinkled. "There may not be that many entries, and most of those will go out fast. Chess is not as popular here as it is in some places, and I don't think many are up to your level of play. You may defeat them handily."

"I'm thinking about entering the horseshoes," Uncle Sam said, "but there will be fierce competition and some very good players there."

"We need to support the school," Aunt Ivy said, "so I think all of us should do something."

"What are you planning on doing, Mama?" Sammy asked.

"Going to the food booth, doing some cake walks, and, if I can talk your father into it, going on a hay ride."

Uncle Sam looked at Aunt Ivy, and his eyes softened. "I'd love to go on a hay ride with you, dear."

"You may be asked to furnish and drive a hay wagon, Papa," Hope told him. "I gave them your name as a possibility. You would have to drive for only part of the time, though."

"Then Ivy and I will just have to cuddle on the driver's seat."

"Papa!"

"Rachel, Miss Thomas asked that you come by and see her after school tomorrow," Hope said when she got home from school Monday.

"Do you know what it's about?"

"She didn't say."

"I'll take you," Patrick said. "I'll pick up Sammy and Hope and we'll wait on you."

# CHAPTER FIFTEEN

# Teaching

MISS THOMAS LOOKED UP AS Rachel walked into the room. "Thank you for coming by, Miss Moretz. I've had a family emergency come up, and I'm going to need to leave as soon as possible. I don't think I'll be able to return. I was impressed with you the day you came to school with Hope, and I wondered if you would consider helping out, at least until another teacher can be hired. Mr. Hatley, who teaches the third-level class of ten-, eleven-, and twelve-year-olds, wants to move up, and you'd have his class. This way you wouldn't be teaching your cousins, either. You'd be paid, of course. I want to leave over the weekend, so you'd start Monday."

"I'm not sure about this." Rachel needed time to think it over.

"So far, there's not many students in the class. Of course some of the boys may still be helping out in the fields and come in later. Right now there're only five girls and four boys. My class is much larger, but we didn't want to move anyone down. You'd really be helping us out."

"Could I talk it over with my family and let you know tomorrow?"

"Of course, dear. That would be fine."

"What do you think I should do, Patrick?" Rachel asked after she'd explained the situation. "I'm not sure I want to teach, and I wouldn't have time to cook much."

"I think it's something you need to decide. I'll support you either way, and I'm sure Mama and Papa will too. Why don't you pray about it? Surely we can survive without your cooking for a short time, although it may be difficult." He grinned and winked.

"I'd like you for a teacher better than Miss Thomas," Hope said.

"I'd rather she stay home and cook," Sammy said.

Rachel prayed about the teaching position, just like Patrick suggested. "You'd really be helping us out." The words echoed over and over in Rachel's mind. She felt torn. She didn't feel qualified, but maybe she should try to help them out.

After a fitful night, she still hadn't come to a decision. She prepared breakfast, ate quietly while the family talked, and went outside to do some thinking when Patrick left to take Sammy and Hope to school.

She wondered how long it would take them to find another teacher. If she took the class, would they even look hard? She wouldn't want to be teaching while Mama and Papa were here, or all year, for that matter. Maybe she could agree to teach for one month while they looked for another teacher. This seemed to be a reasonably good solution.

She told the family at the dinner table. She would ride in with Patrick to pick Sammy and Hope up and give Miss Thomas her answer. She would also ask to go to the class Friday to observe. That way she would get to know the students a little before she started, and she could pick up the books and schedule.

After observing the class for only a short time on Friday, Rachel could see why Mr. Hatley chose to move up. The students were very unruly. In the first thirty minutes, a girl's hair ended up with something sticky in it, and someone shot a spit wad across the room. No one saw who the culprit had been, or else they weren't telling. The rest of the day went no better.

Rachel left with an armload of books to use to make lesson plans over the weekend and a feeling of trepidation. What had she gotten herself into? She decided she needed to put prayer time at the top of her list of things to do.

Rachel cooked Saturday, but she did little else around the house. She planned her lessons. She even fixed a stew for supper and worked at the kitchen table while the stew simmered on the stove. By the time she crawled into bed, she felt she'd done as much as she could to prepare.

She hoped to spend tomorrow afternoon with Patrick. Talking with him would help dissipate fears, calm her, and give her courage to face a class of rowdy students.

"Can we go to the woods today?" Sammy asked as they started out on a Sunday afternoon walk.

"*May* we," Patrick corrected. "What about it, Rachel? Feel like a tramp through the forest?"

"Sure." Anywhere would be fine, as long as she was with Patrick.

"Are you worried about tomorrow?" Patrick asked her as they picked their way through a scattering of saw briars.

"I am some. The class seems to be hard to control, and I'm sure they'll test me, because I'm new and a female."

"I think you can handle them. You have an independent spirit that comes from growing up in the mountains, and you're not timid or weak willed. You'll do fine."

"I hope you're right. At least, I'm aware of potential problems and I can be vigilant and alert."

"I wouldn't be surprised if you don't have the girls trying to please you and the boys infatuated with you before the first week is out."

"I'd prefer to be here on the farm with you, but I felt the need to help out. At least, I told them I could teach only for a month. That should give them time to find someone else, and I want to be free to enjoy all of Mama and Papa's visit. Surely I can survive for a month."

"Knowing you, I'm more afraid you'll get attached to the children and have a hard time leaving them."

"You might be right, if they were better behaved, but I can tell this class is going to give me a hard time of it. Just be praying for me."

"I always do, but I'll pray specifically for your day at school Monday. You know, if there's anything I can do to help, all you need to do is ask."

"Teach for me Monday, then." She laughed.

"I know you're teasing, but if you seriously needed me, I would."

The look Patrick gave her almost melted her resolve to wait and seek her parents' advice before she told him she loved him. Her love was so strong it was hard to contain. Like mighty floodwaters, it wanted to burst forth and sweep her with it.

But suppose Patrick didn't love her in the same way? What would such a declaration do to the easy friendship they shared? Suppose their parents had strong objections to them marrying? No, she'd better wait. Her parents would help her decide how best to handle the situation.

"Would you like to marry in the near future, Patrick?" she asked as they sat on a fallen tree and watched Sammy start a "fort."

"If I found the right woman and she wanted to marry me, yes, I would. I'll be twenty-five my next birthday. I still have time, but I would like to start a family."

"How many children would you want?"

"That would partly depend on how many my wife wanted, but personally, I'd like four or five."

"You'd make a great father. You're really good with Sammy, and I hear you were really good with me all those years ago."

"I remember those years well. I was seven when I came to your mountain farm. You weren't born yet, but I can remember when you were. I was eight by then."

"Tell me what you remember."

"I became upset when your mother was in labor. I didn't understand what was happening, but I knew she was in pain. Mama stayed with me most of the time to reassure me. Granny Em helped with your birth. When Aunt Leah cried out, Hawk went to her and stayed by her side, until you were born."

He looked at her and continued, "You fascinated me from the very first, and I would sit by your cradle and watch you sleep. One day, when I extended my finger, you grabbed it in your tiny hand, and I think you grabbed my heart. I felt sure you were supposed to have everything you wanted."

He smiled. "I can remember sitting on Aunt Leah's bed, and she'd let me hold you. I felt so big and important with you in my arms. When you started sitting up and then crawling, I'd play with you and watch after you to make sure you came to no harm. When your face would light up or you would get excited when I came into the room, my heart jumped with joy.

"Then, you started pulling up and standing, I'd take both your hands in mine, stand behind you, and help you walk around. We may have put in many miles like that. I did it so much that you were walking well on your own by the time you had your first birthday."

"I wish I remember more of that time." Rachel spoke her thoughts aloud.

"You were a happy little girl. I'd do silly things to amuse you and you'd laugh and laugh. I'd say, 'Who's your best friend, Rachel?'

and you'd say 'Paddy,' which seemed to be as close as you could get to saying 'Patrick.'"

"But then you had to leave, didn't you?"

"Yes. My parents married, after Papa came back from the war, and we left to come here. You and I stood arm in arm before they put me in the wagon. It hurt so much when I had to leave you, I must have cried for over an hour straight on the way down the mountain. Mama held me and tried to comfort me while Papa drove the wagon. I cried myself to sleep for weeks from missing you. I don't think anyone knew that."

He looked at her and smiled, but she couldn't speak. She worked hard to control the lump in her throat that threatened to become tears. She had heard some of this before in bits and pieces from Mama and Aunt Ivy, but she had no idea the extent of what Patrick had felt then.

"You do have a clear memory of it," she said after she'd collected herself. "I wish mine were clearer."

"You were only two when I left, so I can see why it isn't."

"Perhaps I remember subconsciously. Maybe that's why we immediately fell into such a deep friendship."

"I . . . I . . . could be."

Where did that hesitation come from?

He looked at her with an important question in his eyes, but she couldn't decipher it. He seemed to be searching for something he couldn't find. She needed to look away, but she never could, not when his intense blue eyes locked onto hers. Sometimes she felt like she might drown in those eyes.


Rachel got up early Monday morning. She had breakfast ready when Patrick came down, and he was the first one up.

"You're up mighty early." He gave her a broad smile. "Did you sleep all right?"

"I did once I got to sleep. I'm just anxious about today."

"Need a hug?"

He put out his arms, pulled her into a quick hug, and then released her. In its quickness, it didn't shake the earth beneath her as much as the last one had, but she still felt an exciting thrill run throughout her body. Patrick's hugs had the power to right her world.

"Do we need to wait for the others, or can we go ahead and eat?" he asked.

"Let's eat it while it's hot. I'm sure they'll be down shortly. I want to go freshen up and change dresses before we go. I didn't want to cook in my good dress."

They sat across from each other and ate. Rachel liked the intimate feeling.

"This is nice," Patrick said. "I don't think we've ever eaten just the two of us before."

She looked at him carefully, but couldn't tell how he meant the comment. It almost sounded like something a beau would say to his girl, and it gave her a warm, tingly feeling.

They had just finished when the others came down. Patrick got up to go milk.

"Someone must be eager to get to school today," Uncle Sam teased.

"Anxious would be the better word," she told him.

She packed their dinners, and Patrick hitched up the team. Why did she feel as if she were going to her own execution?

The children came in talking and pushed and shoved into their seats. They did seem to be listening when she spoke, however. "I would like it very much if you would walk quietly to your seats each morning without bothering anyone. This is what I'll expect of you. If you do, I will make sure you get out to recess on time. If not, I will subtract the time it takes for you to settle down off your playtime. Do you understand? Are there any questions?"

She noticed two of the boys were interested in her every move, especially when she moved toward her desk. She knew something was up.

"You may remember from Friday, my name is Miss Moretz, and I'll be your teacher for the time being." Rachel thought it would be better if they thought she was their regular teacher for now. They would be harder to handle if they thought she was a substitute.

She wanted to write her name on the blackboard for the children to see, but she didn't see any chalk. She opened her desk drawer and a snake started to crawl out. It was a pretty corn snake. Rachel picked it up, and it wrapped around her arm.

She looked at her students and most sat with their eyes wide and their mouths open. She took the chalk from the drawer and wrote her name on the board.

"As I was saying, I am Miss Mortez. Did Mr. Hatley call you by your first or last names?" She pointed to a girl in a front seat.

"He called us by our first names, Miss Moretz."

"Thank you."

A boy raised his hand. "How long are you going to keep that snake on your arm?"

"I need to learn all your names first, and then this snake's going to help me teach the class before we take him outside and release him at recess."

Another boy raised his hand. "Miss Moretz, are you going to take minutes off our recess today because we were noisy coming in?"

"No, I'm not. I don't think that would be fair, because I hadn't warned you yet or told you what I expected. Now, I want you to stand beside your desk one at a time, then tell me your names."

They did so, and she repeated their names after them. As she did, she tried to remember their first names. She would learn their last names later. The girls were Mary, Nancy, Louise, and Penelope, and Henry, Alfred, Nelson, and Johnny were the boys. It didn't take long to learn eight students.

"Now, I want to thank the two boys who brought me this snake." She saw them look at each other and her in surprise. They were wondering how she knew, and she tried not to laugh at them. "I'd planned to hold reading lessons this morning, but this is a wonderful opportunity for a science lesson instead. This is a corn snake. It was very scared from being caged in the desk drawer, so when I first took him out, he squeezed my arm very tightly."

"A corn snake is a constrictor." She wrote the word *constrictor* on the board. "That means it squeezes the life out of his prey and then eats it. This one won't do that to me, because I'm too big for it. There are constrictors that grow big enough to kill a person. One such snake is the boa constrictor from Central and South America. Another is the python, which is found in Africa, Asia, Australia, and the Pacific Islands. Even though constrictors can kill, they aren't poisonous."

Every student sat enthralled with the lesson, so Rachel continued to tell them about snakes. She told them about the cobras in India and the snake charmers there, and she told them about local snakes.

"I wasn't too afraid to handle this snake, because the boys who put it in my desk had probably already handled him. I want to caution you not to do this. You might not recognize a poisonous snake from a nonpoisonous one, and even a snake that isn't poisonous can bite when it gets scared, and the incision can become infected. Do you have any questions?"

"Would you go back over the poisonous snakes here?" Mary asked.

"Certainly. The most common one is the copperhead. Like most snakes, it blends into its surroundings and is very hard to see. In the Uwharrie Mountain area, I understand there are some timber rattlesnakes. They make a noise to try to scare away an adversary before they strike. There may be a few water moccasins, but most of them are farther east. The water snakes you see around here are more likely to be nonpoisonous."

She looked over the class. "You've been an excellent class this morning, and I'm proud of you. If you will spend the next twenty minutes writing me a paper on what you've learned about snakes, we'll go out a little early for recess and release our corn snake in the woods behind the school."

Rachel walked around the room and watched them work. The morning had gone well so far. It was hard to believe it was almost time for recess. The impromptu lesson on snakes had certainly held their attention, and she knew every student had learned something. It had actually been better than the reading lesson she'd planned. With the snake lesson, she'd been able to teach the whole group at once, while the reading lesson would've required she divide them in groups. At times it would have been hard for her to watch everyone, and there'd have been more chances for misbehavior.

*Thank Thee, Lord, for the opportunity to turn naughtiness into something positive.*

She had Nancy collect the papers, and then Rachel lined the students up to go outside. She gave them the choice of following her to release the snake or beginning to play. Every child chose to go with her.

She pried the snake from her arm and gave it a push toward the woods. They watched it quickly crawl away, glad to finally obtain freedom.

"Why weren't you afraid of that snake?" Alfred asked her.

"I grew up on a farm in the mountains and learned to appreciate nature. My father taught me whatever I wanted to learn. I've fished and gone hunting too."

"Wow! You're not like the other teachers. You make learning sort of fun."

For reading class, she had each student read what they'd written about snakes. Not only would she be able to assess how they could read and write, but it would help reinforce the lesson and correct any misconceptions.

When she announced dinnertime, several of the students asked her to come outside and eat with them. She'd planned to eat her dinner peacefully in the classroom, but she felt honored they wanted her to eat with them, so she went.

Another class ate at the same time, and she heard some of her students tell them all about the snake lesson. She smiled to herself at the amount of information that poured from them.

"You should have seen Miss Moretz," Johnny said. "She wasn't a bit afraid of that snake. She let it ride around on her arm until recess."

The arithmetic lesson began okay, but when they were assigned problems, Penelope kept grabbing the lower part of her leg and saying something was stinging her. Rachel looked and saw small red dots, but she couldn't find a bee or insect. Then, she saw Henry's foot moving back. He sat behind Penelope.

"Henry, please stand up." He started to bend over. "No, stand beside you seat now."

By then, Rachel had moved beside him. She looked down, and he had a straight pin wedged between the sole and the toe of his shoe. She picked up his work and moved him to a small table in the corner.

"Give me the pin," she told him.

"I'm sorry, Miss Moretz." He handed her the pin.

"Do you also need to apologize to someone else?"

"I'm sorry, Penelope."

"Did you know you also disrupted the entire class?"

"I'm sorry, everyone."

"We'll need to discuss this after school today. Please stay when the class is dismissed for the day." He nodded and started doing his math.

"Henry, I am very disappointed in how you behaved in arithmetic class today. I expected better from you."

He hung his head. She hoped she could get him to understand.

"It shouldn't be fun to cause someone pain. You really hurt her, and those pricks could become infected. She could even get so sick her muscles began to stiffen up, and she could die. Wouldn't that be a huge tragedy? Think how you would feel. Penelope is the youngest girl in class, and she would never hurt anyone."

Rachel saw the worried look on his face. "Now I know you didn't mean to really harm her, but sometimes pranks can turn into something serious. School is hard enough without the students making it harder on each other. I hope and pray all the students in my class will try to make things better for each other, instead of worse. Do you understand what I'm saying, Henry?"

"Yes, Miss Moretz." He looked pretty stricken. "I really am sorry, and I promise never to do it again."

"I believe you, but I hope you won't make any more poor choices, either. I would like to see you become one of the responsible leaders in my class. That's all, Henry. You may go, but if I have any more trouble out of you, I will have a conference with your parents."

Henry was leaving when Sammy and Hope came in. She'd told Patrick to pick them up at least a half an hour later than usual. She wanted to get her room in order for tomorrow.

Hope and Sammy helped, and she could soon pack up her things. She would readjust her lesson plans for tomorrow to include those she hadn't gotten to today, so her planning tonight shouldn't be lengthy. She would also check their papers on snakes.

"I can tell it went well by the look on your face," Patrick said as he helped her into the wagon.

"It went much better than I expected. Having such a small class certainly helped."

"Everyone was talking about her snake lesson today," Hope said. "All the boys and some of the girls in my class feel cheated, because she and Mr. Hatley switched places."

"They said she carried a snake around most of the morning," Sammy added. "Was that true, Rachel?"

Rachel told them how the snake had been put in her desk as a prank, and how she had turned it into a lesson. When she described the dismay on the two boys' faces, Patrick roared with laughter. "I can just imagine you carrying a snake around the classroom on your arm as you hold your students mesmerized," he said. "I knew you would do a fantastic job. It makes me want to be in your classes."

"Me too," Sammy said. "Will you teach next year so I can be in your class?"

"I'm not even supposed to be here all of this year, much less next year."

"Oh, yeah. I forgot, but I want you to stay."

"I second that," Patrick said, "although you wouldn't have to teach."

The next morning, she went into her classroom to find a jar with a tadpole and a small frog sitting on her desk. She started jotting down notes on amphibians. Apparently someone wanted the science lesson today to be on frogs. At least they'd not hidden it somewhere as a prank. She hoped it would hold their attention as well as the snake had yesterday.

She also had a new student, Dennis. Apparently he'd heard about the new teacher and decided to return to school as soon as possible.

"I wouldn't be surprised if you don't end up with a large class," Patrick said that afternoon.

Hope was happy, because Charles had also returned to school. He came to Rachel's room with Sammy and Hope after school and helped her straighten and clean.

CHAPTER SIXTEEN

# Fall Festival

MR. HATLEY HAD ALREADY MADE preparations for parents to handle her class's part in the fall festival. Rachel didn't have to do anything, although she did bake some cakes for the cake walk.

The first week of school had passed quickly, and the festival had been scheduled for four o'clock on Saturday. Parents planned to sell chicken stew for supper, and Uncle Sam decided they'd eat there to support the school.

It seemed everywhere she walked, parents came up to tell her either how much their child was enjoying her class or ask if their child would be able to have her for a teacher in a coming year. She didn't know quite how to handle the compliments.

Patrick's teasing didn't help. "You're becoming quite famous and sought after in the community, Miss Moretz."

She just shrugged and didn't reply. She and Patrick walked around, played a few games, and did the cake walk for couples or pairs. She saw Hope and Charles doing some activities together too.

"Let's check out the chess tournament," Patrick told her. He seemed to be determined to have her play.

There weren't many entrants in the chess tournament, so the checker games were set up in the same room. Many more had entered the checker contest.

"If I play chess, you need to at least enter the checkers contest," Rachel told Patrick.

Patrick paid their entry fees just before the tournaments began. Rachel was the only woman entered among the eight chess contestants. Julius was one of them.

Rachel had no trouble defeating her first opponents. Julius maneuvered so he didn't have to play her in any of the first rounds. They were the last two players left, however.

"I wouldn't have entered if I'd known you were entering," he said through nearly clenched jaws.

She could tell he was torn between wanting to beat her badly and forfeiting so he wouldn't have to play her at all. After a long pause, he chose the latter.

"I refuse to play a woman," Julius told the officials.

Rachel took his arm to stop him from rushing away. She saw Patrick watching her, instead of making his checker move.

"Please don't be so angry with me," she whispered. "Can't we be civil? I liked you Julius, but I realized we'd have eventually made each other miserable if we'd married. Can't we be friends or, at least, not enemies?"

He jerked back and left without a word. She looked up to see a worried look on Patrick's face. She accepted her plaque from the official and went over to watch Patrick win the checker tournament.

"What did you say to Julius?" Patrick asked as they went to put their plaques in the surrey.

"I tried to tell him not to be so angry and resentful. He seems to have so much animosity for me. I guess he can't handle feeling rejected, but I didn't want it to be this way."

"You may be right, but he could be treating you like this because you're part Cherokee."

Rachel hadn't considered that. She looked at Patrick. "My Cherokee heritage doesn't bother you, does it?"

"Are you serious? I'm hurt you would even ask. You should know me better than that. It wouldn't bother me if you were part colored, although I'm afraid it would be a huge problem with most people. I like you for who you are as a person, Rachel, not for what you are."

She wished she could take his hand or fall into his arms, but she hesitated to do either in public. Instead, she gave him a big smile.

He smiled back. "Come, let's go get some supper." His touch on her back would do.

After supper, they went on a hayride. The sky had just started to turn to dusk, and the evening had become cool. They didn't know the driver of the wagon they climbed into, but it had plenty of room. They were able to take seats in a corner with their backs against a high wagon side, where the loose hay had been packed up to form a comfortable backrest.

Immediately Patrick reached under the hay and pulled her hand into his. Since their hands were covered in hay, no one would notice in the dimming light.

"If you want a hay ride," the driver announced to those standing around, "you'd better pay and climb aboard. This is going to be my last trip."

Others started boarding the wagon until it grew so crowded that Rachel had to press against Patrick to keep from being squeezed too close to the man on the other side of her. Patrick put his arm around her to make a little more room for them.

Rachel had been growing chilly, and Patrick's closeness warmed her. As they started to move at a lumbering pace, she felt secure and at peace.

Into the ride, she leaned her head back to see the stars and found her head on Patrick's shoulder. After star gazing for several minutes, she turned her head toward Patrick and snuggled into him. She felt his arm tighten around her, and she wanted the ride to last all night.

"It's time to go home," he said.

When he'd handed her down from the wagon, she looked around and people were leaving. The rest of the family chattered about what they'd done at the festival on the way home, but Patrick and Rachel said little.

Rachel's days fell into a pattern. Sometimes a student would bring in something for a lesson, and sometimes she would, but more often, they'd use the text books. Yet, the snake had grabbed their attention so thoroughly and Rachel's handling of it seemed so unusual, the students seemed interested in whatever Rachel did.

She encouraged this. She stood on her soapbox, otherwise known as a chair, when she read them an essay. She acted out soliloquies, like Juliet and Lady Macbeth. The students did skits of portions of literature and read material often far above their level, but they helped each other.

History had always fascinated Rachel. They compared the differences in the two ship's logs Columbus kept, did skits on the Jamestown Colony, had mock trials from the Boston Massacre, and debated why the nation needed a new constitution after the Articles of Confederation.

Rachel had as much fun as the students did because teaching like this was fun, and Patrick helped too. He would often find the tangible lessons she took to school. He helped her gather materials to do experiments and helped plan math lessons her students could relate to. He even helped her check papers if she got behind.

The days flew by, and Rachel found a month was not nearly enough time to use all her ideas. Patrick had been right—it was hard to leave her students, yet she felt good she was leaving a much better class than the one she had entered. Regardless, the last minutes were filled with hugs and tears.

Friday, November 19 had been her last day at school. Thanksgiving would be the following Thursday, and Mama and Papa would be there on Tuesday. Rachel couldn't wait.

---

Patrick liked sitting down again to dinners Rachel had prepared. Her cooking had spoiled them, and it'd been hard to eat Mama's mediocre fare. Annie had cooked dinner on Tuesdays, and her meals were better than Mama's but not as good as Rachel's.

He knew Rachel was excited about her parents' visit, and he was happy for her, but he still had reservations. It made sense to him that they might end up taking her back with them, despite what Rachel had said. Rachel had come to mean more to him with each passing day, and he didn't know what he would do when she left. He wanted that day to be as far away as possible.

When he thought of their Sunday afternoons together, he almost began to hope she had begun to love him too. He hated to see winter come, because they'd have less chance of having private moments.

Then, there was the hayride. With her snuggling against him, he never wanted the hayride to end. Even thinking about it made his blood race and his longing nearly overwhelm him. That night he'd been certain she'd fallen in love with him, and he decided to declare his love for her on Sunday afternoon. However, when morning came, he feared it was only wishful thinking. He felt that telling her he loved her when she didn't have the same feelings would put a strain on their friendship and send her back to the mountains that much earlier.

Even if Rachel wanted to marry him, it was possible her parents would take her home as soon as they learned about the couple. He wasn't sure how his parents would react, either.

*Lord, this is all so complicated I'm at a loss. I put it in Thy hands, but I pray for a resolution soon. It's so hard to live with this uncertainty. May Thy will be done, and help me to live with whatever that is. Amen.*

The Moretzes drove up just before supper on Tuesday. Rachel had already prepared chicken 'n dumplings and persimmon pudding. Patrick stood on the front porch and watched as she ran into her parents' arms, and the three of them stood embracing. As they walked toward the house, his aunt's and uncle's eyes turned on him in a searching look. They were friendly, however, when they spoke to him, and Uncle Luke shook his hand. Patrick breathed a deep sigh and followed them inside.

---

Rachel could barely contain her joy. Not only had she missed her parents, but she couldn't wait to get them alone, so she could talk with them about Patrick. After the hayride, she had begun to hope Patrick did think of her as more than just a friend. However, she couldn't be sure.

At supper, Patrick entertained her parents with accounts of her teaching experiences. He made her sound like some sort of miracle worker.

"I just taught the class like you've taught me at home," she told them. "I made their learning as real as I could and as much fun as possible."

"We're very proud of you," Papa said. "Do you think you'd like to pursue a career in teaching?"

"I really enjoyed the month I taught, but I think it would be much harder to keep the children as interested a whole year. I also missed being at the farm. I like being outside too much to want to be stuck in a schoolroom most of the day."

"We certainly missed her being at the farm and her cooking," Uncle Sam said. "After the dinners she cooked for my workers at harvest, I've had men begging to be hired next year. I didn't have the heart to tell them she wouldn't be here."

"If not teaching, what are you interested in doing?" Mama asked her.

"I'd like to marry and have a family, and I know they hire only single women to teach."

"Oh, is there someone you're interested in?" Mama asked, then glanced across at Patrick.

Rachel dared not look at Patrick. "I'm not talking about getting married right away." She laughed.

Mama gave her a look that said Rachel hadn't answered her question, but she didn't say anything. Rachel knew her mother would wait to bring up the issue again in private. She sent her mother a grateful look.

Patrick had moved in with Sammy, so her parents could have his bedroom.

"Come help me unpack," Mama said to Rachel after supper.

"Go ahead, Rachel," Aunt Ivy said. "Hope and I will take care of cleaning up here."

"I can tell you're interested in someone," Mama said as soon as they'd closed the door to the bedroom. "Who is he?"

Rachel took a deep breath and hesitated. It was hard to know where to begin.

"It's Patrick, isn't it?"

Mama was so perceptive. Rachel should have known she couldn't hide anything from her. She looked into her mother's eyes, trying to ascertain how the older woman felt about it.

"It is. I didn't intend for it to happen, but I've fallen in love with Patrick. I've probably been in love with him for a long time, but I just admitted it to myself a month or so ago. Are you terribly shocked or disappointed in me? I know we're related, but we're only half cousins."

"No, darling. I suspected this from your letters. I'm not shocked, either. I just want you to be happy, and Patrick is a wonderful man. I don't think you could have found a better one."

"Do you think Papa will also approve of me marrying Patrick?" She needed both of her parents' approvals.

"I do. We've talked about it, and we want your happiness."

"There's still another problem. I'm not sure Patrick loves me in the same way. He might just consider me a very good friend."

Mama laughed. "I don't think so, dear. Haven't you seen the way he looks at you? I'd be very surprised if that young man isn't head over heels in love with you already."

"What do I do, though? He's said nothing. Should I wait for him, or should I say something first?"

"Let's include your father in that conversation. We'll get together sometime tomorrow and discuss the situation."

"Oh, thank you for coming, Mama. I feel so much better now." She leaned into her mother's arms for a hug.

Wednesday morning the temperature wasn't so cold, but the wind blew strong, and it was uncomfortable outside. After all the morning chores were done, Papa announced to the others that he, Mama, and Rachel were going to walk to the barn to discuss some family matters.

Rachel noticed Patrick's face fall, and his eyes had almost a look of panic. The poor guy probably still suspected her parents would take her back with them. Maybe Mama was right. Maybe he did love her.

Rachel and her parents walked to the barn and sat on some wooden boxes or the milking stools. It felt comfortable in there, out of the wind.

"So, your mama tells me you're smitten with Patrick," Papa began with a smile.

"I love him, Papa."

"I take it you are sure of this." His face held an amused expression.

Rachel let out a sigh. She knew for sure now Papa wouldn't oppose her on this. "Without a doubt, but I don't know how he feels or if I should say something first."

"That's what your mother told me, and I agree with her. I'm pretty certain Patrick is in love with you too. I'm surprised you haven't seen it. He doesn't hide it very well."

"What should I do, Papa?"

"Tell him how you feel. Waiting won't change the situation. If we're wrong about how he feels, and I don't think we are, you can just pack your things and go home with us. Being away from him and having a loving family around you will help you endure your grief."

Rachel knew she must look stricken. She'd rather say nothing and have Patrick for her best friend than to lose him completely. Their relationship had been special as just one of friendship.

"Don't let fear take hold of you." Mama patted her hand. "I can understand your apprehension, but trust in Patrick. I don't think he'll let you down."

Mama was right again. This was Patrick, the man who'd always protected her and come to her aid. He wasn't likely to hurt her. If he didn't want her for his wife, he would still be kind and gentle.

"I know how you feel, Rachel," Papa said. "I remember very well how it was in the beginning for your mother and me."

His dark eyes gave Mama such a loving look, her own heart thumped at the intensity. Mama reached out her hand to him, and Rachel felt she was intruding.

"When should I tell Patrick, then?" she asked.

"Didn't you say you and I would spend the afternoon baking for tomorrow?" Mama asked. "We'll have dinner and supper to fix too. I would suggest you wait until tomorrow after our Thanksgiving dinner. Then, you can really give Patrick something to be thankful for." Mama's smile looked mischievous.

"May he and I be alone somewhere? We've never done that before."

"I think that would be okay under the circumstances for this one time," Papa said. "Your mother and I trust both you and Patrick."

Rachel hummed as she and Mama cooked for the rest of the day, as her excitement grew. She'd never known Mama and Papa both to be wrong about something when they felt so sure. The more she thought about it, the more she believed that Patrick might just love her.

Patrick came to the supper table with a solemn face. Rachel wished she could tell him she wasn't planning to go back to the mountains now, but if he wasn't in love with her, she would leave. She searched for something she could say to him to take away his worry.

If she told him they would talk tomorrow, he might think she was planning to tell him good-bye, and she didn't want to say too much in front of Uncle Sam and Aunt Ivy. In the end she couldn't think of anything to say, so she gave him what she hoped was a reassuring smile.

# CHAPTER SEVENTEEN

# Thanksgiving

"THIS WAS SOME FEAST," UNCLE Sam said when they'd finished eating Thanksgiving dinner. "Rachel and Leah together cook so well I can't stop until I'm too stuffed for comfort."

"I'm one very lucky man," Papa said and looked at Mama.

"Well, I'm not complaining, either," Uncle Sam said. "Ivy and I have been very happy. I have no regrets. I never doubted she was the one for me."

"Well, since Rachel and Leah cooked all this, Hope and I will do the dishes," Ivy said.

"The weather is mild today." Rachel looked at Patrick. "Papa said you and I might go for a short walk. Do you feel like it, Patrick?"

"Sure." He looked pleased. "Where did you want to walk?"

"Let's go down to the stream and sit on the log."

They walked side by side for a while, but Rachel could see the suspense weighed heavily on Patrick. Finally, he asked, "Did you and your parents have a good discussion yesterday?"

"We did, and I wanted to talk to you about it."

"They're taking you home now, aren't they?" He tried to keep his voice steady, but he looked as if his whole world had crumbled into dust.

"You know I'd never want that, don't you? You'd be looking at one unhappy woman if that were the case."

"Then what did you talk about that couldn't be said in front of everyone?"

They'd come to their place beside the stream, but they had yet to sit down on the log. Rachel hesitated. How could she say this?

"I can't imagine what's so hard to say," Patrick said. "Surely Uncle Luke hasn't arranged a marriage for you. He seems too close to you to do such a thing."

She put out her hand and touched his upper arm. She'd better just say it. "No, we talked about the fact that I've fallen in love with you, Patrick."

Patrick just stood there with a stunned look on his face.

Why didn't he say something? "Are you upset with me? Don't you have feelings for me?" Rachel felt tears forming.

"Did you say you *loved* me?" He sounded incredulous.

She nodded.

"As a woman loves a man and not just as a friend?"

She nodded again, but her eyes were beginning to pool with tears as she searched his face for some clue of how he felt.

"Oh Rachel!" He pulled her into his arms. "You just made my dreams come true. God has just given me my heart's desire. I've been in love with you since almost the moment you walked through our front door." He pulled his head back and looked into her eyes.

She had to sit down then.

He sat down beside her. "What did your parents say?"

"They weren't all that surprised. They said they read between the lines of my letters. Perhaps that's why they came now."

"And they don't object to you marrying your half cousin?"

"No. Cousins do still marry, you know."

Patrick leaned back. "Learning you love me and having no objection from your parents is more than I dared hope. So there's no obstacles to us marrying?"

"Just finding out how your parents feel and the fact you haven't asked me yet."

He looked at her carefully again, and then took both her hands in his. "Rachel Moretz, I love you beyond anything words can express. You're an integral part of who I am. Will you please do me the honor of becoming my wife?"

"I'm so deeply in love with you, I can think of nothing else. You are woven into the fabric of my very being. I would love more than anything to marry you, Patrick Whitley."

He took her into his arms and kissed her. Time stood still. In that moment, nothing existed but her and him and God. She'd never felt so strange, so full of ecstasy and so out of control all at the same time.

Even after the kiss ended, she clung to him, and he held her. She had no power to move or to say anything.

"Oh, my darling," he whispered in her ear before he pulled away and took her hand.

They sat watching the creek wash by. Rachel could feel her strength gradually returning, but she felt giddy and more alive.

"So when did you figure out you loved me?" Patrick asked.

"One Sunday when we were sitting in church, after Julius and I had parted. I was thinking about what a special friendship you and I share and how much we have in common. I had wished I could find a man like you to marry. All of a sudden it hit me. I'm sure I'd loved you for a long time, but I didn't realize it until then."

"Why didn't you tell me right away?"

"Probably for the same reason you didn't tell me. There was a lot to consider. I didn't know how you felt about me, or what our parents might think. Not long after I knew how I felt, I got the letter from Mama and Papa saying they were coming for Thanksgiving, so I decided to wait and talk to them. I knew they'd have good advice."

"When and where do you want to have the wedding, and where do you want to live?"

"I'll live wherever you want, Patrick. I love the mountains, but I love you so much more. It would be fine with me if we stay here, but if you have something else in mind, that would be fine too. I'd love to be married before winter comes, but I'm not sure that will be possible. Let's talk to our families and have them help us decide what's best. We'll also discuss where the wedding will be held with them. I see three possibilities: here, Watauga County, or Salisbury."

"You know, I was so afraid you were going to marry Julius. I lived in agony during that time. The only thing that helped was the fact that you confided your feelings with me. At least I knew you weren't deeply in love with him yet."

"I would have never loved him. I'm convinced I was in love with you at the time, but I didn't know it yet. I'm sorry that I hurt you, though."

"It's fine and worth every moment, now that I have you, but that fact still doesn't seem real. It seems too good to be true."

"You know my relatives for four generations now have had problems getting together with their love, but each one has ended up with a great love."

"Maybe adversity helps us appreciate the blessings all the more. I know I'll thank God for you for the rest of my life."

She stood up. "Should we go talk with our family now?"

"Yes, but first I need to ask your father for your hand. Then we'll see what my family says."

He continued to hold her hand as they walked slowly back. Rachel really hoped they could marry soon. Now that she knew for sure Patrick loved her, she couldn't wait.

"You know the Sunday we almost had an argument was my fault," she told him. "I didn't want to let it slip that I loved you, but I hoped you'd tell me how you felt about me."

"You had me confused there for a while, but I did something similar. I'd been hiding how I felt about you for a long time, and it's very hard for me to keep a secret from you." He paused and looked at her lips. "I'd like to kiss you again, but I'd better not."

"If you did, you'd have to carry me back." She laughed.

"Are you saying my kisses leave you weak kneed?" A grin spread across his face.

"That and so much more."

He put his arm around her waist until they got in sight of the house. When they entered, her parents looked at her expectantly. She smiled at them to let them know everything was fine, and they gave her a knowing look.

Patrick turned to Papa. "Uncle Luke, I'd like to show you something in the barn, if you have time."

"I have plenty of time."

Mama and Rachel heated up leftovers for supper. Mama didn't ask anything about Patrick. She already knew the answers from reading their expressions.

Patrick gave her a quick nod and smiled when he and Papa returned, so she knew Papa had been agreeable.

After the family devotion, Patrick looked at his parents. "Rachel and I have something we need to discuss with the family. We've fallen in love and want to get married."

Aunt Ivy turned pale. "Impossible! You can't marry your cousin."

"Mama, you planned for Papa to marry his cousin, when you thought it was the only way he would get this farm. Violet was his full cousin. Rachel and I are only half cousins."

"Well, I'm used to thinking of Rachel as family." Aunt Ivy seemed to have calmed down some, but she still looked uncertain. "And besides, you are a lot older than she is."

Mama went over and hugged her sister. "Ivy, this isn't a bad thing. Rachel has always been mature for her age, and eight years is not all that much."

"You and Luke approve of this then?" Aunt Ivy searched Mama's face.

Mama smiled. "I wouldn't want to stand in the way of true love, would you?"

Ivy burst into tears. Uncle Sam stood and went to her. "Let us have a minute alone," he said, as he led Aunt Ivy out. "We'll be back, and we can discuss things then."

"Don't worry," Mama said to Patrick. "Everything's going to be fine. Sam will help Ivy get her thoughts untangled."

They weren't out of the room long. When they came back, Aunt Ivy looked more composed. "I take it you and Luke are supporting this, Leah?"

"Yes, we support Rachel and want her and Patrick's happiness."

"Sam tells me I've overreacted. He's not as surprised as I was. If everyone else is for this, then I'll get use to the idea."

"Rachel wants your help in figuring out when and where we should get married," Patrick said. "We'd like to marry before the bad part of winter, if possible."

"That doesn't give us much time," Aunt Ivy said. "We won't have time to make you a dress."

Rachel said, "If it comes to a choice between having a new wedding dress and marrying Patrick sooner, I'll choose marrying Patrick sooner."

Patrick gave her a look that made her heart race faster.

"Well, I just happened to have brought the ivory silk I was married in," Mama said. "Rachel and I are nearly the same size, so maybe we can refurbish it."

"Mama, you're amazing. That's perfect. I think I've found what I've always wanted, a love as deep as yours and Papa's. How fitting I get married in your wedding dress."

"You can thank your father for thinking of bringing the dress. You know how he's always planning ahead. As he said, we wouldn't have to mention it if it wasn't needed."

"Now the question is, where?" Papa went back to the original set of questions.

Aunt Ivy sucked in a deep breath. "I don't think we've settled on exactly when yet, either."

Mama looked at Rachel. "I have a suggestion for the where. Why don't we have it in Salisbury? That way the boys will be there, as well as Father and Clara. I don't think they would be up to traveling in the cold now."

"I hoped it could be here," Ivy said.

"Father's house is larger," Papa reminded her.

"Rachel and Patrick could stay in a cottage there the night of the wedding, and then come back here alone," Mama added. "The rest of you could do some shopping in Salisbury before you come back."

"That sounds like a good plan to me," Patrick agreed.

"Now, when?" Uncle Sam asked.

"I hate to take over the plans," Mama said, "but we need to hold it before Christmas, if possible."

"I don't mind that," Rachel said.

"That gives us only a month or less," Aunt Ivy said. "Can we pull everything together that fast?"

"It will be a small wedding with just family," Rachel said. "Hope will be my only attendant, and we'll have it in Grandfather's parlor."

"Papa will be my best man," Patrick said.

"Let's have the wedding on December the fourteenth," Rachel suggested. "That's a Sunday and should get everyone settled before Christmas, as well as give us three weeks to plan."

"We'll come home on the following Saturday," Uncle Sam said. "That will put us home on the twentieth and in plenty of time for Christmas."

"Hopefully, the weather will cooperate and we can go home too," Papa said. "If not, we'll have the boys and can spend Christmas with Father."

"We'd better plan to leave on Saturday for Salisbury," Mama said. "We'll take Rachel and Patrick with us to work on the wedding plans. Ivy, Sam, Hope, and Sammy can come whenever they think best."

"Well, that wasn't so difficult, was it?" Uncle Sam grinned and looked at his wife.

# CHAPTER EIGHTEEN

# Married

"SINCE ALL THAT IS DECIDED," Patrick said, "does anyone object if I take my fiancée to the barn to help me milk tonight? I promise not to do anything more than hug her and give her one kiss."

"I remember how well you've always protected Rachel," Mama said, "and by her letters, I know that hasn't changed. I trust you, Patrick."

"I'm okay with it too," Papa said.

"This has been the best Thanksgiving in my life," Patrick told Rachel as they each milked a cow.

"It has been full of wonder," Rachel agreed. "Everything is happening so fast, I'm having a hard time catching up. This morning I woke up not even knowing if you loved me, and now my wedding is all planned."

"Do you have any regrets?"

"None whatsoever. I had hoped we wouldn't have to wait until spring to get married."

Patrick smiled his agreement. "After waiting months for you, I want you as my wife as soon as possible."

"Who'll do the milking and see to the farm while everyone's gone?"

"Papa will ask a neighbor. It won't be but a few days, because my parents won't come until about the eleventh or twelfth, and you and I will be here on the fifteenth. I'm glad we'll have some time alone too. Your mother's a smart woman."

"She always has been. I'm very blessed to have such wonderful parents. I've always prayed I would find a love as deep and wonderful as theirs, and now I have."

They finished milking, and Patrick looked at her with that intense gaze of his. "I know you so well, Rachel. We've been best friends from the very first. Now, I'm getting to discover the romantic side of you, and I find it exciting."

Rachel looked down, embarrassed by what she wanted to say. She said part of it anyway. "Patrick, you thrill me beyond measure. I don't even think we'll have those explosive arguments your parents can have. I think we work together too well for that."

"Come here and let me take you in my arms. I want to hold you close and never let you go. Maybe soon, I'll even begin to believe I have your heart, and you really do want me."

Patrick held her close for a long time. She loved the feel of him. When his lips found hers, she had to hold to him for support. She'd had no idea that so much emotion could be delivered in a kiss. Everything ceased to exist, except their love, but that was more than enough.

He held her for a minute longer after the kiss ended, which was good. Her legs didn't want to work properly. Patrick turned and picked up both milk buckets, and she followed him to the house on shaky legs.

The trip to Salisbury went well. The day had turned warm, and the sun shone brightly.

Grandfather and Clara were elated with the wedding plans after the initial surprise wore off. Rachel eagerly hugged her brothers, and they hugged her back. They must have missed her some.

Sunday turned into a raw, wet day, with a drenching rain falling. They all went to church, but they stayed inside, ate, rested, and talked afterwards.

Although Monday came with clouds and cold, no rain, sleet, or snow fell. Grandfather and Patrick went out to take care of some things related to the wedding, and Clara, Mama, and Rachel did the same. Papa stayed home with the boys.

They went to the dress shop they'd always used. Mama chose a new dress, and the seamstress agreed to alter Rachel's gown to suit.

The days passed quickly in a flurry of activity. Grandfather secured the preacher, and the women decided on the food. Rachel chose a few flowers, but they were so expensive, since they were out of season and had to come from the hothouse, she chose carefully. There would be Christmas decorations, too, so they wouldn't need many.

She and Patrick spent the time from supper to bedtime together, but they didn't see that much of each other during the day. They did get to finally play each other in a game of chess. Mama and Papa paired off at the same time, and Mama won. Patrick and Rachel had a stalemate.

"I admire the four of you," Grandfather said. "I learned very quickly not to play Leah or Luke. I see I can now add Rachel and Patrick to that list."

"It's good to have a well-matched mate on the cold winter evenings," Papa said, and Mama smiled at him with a knowing look.

"Well now, I have that," Grandfather said as he looked at Clara.

Aunt Ivy, Uncle Sam, and Sammy came on the eleventh. Ivy and Hope had already made themselves new dresses.

Grandfather still had his little cottage, and Patrick would move in it to let his parents have his room. Rachel and he would spend the night there after the wedding.

The wedding was lovely. The seamstress had reshaped Rachel's gown to look like a new creation. She knew by the expression on Patrick's face when she came in on Papa's arm that she looked her best.

As she and Patrick stood together to say their vows, Rachel felt love surround her. She had the love of all these people, especially Mama's and Papa's, the love of God, and the love of this incredible man.

When the preacher pronounced them man and wife and Patrick kissed her, she had never felt so much joy and so fully blessed.

She turned to find Mama with tears in her eyes, holding onto Papa. She smiled through her tears.

"They're happy tears," Papa told Rachel and held his wife closer.

Rachel enjoyed the reception. The food was good and only family being there made it special. She couldn't imagine a better wedding.

Grandfather had hired a violinist, who played soft music. When he played a waltz, Patrick pulled her to him and led her across the floor. Their every movement was in perfect harmony. She should have recognized when they danced at Hope's party that Patrick was the man for her. Well, she had him now. When the dance ended, she saw Mama and Papa, Aunt Ivy and Uncle Sam, and Grandfather and Clara had also been dancing.

Patrick and she left the others still celebrating. They said their good-byes. The ones to Mama and Papa were the hardest. Grandfather sent his driver with the enclosed buggy to take them to the cottage. Patrick pulled her close and kissed her again.

"Are you concerned about tonight?" he asked her.

She shook her head. "I trust you completely, Patrick. I just hope I don't disappoint you."

"I promise you, you won't. If you trust me, then you can believe that."

She and Patrick woke up at the same time. The room had just started to lighten. Patrick pulled her into his arms and kissed her thoroughly.

"Still think you could ever disappoint me?" he asked, smiling.

"I should have known we'd be well matched, because we have been in everything else."

"I honestly didn't know there could be so much love and happiness, Rachel. The reality of you is so much better than my imagination could ever envision."

"You've made me very happy, too, Patrick. Once I wrote down the qualities I wanted in a husband, and you have every one of them, plus a few more."

He turned toward her and she encircled his neck with her arms. "I'll never get enough of you," he whispered in her ear.

Grandfather's driver delivered them to the farm late that afternoon. They tried to get him to stay, but he said he had orders to stay overnight in Albemarle and return to Salisbury tomorrow.

It seemed strange to be in the house alone. Patrick went to milk, while Rachel prepared them some supper.

Patrick had said to make it simple, so she fried some cornmeal cakes and served each with a fried egg on top, like Mama used to do when she needed a quick meal. Patrick loved them.

"Will we always live here?" she asked him as they cuddled in front of the fireplace.

"We probably will this year, but I own the property in Anson County that was once Fair Oaks. The plantation house is no longer there, but there's a lot of acreage. Mama said Father would want me to have it."

"You still call Lawrence Father?"

"Yes, he was the only father I knew for over seven years. He certainly treated me as his son. I have nothing but love and respect for him."

"Are you thinking about us building a house on the property and living there?"

"I'm thinking about it, if you like the idea, but I haven't made any decision. I thought we might take a trip there just before spring planting and see what we think. I could even sell some of the property, but we received so much money as wedding presents, we'd have enough for a start with what I've already saved."

"Wouldn't it be hard to start a farm without help?"

"I'd have to hire some help. What do you think?"

"It would be worth looking into. I can see advantages and disadvantages of moving there or staying here. I'll look forward to a trip there with you in the spring."

Their days of having the house all to themselves went too quickly. The rest of the family came back on Saturday afternoon. They brought in more presents.

Everyone at church seemed shocked by the news of their marriage.

"Well, I tell you, I am stunned," Blanche said. "I never dreamed that's the way things were."

"We didn't either, until Thanksgiving," Rachel told her.

"My, that was a fast wedding, wasn't it?" Blanche raised her eyebrows.

"Only because my parents had to return to the mountains."

"Well, I guess we'll see." She turned away.

"Did she mean what I think she meant?" Patrick asked.

"Yes, she was insinuating we had to get married quickly, but she'll soon see that's not true."

Rachel closed her eyes. Regrettably, gossip could burn like a wasp's sting and leave its welt for a much longer time. But nothing they could say or do would likely help.

"Don't let people like Blanche ruin our happiness," Patrick whispered and took her hand.

"I won't," she told him and squeezed his back.

After the service was over, Julius gave Rachel a look of pure hatred, which did shake her. She had hoped he would either move away or find someone else to marry. He'd certainly seemed much nicer when he'd been courting her, but apparently she'd misjudged his character.

Patrick must have noticed Julius's glare too, because he put his arm around Rachel and pulled her close.

"This is worse than I thought it was going to be," Aunt Ivy said. "The gossip is bound to get worse before it gets better."

Uncle Sam looked at her. "It's nothing but lies."

"Yes, but lies have a way of gaining validity when repeated often enough," Aunt Ivy countered.

Charles came by after school Monday. He rode his horse and looked cold, even with his coat, hat, and gloves.

"Congratulations on your wedding," he said. "I hope you'll be very happy."

He presented them with a wood carving of a pair of lovebirds. They were beautiful, and Rachel was touched.

"Could I speak with you, Mr. Whitley?" he said to Uncle Sam. "I'd like to ask your permission to call on Hope. I plan to attend school through the winter, but I'll quit in the spring to help my pa, and I won't be going back. I'm the youngest, but all my older brothers have places of their own, so the farm will be mine someday."

"If it's agreeable with Hope, you have my permission."

Hope bubbled with excitement. Charles began to come up somewhere in almost every conversation she had.

Christmas was a joyful time. Rachel cooked breakfast, and afterwards they opened presents. With the extra shopping in Salisbury, everyone was well pleased. Patrick gave Rachel a gold chain and heart-shaped pendant with "Rachel" engraved on one side and "Patrick" on the other.

Dinner was almost as lavish as the one at Thanksgiving. Rachel baked a cherry-chocolate cake using some canned cherries Mama had brought down. The cherries in the mountains grew bigger and sweeter than the few small ones that grew around Big Lick.

Everyone went up to take a nap afterwards, but Rachel and Patrick didn't sleep. Rachel lay in his arms and they talked, kissed, and held each other close.

Charles came in the afternoon. He brought Hope one of his carvings. He'd left the back of the piece of wood rough, but had carved it in the shape of a heart with a flat front. There he'd carved "Charles & Hope." He'd stained it so the lettering stood out.

Rachel had helped Hope knit a gray scarf, mittens, and winter cap for him. He stayed and ate leftovers with them for supper.

"How far is it to the Hinson farm?" Hope asked her father after Charles left.

"Not that far, about three miles, I'd guess. Why? Are you worried about him traveling in the cold?"

Hope blushed. "I just wondered how hard it would be for him to come."

"And how often he'd be able to?" her father teased.

Aunt Ivy gave her husband a hard look. "Don't tease her so, Sam."

The family did little to bring in the new year. This was a leap year, and they heard guns being fired in the distance at midnight, but neither Uncle Sam nor Patrick took part in the revelry. Patrick kissed Rachel instead. That was all the fireworks she needed.

Rachel cooked the last of their turnips, some greens, pork, cornfield peas, and cornbread for dinner. Charles joined them.

The rumors and lies got worse. Hope brought most of them home from school. Some were wrapped around bits of truth, but most were nothing but lies. Rachel heard people gossiping herself.

Of course there was the one that said Patrick was forced to marry Rachel, because he got her in a family way. That's why her parents had made that unexpected trip here over Thanksgiving. It must have also been why Rachel would teach only a short time. Why, Rachel wouldn't even go to dinner at Julius's house without Patrick, and of course, his parents were right there. In addition, everyone had seen how Patrick rarely left her side and how protective he was of her. Something had to be up for them to run off to Salisbury like that for a quick wedding.

"Cousins marrying is another thing," one of the gossipers said. "I know it was done in the past, but times are modern now. It's just not the thing to do."

"Did you hear Rachel's been treatin' the colored like they's as good as anybody else?" another said. "I heared from a good source that she even had their harvest workers settin' at the family table. She cooked special for them too. Heard tell she has enough colored blood herself to be counted as part of the Negro race. She's a fourth, you know, but it's on her father's side. That means she's married into a white family now. She tries to pass herself off as part Injun, as if we're going to believe that!"

There was even the rumor that Rachel was a witch. Some told how the cows would stop giving milk or go sour if she came near. Sometimes, those brown eyes of hers would take on a strange, evil look, and you'd know she was placing a curse on somebody. That's probably why Patrick ended up marrying her. She'd cast a spell on him, or why else would he be so besotted with her? It was a known fact that she taught her class one day with a snake wrapped around her arm. What more proof did anybody need? She'd probably cast a spell on the whole class. That's why they hadn't given her any trouble like they had Mr. Hatley.

The slurs went on and on. Rachel suspected Julius and Blanche instigated many of them, but once the false chains started, many in the community became links.

"I thought we could ignore the malicious gossip and go on with our lives," Patrick told his father, "but this is getting completely out of control. I hate that it's hurting Rachel, and I can't stop it."

"I thought it would all quickly blow over," Uncle Sam said, "but I was wrong. It's certainly not everyone. There're still a lot of good people with plenty of sense, who know better, but the group of troublemakers are loud and persistent."

"If this doesn't stop soon," Patrick said, "Rachel and I are going on a honeymoon. We'd go stay with her parents right now, if it wasn't the middle of winter. I may take her there, regardless, if this doesn't let up. We could stay with her grandparents in Salisbury if the weather got bad."

"I don't think running away will solve anything," Aunt Ivy said. "Rumors have a way of following."

Rachel said nothing about the gossip in her letters to her parents, but Aunt Ivy must have. Mama wrote her, very concerned, and said they were praying for her without ceasing. *Read your Bible, pray, and give it to God*, Mama advised. *I know Patrick is your support too. I'm sure he's very distressed that he can't protect you from this.*

Rachel smiled. Mama was right about Patrick and about depending on God. God knew the truth, and He would see them through this evil spreading the lies.

Patrick gave her a beautiful store-bought card and a bottle of perfume for Valentine's Day. For the most part, they exchanged gifts and celebrated the day privately, with just the two of them.

She made him a card that told of her love, baked him a cherry-chocolate cake, which he had loved, and gave him a copy of poems by Elizabeth Barrett Browning. She read aloud "How do I love thee? Let me count the ways . . ." for him.

Rachel's birthday in February fell on a Thursday, just as Thanksgiving, Christmas, and New Year's Day had. Patrick had Annie come cook her birthday dinner, but they kept the celebration simple, with only the family and Charles, who brought her a small carved cross on a stand. Patrick gave her a gorgeous chess set with medieval figures carved from onyx and ivory. The rest of the family gave her fabric and books.

"I thought you needed a chess set of your own," Patrick told her, "especially if we ever move from here."

"I love it. You and I need to play a game on it today."

The rest of the family thought the winter was rough, but it seemed mild to Rachel. She barely needed more than her shawl on most days. They'd had an ice storm and one light snow, but they both had melted within three days.

Rachel and Patrick had been going out and cutting more firewood on some of the milder days. Gathering the wood warmed them as they worked.

She also went out to hunt with him several times. It surprised Patrick that she could shoot as well as he, and she brought down as much game as he did.

She liked helping him with the outside chores. It felt good to be able to finally go off alone together, and she cherished those times.

The largest snowstorm of the year hit toward the last day of February. On the twenty-ninth, the storm began around suppertime with large, floating flakes. It must've snowed on and off throughout the night. They woke up to the wind whistling and the snow falling in thin, biting slivers.

The house had grown so cold that Patrick hurried up to start the fires. He told Rachel to stay put, and he'd come back to bed to get warm until the fires started to knock the chill off the rooms downstairs. Then, they'd get up.

Rachel cooked a hot breakfast of oatmeal and everyone ate seconds. She went to the barn to help Patrick milk, despite his protests that she should stay in the house.

"This is nothing to the winters I'm used to," she told him. "If you can go, I can too. Besides, I appreciate our time out there together."

The day cleared between dinner and supper and left about a foot of snow. By the next morning, the sun was up, and the snow began to melt away.

From the bedroom upstairs, Rachel could hear the globs of snow scoot across the roof and plop to the ground. It didn't snow nearly as much here, but when it did, there was much more melting, sliding, and plopping. The snow stuck around longer and melted much slower in the mountains. This wouldn't be around much longer.

# CHAPTER NINETEEN

# The Ku Klux Klan

ONE NIGHT IN MARCH, A small group of men rode up to the farm. They wore robes, hats with pointed hoods, and hideous masks to hide their faces. Even more frightening, they carried burning torches.

"Stay out of sight," Patrick told Rachel as he and Uncle Sam grabbed their guns and stepped out on the porch.

"We hear you folks've become colored lovers," one of the masked men said, only he used a more offensive word. "In fact, word is your son married one of them."

"You heard wrong," Uncle Sam said. "My son's wife is one-eighth Cherokee, and there's not a drop of colored blood in her."

"You can't deny her father fought for the Yanks in the war. He wouldn't have a slave around him, either, but he insisted to have them freed first."

Rachel couldn't imagine where they'd gotten that information. Maybe it was someone who knew Grandfather in Salisbury.

"You know I fought for the Confederacy," Uncle Sam said.

"Heard she's also a witch," another said. "Either one of those is a hanging offense."

"If you really believed she's a witch, you wouldn't be riding out here," Uncle Sam said. "You'd be too afraid she'd cast a spell on you. You know very well all of this is just a pack of lies."

"We'll shoot anyone of you who tries to lay a hand on Rachel," Patrick said.

With that statement, Rachel got another rifle, but she stayed away from the windows for now. She could step to one and help the men out, if need be. In the meantime, she prayed.

"We just came to warn you this time," the first one said. "You better get your family in line, Whitley. The next time we have to come, we won't be so nice."

And with that, they rode away.

Rachel couldn't stop trembling. When Patrick came back in, he put his arm around her and led her to the sofa.

"She was okay while this was happening," Aunt Ivy said.

"That's the way I am." Rachel smiled. "I'm fine during an emergency, as long as there's something I might do to help, but I grow weak and shaky when everything's over."

"I thought the Ku Klux Klan had disbanded and ceased to exist around here," Patrick said.

"They're not meeting formally or holding rallies," Uncle Sam said, "but they come to terrorize when they feel the need. Some of them are moonshiners who've joined just to have the others help protect them from the revenuers."

"This has gone way too far," Patrick said to his father. "As soon as we can, Rachel and I are going to her parents. I'll pay for Willie or someone to come help you with the planting. I'm not going to risk Rachel's well-being."

"Now, don't make hasty decisions," Uncle Sam said. "Those men were just trying to scare us. They're all talk and threats. I don't think we need to worry."

Patrick didn't look convinced. "Rachel and I will discuss this and decide."

They went to bed, and Patrick held her. "I can't believe we were paid a visit by the Ku Klux Klan. I'm so sorry you had to endure this."

"Are there many members of the Klan around here?"

"Way too many from the look of things tonight. Many of the county's lawmen are probably involved, so there's not much recourse, except to handle things yourself."

She snuggled closer. "I'm scared for you and your family. I was so afraid tonight that something would happen to you or Uncle Sam. I prayed as hard as I knew how."

"I think you prayed with the rifle in your hand." She could hear the smile in his voice.

"If they'd fired on you, I would have broken out a window and done my part. I'm thankful it didn't come to that."

"I am too. What do you think we should do, darling? Do you want us to go stay with your parents for a while?"

"I don't know. I would like to go, but I don't like the idea we'd be running away."

"I'd run as far as need be to keep you safe."

"I'm glad you never mentioned me staying in the mountains without you. Thank you for that."

"Rachel, I would never choose to leave you. It would be like tearing out my heart and leaving it behind."

"Let's give things a little more time and think them over. If there's any hint of more danger, we'll leave right away." She moved her lips to his.

Patrick wanted to go to Anson County and look at his property for his birthday. They'd already planted the early part of the garden, and Uncle Sam said he could wait until Patrick returned to plant the rest and the fields. In the meantime, he would work on getting some of the ground prepared.

They planned to be gone three or four days, and they'd stay in the hotel in Wadesboro. Rachel looked forward to the trip. She always liked to spend time alone with Patrick. She'd packed them a picnic and they ate it on the way.

Patrick wanted to go to his property and spend most of the day there tomorrow, so they drove to see Patsy and Moses first. Besides visiting, Patrick wanted to talk with Moses about them possibly moving here and farming. Of course, Moses couldn't speak since a former master had cut out his tongue, but he could write well enough to be understood.

Patsy stared at Rachel for a minute, as Patrick set her down. Then, she came running and gave Rachel a hug.

"Oh, look at you, Miss Rachel," Patsy said. "You're all grown up, and so pretty. It's been way too long since I've seen you."

Patsy noticed Patrick and stared at him too. Moses was already vigorously shaking Patrick's hand with recognition on his face.

"You remember my husband, Patrick, Ivy's son," Rachel said to her.

"My, yes! Yes, I do. He's turned out to be even more handsome than that father of his. How are you doing, sir?"

"You don't need to call us sir or Miz, Patsy. We're practically family."

"You'd better let me call you that here. I don't know what would happen if we don't show proper respect to the whites. I'd be in deep trouble. I know it's not what you want, but I'd better keep in the habit. I wouldn't want to let something slip in the wrong person's hearing. I get strange stares as it is for forgetting and speaking proper English."

Moses tapped his wife on the shoulder and pointed to their house. He turned and headed in that direction.

"My, my, where are my manners? I just got too excited at seeing y'all. We don't need to keep standing out here. Come on to the house."

The house was an average-sized, single story home with a front porch. It was weathered gray, because it'd never been painted. Inside, however, it was very nice and finished. The interior was every bit as pretty as Aunt Ivy's. Rachel realized Patsy and Moses couldn't give the appearance of being anything but poor. Like Papa had feared, slavery may have ended, but bigotry had not.

Rachel told them about their episode with the KKK. Patsy's eyes got big as she listened. "They're all over here too. They used to be a lot more active about ten years ago. Still, we know several colored families who have had trouble with them. They hanged one man for talking too friendly with a white woman. Those men are scary."

Patsy and Moses had five children. Ezra had just turned sixteen, Aquila was thirteen, Callie twelve, Isaiah ten, and Jeremiah nine.

"I'm not all that surprised by you two marrying," Patsy said. "You were almost inseparable before Patrick moved away. I never saw two children so attached to each other, unless they were twins. The others were always saying how you acted more like brother and sister, but I never saw siblings who didn't bicker and fuss half the time. You weren't like that."

Patrick asked Moses and Patsy some questions about his land and possibly starting a farm. Patsy answered what she knew and Moses wrote out the answers to the others.

"Well, we best be going," Patrick said. "We want to get to Wadesboro before dark."

"You're welcome to eat supper with us," Patsy said. "I would invite you to stay, but I don't think we could get by with that, and it might make trouble for you too."

Patrick gave her an understanding look. "Thank you, but we'd rather get settled in our room before we eat. We'll come back and see you again before we go back."

"You make sure you do. Come as often as you can. It is so good to see you, and if we can help in any way, you just let us know."

"I'll take you up on that if we decide to move down here."

"I remember Patsy and Moses well, but I don't remember Moses' last name," Patrick said as they drove away. "Everyone always just called them by their first names."

"When they got married, Moses took Mama's maiden name, Morgan. Jasper, Moses' father, did also, as well as Bertha. I don't know about the other slaves from Gold Leaf. Moses said he didn't want the name of any of his other masters, especially the one who cut his tongue out."

Patrick gave a slight nod. "I can certainly understand that."

Their room at the inn was small but cozy. Patrick stabled the team, while Rachel unpacked their things. When Patrick returned they had a quiet, leisurely supper and retired.

The following day was Patrick's birthday. Rachel had the inn pack them a special picnic dinner, she took his birthday gift, Patrick packed the saddlebags, and they left to ride to the property.

They walked out of town, leading their horses. Rachel had worn her riding skirt, but Patrick was afraid to let too many people see her riding astride. When they were out in the open, Patrick helped her into the saddle.

"Fair Oaks was once a big plantation with a splendid house," he told her as they rode up. "All the buildings were destroyed in the war, but the land is still there. The fields have grown up, but it wouldn't take too much to clear them again. A river runs through the back of the property, and there's woods for hunting."

"When was the last time you saw it?"

"Not long after my eighteenth birthday. My parents and I came down to check on it, and Mama put it in my name. We've been paying the property taxes each year."

The foundation and chimneys were still there to mark where the huge house had stood. They slowly rode around and discussed what they saw and what they might do with it. Even in its present state, the land seemed inviting.

"I see there's red clay here, just like in Stanly County," Rachel said.

"Yes, you'll find red clay until you get a little more east, and then the soil turns sandy. I wish we could have that black fertile soil you have in the mountains, but with a little care, this farm's okay."

They rode to the river near dinnertime and had their picnic there. Rachel gave Patrick her gift, a small revolver with a horn insert in the handle.

"I thought you might carry it in your pocket when you didn't want to take a rifle or shotgun," she told him

"I love it. Thank you darling. But if I never got another gift the rest of my life, you would be gift enough."

They relaxed on the blanket, and Patrick kissed her. At times like this, she liked the idea of them having their own place.

"What do you think about the place?" Patrick asked her as they left.

"I liked it. I can see it has potential."

"If we're going to start our own farm from nothing, I'd like to do it soon. I'm also thinking, if I build this, Sammy can eventually get the Big Lick farm."

Rachel would prefer moving closer to her parents, instead of farther away, but she didn't say so. She didn't want to put a damper on Patrick's dreams, and she felt sure she could be happy here.

"In moving, we might leave some of the lies about us behind," Patrick said after a few minutes of riding.

She frowned. "I don't understand where all the lies came from. I haven't done anything bad to anyone. I really did Julius a favor not to marry a man I could never love."

"There's a lot in this world that's not fair and doesn't make sense. People do a poor job of behaving as they should. We just have to give things to God and trust in Him. I've told myself that every day since we were threatened."

On the following day, Patrick wanted to take care of some business, and Rachel chose to accompany him. They saw a lawyer, checked with a builder, and went by county offices. Patrick said he just wanted to gather as much information as possible for now.

"Tomorrow we'll check out of our room, drive out and tell Moses and Patsy good-bye, and head for home. I think we've done what we need to here."

"I've enjoyed this time, Patrick. I'm glad we came."

"I am too. I love being alone with you like this. I can't get enough of it." His eyes twinkled. "That's another good reason to have our own place."

A thought came to her. "Patrick, you said you'd have to hire help if we came here. Do you think it might be possible to bring Annie and Willie here with us?"

"We could ask them if they'd like to come."

# CHAPTER TWENTY

# Abduction

THINGS TURNED VERY BUSY WHEN they returned to Big Lick. Patrick and Sam worked long and hard to plant the fields. Rachel helped with planting the garden and with seeding some of the fields.

She had headed back to the house from a far field to start supper when the riders descended upon her. She screamed when she saw the men in the robes and hoods, but she had gotten only about halfway to the house, and she doubted anyone would hear her. Terror ceased her. One of the men sprang from his horse and put his hand over her mouth. Another quickly gagged her, tied her hands behind her back, and blindfolded her. They placed her in front of someone on a horse.

She had no idea where they took her, but they pulled her from the horse and shoved her into some type of building. Two men stayed to guard her, while the others left. She wanted to ask questions, but it was impossible with the gag. One of the men tied her to a chair. She didn't know how long she sat there, but her legs and hands grew numb. Her mouth became so dry she felt as if she were choking, and her throat felt as if it were coated in ashes. She would have loved to have even a sip of water.

The whole time, she prayed and remembered Bible verses to keep her mind off her situation. They helped her keep her wits.

*Yea though I walk through the valley of the shadow of death, I will fear no evil, for Thou art with me; Thy rod and Thy staff, they comfort me.*

*My help cometh from the Lord, which made heaven and earth.*

*The Lord shall preserve thy going out and thy coming in from this time forevermore.*

*... whoso putteth his trust in the Lord shall be safe.*

She prayed for Patrick too. She knew he would be frantic after he found her missing. Had he heard her scream? Would he guess what had happened?

———————————

Patrick heard a distant scream. He dropped everything, grabbed his rifle, and took off running. His heart beat so fast he could hear the blood rushing through his temples, but he barely noticed in his rush to get to Rachel.

He saw Rachel's straw hat, stopped to pick it up, and looked around. The dirt was scuffed up, as if there'd been a struggle, and there were signs of several horses' hooves.

*Oh Lord, no!* He ran to the house and found himself almost too out of breath to speak.

"M-a—ma, h-have you seen Rachel?" he panted.

"No, son. What's wrong?"

Patrick didn't stop to answer her before he rushed out again. He was on his way back to the field to get his father when he saw Papa coming. He hurriedly told him what he knew.

"Calm down, son. You can't help Rachel by falling apart."

"What can we do?"

"I don't know. It would be foolish to try to go after her. We wouldn't know where to start."

What was wrong with Papa? He was supposed to know what to do or at least have some ideas!

"Papa, this is my wife we're talking about! She's been abducted and we can't just stand here and do nothing. Should I go talk to Blanche or Julius? Do you think they might know something?"

"I doubt if they'd reveal anything, if they did. Tell you what, you go get the things I left in the field and put them up. I'll go over and talk with Blanche's father. He's not a bad fellow, and I think he'll tell me if he's heard anything. Don't worry. I'll hurry."

Papa saddled a horse and took off, and Patrick went to the field as Papa requested. He did what he needed to, but he did it by rote. His mind stayed on Rachel.

*Dear Lord, please protect her. Wrap Thy arms around her and keep her safe. Bring her back to me before tonight, I pray. Amen.*

He stopped and wept before he went back toward the house. He knew he was supposed to be strong, but he had to let the tears flow, or he would explode with grief.

He should have taken Rachel away from here when the first incident occurred. They should've packed up and gone to stay with her parents in the mountains. They would've been happy there, and Rachel would be safe now and by his side.

He shook his head. Regrets wouldn't help Rachel. He needed to do something to rescue her.

At a loss as to what to do, he went into the house. Papa must have briefly told Mama what had happened before he left.

"I'm so sorry, Patrick," she said as he came in.

He nodded. He didn't think he could talk at the moment. Mama came to hug him, but he shook her off. There was no comfort for him now. He didn't want comfort. He wanted Rachel.

There seemed to be nothing else for him to do, so he sat down and watched the clock. A minute seemed an hour. Ten minutes seemed days. Watching the clock wasn't helping.

He went out and sat on the porch to watch for Papa. He prayed and prayed again.

Finally, he saw his father riding up at a brisk pace. Patrick met him and held the horse.

"Mr. Furr didn't know much," Papa announced. "He'd heard rumors the KKK was going to take someone soon, but he didn't know who, and he doesn't have any idea where they would have taken Rachel if they did. He said the group was too secretive to divulge much. Most of their members don't even know where they're going or what they're about to do, until it's time to go."

"So what do we do now?"

"There's not much to do, except wait and pray."

"Papa, don't tell me that. This is Rachel! How would you feel if Mama had been taken?"

Papa's face contorted. "I know you're hurting, son. Your insides are being torn into a thousand pieces. I wish there was something I could do to help, but there isn't. We just have to wait . . . and trust God will bring her back to us unharmed. He loves her, too, you know, even more than you do."

———

Rachel heard other men return. "It's getting' about dark enough now," one of them said.

"Listen to me, woman," another said. "It's come to our attention you've gone visitin' coloreds"—only he used another word—"in Anson County. You just don't learn, do you? Here we are tryin' to keep them in their place, and you go tryin' to be their friend. We just ain't gonna stand for that. On top of it all, you go traipsin' all over the place straddlin' a horse like a man. What's wrong with you, woman? There's not a decent bone in your body, is there?"

How did he expect her to answer anything with her mouth gagged? She wished she knew what they were planning. Nothing good, she felt certain, and her stomach knotted up. She prayed once more.

They roughly put her in front of one of them on a horse again. This man held her too tightly, and his hand had inched up to touch inappropriate places. She became nauseated.

She could sense a difference in this man than the one who had brought her here. There was almost something familiar about him. Could it be Axel or Julius? She couldn't think of another man who might hold a grudge against her.

The man breathed down her neck, and it sent cold shivers down her spine. *Lord, I'm relying on Thy promise to never leave me and to keep me safe. Help me, I pray.*

Rachel tried to reason with herself. If they were going to ravish her, surely they would've done it in the place she'd been held. She grasped that glimmer of hope.

She couldn't tell how far they rode, but they must still be somewhere in the Big Lick area. They stopped, and a man jerked her off the horse. She fell and hit the ground. The man on whose horse she'd ridden jumped down. She heard his feet hit the ground, and he must have been the one to snatch her up.

He led her a short distance and turned her to face him. She could tell, because of his hands on her shoulders. By what little she could discern, he seemed more cultured than the others. The way he held himself and the soapy smell of him was different than the others. She kept waiting for him to talk, but he remained silent.

Someone untied her hands, pushed her back against something, and retied her hands behind her but also around a post or something. Were they going to leave her here? If they were tying her to use a whip, they'd have tied her with her face toward the post. If they were going to hang her, they wouldn't have tied her to anything. Were they planning to burn her at a stake? They'd accused her once of being a witch.

"Teach her a lesson, Judge," someone said and laughed.

A man—he smelled like the same cultured one—placed his hands on the sides of her face and head and held them in a vise grip. Suddenly, hard lips were covering hers and consuming her through a large hole in his hood. One hand moved slightly and held her hair at the scalp, so she still couldn't move her head. The other hand groped her while the force of the man's mouth pushed her head into the post, until she thought her head would split. A tongue filled her mouth and probed so far, she thought she would gag. Teeth jarred against her teeth. She tried to bite down, but she couldn't. The man was using too much force. Instead she stiffened her mouth and jaw. His body pressed into her and held her against the post, until she couldn't even kick. She couldn't breathe.

He pulled away and she almost crumbled. Her lips burned and her mouth hurt. She could feel them swelling already, and places on her body felt bruised.

"She's a plucky little thing. I'll give her that," one of them said. "She hasn't shed a tear."

"Aw, she liked it. Can't you tell?"

The same man, the one they'd called Judge, stood before her again. She could sense his form and bearing. He started to run the back of his fingers down the side of her face. She jerked to the side, away from his hand, but he held her head with his other hand and did it again. This time his touch was gentle, however. He gently held her head in his hands and brushed his lips across her forehead.

She kicked out, but only glanced the side of a leg before he backed away. The other men laughed.

"That's enough playing with her," the man who'd done the most talking said. "We'll leave her for her friends to finish off. You like them black devils, but we'll see how much you like them after tonight."

They took the blindfold off her. She could see about a dozen men in those awful robes and hoods. One was already on his horse, and he was the farthest away from her. She knew instinctively he was Judge. She tried to see his eyes, but it was too dark, and he was too far away.

"I'm going to take the gag off you, but I'd not do any screaming if I were you. I'd be quiet as a mouse. You're in the n----r section. You can't even imagine what those devils will do to you when they find you."

With that, he took her gag off, and all of them quickly mounted and left. She tried to see where she was, but it was too dark to see much. It appeared she was tied to a tree.

Should she call for help or wait for daylight? It might be safer for her once the day came. She prayed for guidance and thought of Patrick. She needed him so badly right now.

"Help!" she cried at the top of her voice. "Someone, please help me!"

At first no one came, and her throat felt so raspy and dry, she had a hard time calling out. She started just crying for help at intervals.

Then, she heard footsteps. Three colored men appeared and looked at her warily.

"What's ya doin', girl?" the largest one asked.

"The Klan abducted me and tied me up. I'm Rachel Moretz, and I need to get home." The words came out scratchy, but she thought they understood her.

The men's eyes got even wider, and they started backing off. Were they so scared of the Klan they were going to leave her like this?

"Is dat you, Miz Rachel?" Someone else had come up.

"Willie?"

"Yes, Miz Rachel. Abner, ya goes and gets my Annie real fas' like. I's goin' ta get you loose now, Miz."

Willie took out a pocket knife and cut her loose. It felt good to rub her wrists.

"I's not goin' to touch ya Miz Rachel, but I done sent fo' my Annie, and she'll sho' take cear of ya."

"Oh, thank you, Willie. I'm so glad to see you. I know God must have sent you to save me."

"I's don' know 'bout dat, Miz Rachel."

Annie came and wrapped Rachel in her arms. Willie sent someone to borrow a wagon and mule, and they were back sooner than Rachel expected. The three of them climbed into the wagon, and they headed toward the farm.

*Thank you, Lord!*

---

Patrick was so distraught he couldn't think. He'd sit for a few minutes and then pace the floor. He prayed in spurts. He often found it difficult to put a coherent thought together.

*Oh Rachel, Rachel, I need you so much! God, send her back to me. Please, please!*

He didn't think he'd survive the night if she didn't come home soon. His parents had tried to comfort him, but they'd only made matters worse, and they'd eventually left him alone. They'd gone to their bedroom, but Patrick knew they weren't asleep.

He couldn't stand to go to his bedroom. Everything there cried, *Rachel*.

He paced the floor when all of a sudden he heard something. He ran outside to see a wagon with two mules pull up. He recognized Willie first, because the wagon had pulled up with the driver's side facing him. Willie jumped down, and he saw Rachel.

Patrick had her in his arms before he had time to think. He just held her tightly against him and put his face in her hair.

*Thank you, Lord! Thank you!*

He felt tears slide down his cheeks, but they were happy tears, tears of release. He didn't know how long he held her, but he looked up to see Annie there too.

"Come in and tell me what happened," he told them.

When he led Rachel into the house, he noticed her swollen lips. *Oh God, don't let anyone have hurt her.*

His parents came downstairs to see what was going on, but he wouldn't release Rachel. Mama hugged her with him hanging on to her too.

They sat down and Rachel told her story. She hadn't been hurt until the very last, and then it was with a rough kiss. She assured them she was otherwise all right.

Patrick would still like to get his hands on the scoundrel who had kissed her so roughly. Instead of his blood racing, like it had, it now boiled.

"Did you recognize anyone?" Papa asked Rachel.

"No. They called the one who kissed me Judge, but that's probably not his real name. They had me blindfolded, and when they released me, all I saw were men in hoods and robes."

"Willie, I don't know how to thank you," Patrick said. "If you ever need anything, you just let me know. I'd be glad to pay you a reward for bringing Rachel back to me."

"Naw, sir. I jus' glad I's could hep."

Willie and Annie left, and Mama offered to get Rachel something to eat, but she declined. Patrick led her upstairs. He helped her into her nightdress and noticed bruises starting to form from the rough treatment. He got her a glass of water and a cold, wet cloth for her lips. Finally, he undressed and lay down beside her.

"Is the rough kiss all they did to you, Rachel? I just realized you might not want to say more in front of the others downstairs."

"That and while he kissed me he touched me in places he shouldn't, but he didn't move my clothing or do anything else. Oh Patrick, it was awful, but it could've been so much worse. I'm so thankful to be home with you and to be relatively unhurt."

He would have liked to kiss her lips, but, from the way they looked, it would be some time before he could do that. Anger that someone had treated her like this surfaced again, but he reminded himself to be thankful that's all they did and that he had her back in his arms.

He gently took her in his arms and held her. He kissed her cheek and told her how much he loved her. It took her a long time to get to sleep, but she finally did. He lay still holding her. He didn't need to sleep. He had Rachel in his arms.

Rachel cried out, and for a moment, Patrick thought she was being abducted again. He must have fallen asleep, for he realized she had called out in her sleep, but she had startled herself awake too.

"Was it a nightmare?" He raised himself up, pulled her into his arms, and gently rocked his body from side to side to soothe her. He kissed her head and told her everything was fine. God had answered his prayers, and he would forever be grateful.

Patrick woke in the morning when Rachel moved and watched her wake up. He never knew love could be so deep and wide and high.

She looked at him and tried to smile, but he could tell her lips hurt. She started to get up, but he took her arm.

"Stay in bed for a while if you want," he told her.

She shook her head. "No, I'll cook breakfast and go to the barn with you to milk. I need for things to get back to normal."

"I guess Papa milked last night. I didn't even think about it. Cook oatmeal or something simple that you can eat. Your mouth looks sore."

Patrick told Papa he was spending the day with Rachel. He needed to be close to her, and she'd probably like that too.

———————

Patrick was being even more wonderful than his usual self. Rachel knew she must have the most fantastic husband ever born. She knew he'd been shaken and frantic when the men took her. If he could have done something to help, it wouldn't have been so hard on him, but he had to sit and wait and do nothing. That was doubly hard for a man like Patrick.

After they milked and gathered the eggs, Patrick told her he wanted to spend the day with her, and she could decide what they'd do.

"I'll need to cook meals and do some chores," Rachel said.

"That's fine. I'll either help or keep you company."

They walked down to the creek first, then sat on their log. It felt right to be there with Patrick.

"I'm so sorry I failed to protect you yesterday," he began.

"Patrick, it was not your fault. I'm sure they must have been watching for me to be alone. If they hadn't taken me then, it would have been some other time. I know very well you would do anything to keep me safe, but you can't be with me every minute."

"I wish I could."

"Well, so do I, but we need to do other things too." She started to laugh, but couldn't. It hurt too much.

"Is it hard for you to talk?"

"A little, but I want to talk. It would hurt my feelings more not to."

"I love you so much, Rachel. I don't know what would happen to me if I lost you. I need you to be whole. I don't know how I'd survive without you, and I know I don't want to find out."

"God saw us through yesterday, though, didn't He? He was with us all the way, He kept me safe and returned me to you. We can give Him the praise."

"You're right, darling. I'm always trying to protect you, but it's not really within my power. Only God can really do that."

When Rachel went in to cook dinner, Patrick went with her. They walked back hand in hand.

She started the meat cooking for a stew, and Patrick helped her peel and dice the potatoes and onions to be added later. She would also add some canned vegetables to the mix.

They sat at the table and read their Bibles aloud and talked about the verses. They prayed a prayer of praise and thanksgiving.

"I'd like to take you to the mountains," he said, "as soon as we get all the fields planted. That should be in a few days."

"I don't think that's necessary."

"You didn't think it was necessary before, and look what happened. I want to go. We'll come back in time for harvest."

"If that's really what you'd prefer to do. It'll be fun to show you all my special places there."

They ate dinner, and Ivy said she'd do the dishes. Working side by side on different rows, Patrick and Rachel hoed the garden.

"We'll go back to Anson County right after the harvest and start building," Patrick said. "I'm thinking we'll build a small house to live in while the main house is being built, and Annie and Willie, or whoever we get as permanent help, can stay in it later."

"When are you planning to leave for the mountains?" Rachel asked.

"Probably the end of next week."

"I loved my day with you, Patrick. Thank you."

"I did it for me too. I enjoy every minute I spend with you. I don't understand couples who say they grow tired of each other. If we are married hundreds of years, I know I'd never get enough of being with you."

Rachel decided to go to church Sunday, although her lips were still swollen and had turned blue and purple in places. She wanted to see Julius's reaction when he saw her.

She hadn't told Patrick she suspected Julius was the man her kidnappers had called Judge. The man's scent and the fact that she'd felt he had a certain level of culture made Julius more likely than Axel. Even his touch had felt more like Julius. She'd wait and have that talk with Patrick when they got to the mountains. She was afraid Patrick would want to confront Julius, and she didn't want to put Patrick in that position.

The day had been cloudy and dreary, although it wasn't rain-ing yet. Wanting to look more cheerful, she chose a peach-col-ored dress. After she got it on, she realized it probably made her wounded face more obvious, but she wore it anyway. There wasn't really time to change.

When they got to church, Rachel spotted Julius right away. She stood where he could see her easily and watched the emotions play across his face. At first, she could see shock. That was followed by a softening of his features, as if he wanted to comfort her, as if he cared for her. Then, his face held guilt just before he turned his head where she couldn't see him as clearly.

Patrick saw her watching Julius, and raised his eyebrows. She looked at her husband, and there was no jealousy in his expression, only a question. "Is everything all right?"

"Yes, everything's fine."

"Julius isn't glaring at you, is he?"

She shook her head. "No, it looked like he was feeling sorry for me instead."

"Well, maybe there's hope for him yet?"

"Maybe."

The women of the church were appalled when Rachel answered their questions about what had happened to her face. She had the feeling some of their husbands would have some explaining to do, or would at least be told what their wives thought of such brutality.

Patrick worked hard to help his father get all the fields planted. He told his parents Wednesday that they'd be leaving for the summer on Saturday.

"Please don't go," Aunt Ivy begged. "What will we do without either of you?"

"You'll do just fine, Mama."

Aunt Ivy looked at her husband. "You're being quiet, Sam. Help me out here."

"I talked Patrick out of taking Rachel to her parents' last time, and look what happened. I'm not going to do that again. Patrick is a grown man. He should decide what's best for him and his wife, and I'll support whatever he decides."

Patrick looked relieved. "Thank you, Papa."

Rachel and Patrick packed up the small covered farm wagon, hitched the four-horse team of Morgans Patrick had purchased, and prepared to leave Saturday morning after breakfast. Rachel had packed them a dinner they would eat on the way to Salisbury.

It was a picture-book day, with deep blue skies, fluffy white clouds, and bright golden sunshine. The late spring flowers bloomed everywhere, and Rachel breathed in the clear air.

Patrick breathed a sigh of relief when they turned west out of Albemarle. She looked at him, puzzled.

"I was so afraid something would happen again before I got you away," he said. "I thought we'd have a little time before there were more problems, but it's good to be out of the area."

"Nothing may have ever happened."

"I couldn't take that chance, Rachel. You're too precious to me."

They went at a leisurely pace. Patrick said the Morgans were good, versatile horses, and they could use them for saddle horses too.

"They're stronger than they look," he said. "I don't think we'll have any trouble with them pulling up the mountains, since the wagon is light and we're not hauling anything too heavy."

"How long will we stay at Grandfather's?" Rachel asked.

"As long as you want. We just need to be back to Big Lick no later than the middle of September."

"I'd like to stay about five days, then."

# CHAPTER TWENTY-ONE

# The Haven

PATRICK AND RACHEL ARRIVED IN Salisbury in time to eat supper. Grandfather and Clara were delighted to see them. Since the Moretzes had a cook and housekeeper, Rachel wouldn't need to do so much here. It would be like a vacation.

They spent the evening talking and visiting. Grandfather shook his head after hearing about the KKK incidents.

"They're just trying to keep former slaves subservient," he said. "You should move here to get away from the Klan. They're around here too, but I don't think they're as active as what you've described. You can have this house or the cottage. Clara and I'd be happy in either, and we'd love having family close."

"We appreciate the offer," Rachel told him, "but both of us enjoy country living too much. Patrick owns Lawrence Nance's property in Anson County. We think we might move there after the harvest is in. In our family, I think Mark is the most likely one to want your property. He's the studious one of the boys, and it wouldn't surprise me if he didn't become a doctor, lawyer, or something."

"I'm sorry you didn't like Big Lick," Grandmother Clara said.

"It's not that," Rachel quickly told her. "Big Lick's a great place. It's a town with three general stores, several other shops, and farms all around, so it's perfect for me. Most of the people are warm and friendly. If it wasn't for two people, I don't think most of the rumors would've even started. Then, the Klan wouldn't have heard them, either. Look, the Whitleys are more typical of the people of Big Lick."

Grandfather looked at Patrick and chuckled. "Well, we know how you feel about the Whitleys, especially one of them."

The following days were tranquil and relaxing. Rachel and Patrick went to church, did a little unhurried shopping, and enjoyed being at Grandfather's.

Shopping showed Rachel a different side of her husband. He was attentive, witty, charming, knowledgeable, and quite intriguing. Rachel laughed so much she was doubly glad her mouth had healed.

They usually went for a stroll in Grandfather's garden at least once a day. The profusion of spring flowers exploded in color, and the garden exuded a serene charm. They could hold hands, sit on a bench, and enjoy a kiss.

"Grandfather used to enjoy doing most of the work out here himself," Rachel told Patrick, "but now it's hard for him, and a gardener does it."

"I love it," Patrick said. "I used to think anything other than vegetables in a garden was a waste of time, but I've just changed my mind. I love coming here with you."

"I'm really proud of you two," Grandfather told them one afternoon when Grandmother was taking a nap. "Every love is different, and I can even say that from experience, but the two of you seem to have found what Luke's mother and I had. I know exactly how happy you are. Clara and I love each other deeply, but it's not the all-encompassing love I had with Sarah."

Patrick loaded the wagon, hitched up the team, and headed toward Wilkesboro with Rachel by his side. She had taken this route with her parents several times.

Instead of staying around Yadkinville this time, however, they made it to Jonesville. They'd left Salisbury early, didn't stop but once on the way, and made good time.

Rachel was glad, because the Benham Hotel was an exceptional place to stay. It had twenty-six guest rooms and a large dining room, where students from the Jonesville Academy often ate. The large white building had a long front porch and a full balcony off the second floor. Rachel also liked the huge rock patio in the back for guests.

"We'll need to leave awfully early from here to make it to your parents' in a day," Patrick told Rachel that night. "Yet we'd make it to Wilkesboro with plenty of the day left. What would you like to do?"

"Let's stay here an extra day, get up very early Monday morning, and try to make it all the way."

They ate breakfast Monday before daylight, packed up, and left just as the sky began to lighten enough for the black of night to turn to gray. They ate a quick dinner in Wilkesboro and continued their journey.

Patrick didn't remember the town. "I hope we can stay longer when we come back through," he said. "I like the looks of the town."

Rachel nodded. "My parents and I like it too."

Patrick and Rachel's horses would have probably pulled them up okay, but the team slowed so much on the steeper grades of the mountain that the young couple got off and walked beside them on those stretches. It had grown late before they made it to Boone, so they decided to spend the night there.

When they made it to the farm by dinnertime the next day, Mama and Papa ran out to greet them.

"Is something wrong?" Papa asked.

Rachel laughed. "Does something have to be wrong for a daughter to come visit her parents?"

Mama laughed too. "I think you're picking up your father's bad habit of answering a question with a question."

After the greetings and hugs, Papa helped Patrick bring their things in. They each had a small trunk, their guns, and their travel bags.

"Your old room is all ready for you. Is that okay?" Mama asked.

"That's perfect, Mama."

"It seems strange for me to be back here after such a long time," Patrick said. "I can remember the things that happened here when I was seven and eight, and I remember watching Rachel and keeping her entertained in the parlor."

"You still watch after me and keep me entertained." Rachel laughed.

They ate dinner with her brothers chattering away. After the meal, the boys went outside.

Patrick told her parents of their trouble. "I brought Rachel here to make sure there won't be another incident like that."

"I'm so glad you did," Papa said. "It relieves me that you're ensuring her safety so well."

They also told her parents of their trip to Anson County, seeing Patsy and Moses, and deciding to move there after the harvest.

"Lawrence would have liked that," Papa said. "He would have been very proud of you, Patrick."

"He was a good father," Patrick replied.

Then began some of the most idyllic days Rachel had ever known. Patrick spent about one-fourth of his time helping Papa and Aaron on the farm while she helped Mama. All four of them spent the other one-fourth of their time working together on the farm, and Patrick and Rachel spent about half their time by themselves.

They went on long walks through the woods and explored the old Cherokee trails. They saddled two of their horses and rode through the area. They went to Boone and explored the stores and shops. As the days warmed, they bathed together in the creek and played like children. They sat in the meadow across from the house and talked for hours.

"I always thought I'd get married in this meadow," Rachel told her husband. "Mama and Papa did, Granny married Hawk here, and your mother and father were married here too."

"Do you regret our wedding? Should we have waited until spring and come here?"

"Oh no! I had a hard time waiting the few weeks we did. No, I have absolutely no regrets where you are concerned, Patrick Whitley. Well, maybe there is one."

"What's that?" Patrick looked stricken, and she reminded herself not to tease him like this.

"I wish I would have recognized how much I loved you earlier, and we'd married in the summer."

He smiled. "But, you weren't ready."

"No, and I'm glad you didn't tell me how you felt about me, when you first knew you loved me. I'd have been upset and confused then. I needed to go through a process to be ready to accept the fact I had feelings for you."

"I wanted to tell you so badly I thought I would burst sometimes, but I kept praying and trying to let God guide me. I think things happened with us in God's timing."

"Yes, and that's why it's all too marvelous for words."

Rachel packed them a picnic one day and led Patrick up the mountain behind the farm. The old Cherokee trail was still clear from family members, who came here even now. She knew Mama and Papa did.

They climbed the path holding hands, and Rachel told him about Grandfather telling Sarah he loved her here and later proposing to her. Then, Papa had brought Mama here just before their wedding.

"It's a special place for lovers," she said. "That's why I knew we had to come."

Patrick grinned at her. "I'm seeing a teasing side of you here I never saw before, but I like it."

"It's the mountain air. Papa teases more than anyone I know, although Mama has her moments too."

Rachel watched Patrick take in the spectacular view and inhale deeply. One could stand in this clearing and see for miles and miles. They could see lush, tree-covered mountains and lovely valleys in every direction.

"It's hard to believe such beauty exists," he said. "No wonder you love it so and have so much beauty in you. I feel like I'm even closer to God here."

He held her in his arms and kissed her, and she felt herself melting into him. They sat on the huge rock and marveled at the view and the peace.

"I've been needing to tell you something, Patrick, and I'm going to trust you not to overreact."

He turned to her with an anxious look, as she knew he would. Without a doubt, she was always his main concern.

"I've come to suspect Julius might be the man who gave me that abusive kiss the night I was abducted."

Patrick stiffened and held her hand more tightly. "What makes you think so?"

"I had this strange feeling I knew him when they put me on his horse to take me to the colored community. It was the way his arms touched me as we rode, and he seemed the right size and shape from what I could tell without seeing. Even the smell of him seemed familiar."

"You knew this from being with Julius when he was courting you?"

"Yes, but not the way you're wondering. He hugged me the time we went fishing with Charles and Hope. That's all. He asked me if he could kiss me, but I refused. He was always a perfect gentleman when he was seeing me, so I could be wrong about this. I have no concrete evidence."

"You did say they called him Judge, and since Julius is a lawyer, that might make sense."

She nodded. "After the punishing kiss, one of the men said I liked it, and Judge started tenderly caressing my face with the back of his hand. It was something I could see Julius doing. Also, he never spoke a word to anyone the whole time. It would seem he was either mute or afraid I'd recognize his voice."

"That certainly makes sense. I saw him and you staring at each other at church that first Sunday after it happened."

"Yes, I was trying to gauge his reaction to my bruised mouth. There was a series of emotions, shock, concern, tenderness, and guilt. When I saw the guilt, he turned his head."

"You're sure of all this?"

"No, I can't be sure, but it's my perception."

"Why, didn't you tell me this earlier?" His voice stayed calm.

"I didn't want you to confront Julius with so little evidence. I was afraid it would put you in a bad situation, and you might come to harm. The guilt of such a thing would have been hard for me to bear."

"And why did you tell me now?"

"I never want to keep anything from you, Patrick. I never intend to, because we are truly one. I just want to wait for the right time to try to protect you, like you protect me."

He pulled her to him. "I love you so much, and you're so amazing to me. I'm very glad we came to the mountains for the summer. It's like an extended honeymoon, and I've learned new things about you. How would you like to spend every summer here?"

"Do you mean it? Can we really do that?"

"I don't see why not. We can leave after the spring planting. Willie, or whoever we hire, can see to things while we're away, and we'll return for the fall harvest. We'll have the best of both places. We'll be in Anson County and miss the cold winters and cool falls here, and we'll not have to endure the scorching summers there. Even when children come along, they'll be out of school in the summers."

"Oh, thank you, Patrick. This sounds too good to be true."

"I have my selfish reasons too. Besides the fact that I love it here, we'll have doting grandparents to see to our children, so we can come off alone like this."

"Are you disappointed we're not expecting a baby yet?"

"Not at all. I would be happy if we were, but I'm enjoying our time alone together too much. I'm glad to have that opportunity to have you all to myself a while longer. What about you?"

"I feel much like you. I'd be excited to have your baby, and it's something I want to do in the near future, but I don't think the timing has been right yet. I'm glad we proved those first rumors of how we had to get married wrong."

"I guess we did prove them wrong, didn't we?"

"Yes, and I was thinking it might have happened when we went to Anson County, but when I was taken by those men, I was glad I wasn't expecting for several reasons."

"Why's that?"

"Oh Patrick, I know you trust me, but I was afraid you'd always have some doubt if I came up pregnant after I was abducted. I was afraid you'd think I lied, in order to shield you from the pain of knowing, when I said they didn't force me. I wouldn't, you know. I'll always be truthful with you. And then also, that turned out to be such a stressful time for me, I could have lost a baby."

He pulled her closer to him. "I believe you'll always be honest with me, because that's who you are. You're too close to God to do otherwise."

They'd talked longer than they'd intended until they realized how hungry they'd become, so they sat in the grass and ate their dinner. Afterward they lay in each other's arms.

As the days passed, Rachel shared more of her family's stories with Patrick. They visited Granny Em's old cabin, which Papa now owned. She led Patrick to the creek and told him how Granny had been fourteen when she had come to this creek and had been taken by four Cherokee braves. The leader had protected her from the one who'd wanted to assault her. He'd taken her to his mother in the village and fallen in love with her.

"That must have been Hawk," Patrick said. "I thought the world of him. He took me under his wing when I was here, especially after Lawrence was killed in the war."

"Yes, that was Hawk. Granny was already in love with Grandpa Edgar at the time, so she convinced Hawk to send her home. Hawk loved her enough to let her go to the man she wanted. Sheila and Connell O'Leary brought her home. Sheila was Hawk's sister."

"Then, after all those years, Hawk came back here to check on Granny Em, and they were married."

"Yes, Grandpa Edgar had been dead a long time by then, about twelve years or more. Granny and Hawk had only about three years together, but they were very happy and very much in love. Did you know Connell and Sheila were Grandmother Sarah's parents? Grandfather and Sarah gives us another love story."

"Yes, I remember your grandfather talking of her. When did she die?"

"When Papa was a young boy. Grandfather and she were married for only about ten years or so, but I think those few years were filled with a lifetime of love."

"And, now there's Rachel and Patrick." He gave her a melting look. "Their love story is the best one of all."

All too soon September was upon them and the nights were turning cool and crisp. Rachel realized that days pass so much more quickly when each one overflowed with joy.

"As much as I hate to say this, we need to be going back to Stanly County," Patrick said one night.

They began packing the next day. The following day, they headed down the mountain, and this time they stopped in Wilkesboro. They checked into an inn and walked around the town after supper.

"Do you think the trouble with rumors, lies, and the Klan is over for us?" Rachel asked.

"I think so, and we'll be there only a few weeks before we move to Anson County."

"Are you planning to do anything about Julius?"

"Not unless you want me to. I'm sure it would be futile to file a complaint. Even if we had more evidence, Julius is a lawyer, and the authorities more than likely support the Klan. I've prayed about it, and I think we should leave Julius to God for now. You know, 'Vengeance is mine, I will repay, saith the Lord.'"

"I think that's wise, Patrick."

———————————

"Wasn't it wonderful to have Rachel and Patrick with us for the summer?" Leah asked her husband.

"It was, but I didn't get to see enough of them. They were always off somewhere by themselves."

"You're exaggerating, Luke, but do you blame them?"

"No, I understand. I like all the time I can get alone with my wife too. It was great to see Rachel and Patrick so happy and very much in love."

"Yes, Patrick has turned into the fine young man I always thought he would."

"And, he's very blessed to have our daughter as his wife, but I was surprised he wanted to come here every summer. I know how hard it is for a farmer to get away."

"Patrick really liked it here those two years he and Ivy stayed with me during the war, and he's very attuned to Rachel's needs and wants."

"Don't I take care of you in the same way?"

"You do, but you do it naturally, because in many ways, we're so much alike and think the same way. Patrick seems to make a concerted effort to care for Rachel. He's always spoiled her."

"Well, it doesn't seem to have hurt her any. She's one of the sweetest women I know. She takes after her mother, I guess."

"Luke, do you know how much I love you?"

"No. You'll just have to keep showing me, I guess." His eyes twinkled in mischief.

# CHAPTER TWENTY-TWO

# The Move

"I REALIZED HOW HARD YOU work, Patrick," Uncle Sam said not long after the couple had returned, "but I didn't realize how much more I'd have to do without you."

"I'd also let Rachel take over just about everything, except the dusting and cleaning," Aunt Ivy added. "I didn't realize she'd been doing so much, either."

"Well, we're back to help with the harvest," Patrick said, "but then we'll be moving to Anson County. Sammy should be able to help more soon, and I want to get our place started."

They'd made it back about ten days before Uncle Sam planned to start the harvest, so Patrick wanted them to go to Wadesboro and hire someone to build the small house they would live in this winter while the main house was being built. They would be gone only a couple of days.

"Why don't you go and take care of business and leave Rachel with us?" Aunt Ivy asked her son.

"Because I'm not about to be apart from Rachel, unless it's absolutely necessary."

Ivy filled them in on the news while they ate supper. Charles had been seeing Hope regularly, and Rachel could tell Patrick's sister hoped for a proposal by Christmas.

Julius and Blanche had gotten married and moved to Asheboro, where he would continue to practice law. Rachel wished them well, but she felt relieved they were out of the area.

The counterfeiting had stopped, and the moonshining was either curtailed or gone more underground. In any regard, it wasn't causing the overt problems it once had.

"I would have liked to help build the house," Patrick told Rachel on the way to Anson County, "but this way, we'll be able to move in sooner. Since it'll be small, it may be about ready by the time the harvest is in."

They found a man Patrick thought would be good to oversee the building of both houses. Patrick would help build the main house when they moved. The little house would have a sitting room and kitchen combined. There would also be a pantry and two bedrooms.

Patsy told Rachel how she'd love having them for neighbors, and Moses smiled broadly. Ezra and Moses both wanted to help with building the big house, since their harvest would be over by then too.

"Well, we've accomplished quite a lot in three days," Patrick said as he and Rachel headed back to the farm. "We'll go back, when the harvest is over."

The Whitleys' harvest went much the same as it had last year, except Annie came to help every day. Her Monday employer no longer needed her.

There were five other men, including Willie. All but one of them had been here last year.

"I's sho' been lookin' forward to Miz Rachel's cookin'," one of them said, and the others agreed.

Patrick and Rachel asked to talk with Annie and Willie in private at the end of the dinner Monday. They went into the backyard.

"Rachel and I are hoping you two can come to Anson County and help us out as soon as we get the farmhouse built," Patrick began. "You'll be able to live in the little house we'll be staying in while the main house is under construction. I want Willie to be the foreman on the place. He'll hire extra workers when we need them, and help me work the rest of the time. Rachel and I plan to go see her parents every summer, after the crops are in the ground. We'll be back in time for harvest. You'd have the place to yourselves, then."

"How much y'all be payin'?" Willie asked.

"To start with, I thought I'd give you one-fourth of the harvest and up to half the garden. There's a river full of fish and a woods for hunting. If you ever want to buy some of the land, we can talk about that too. However, we might as well eat together. I see no reason for our wives cooking two separate meals. If our family gets larger, and we want to change that, we'll renegotiate your pay."

"It sound jus' fine ta me, but lets us do some talkin', an' we'll lets y'all knows."

The first week of the harvest went fine. The good weather held, and the men accomplished much.

Saturday, Rachel had a tub of warm water waiting in the bath shed for Patrick, and she massaged his shoulders and scrubbed his back. She could tell how tired he felt from the week's work.

"What did I ever do before you, Rachel? I can't imagine how I made out."

"You just didn't know what you were missing." She laughed and kissed his cheek.

Monday they got up to rain, and it also peppered down steadily all day Tuesday, so none of the men came. Annie did the laundry on the back porch and hung the clothes there and in the bath shed.

"Willie an' me talked it over, an' we wants ta go wiv y'all to Anson," Annie told Rachel.

"That's wonderful. I had hoped that's what you'd decide." She looked forward to telling Patrick.

Wednesday was cloudy and still wet, but the sun came out by midday, and Uncle Sam breathed a sigh of relief. He hoped they could get in the fields again Thursday.

The fields were muddy Thursday, but the workers came, and they went to the fields. They came in for dinner with mud caked on their shoes so badly, they took their shoes off in the yard and rolled their muddy pants legs up.

"It's harder working in the wet fields," Patrick said. "The mud pulls at our feet, so every step takes more effort."

They harvested the sugar cane and corn first and didn't get to the hay until Monday of the following week. At least, the ground had dried out and the sun rested in a clear sky.

Rachel had dinner ready a little early and decided to go out to the field to see how things were going. She had almost made it to the field when she heard a man yell in pain. She looked up to see the man fall to the ground with a large gash in his leg bleeding profusely. She ran to help.

The diagonal slice appeared deep. It ran over a foot long and gaped open. Rachel jerked off the tie from her hat and tied it just above the wound to help stop the bleeding.

"Patrick, get the wagon quickly. This needs stitches. You need to get him to a doctor."

She tore off the bottom of her petticoat and wrapped the leg tightly to hold the slit together and slow the bleeding. She had Willie bring him some water while they waited.

Patrick came back quickly with the wagon and the men loaded him into the wagon. Uncle Sam drove him to the doctor.

"What happened?" she asked her husband as they all walked to the house.

"Jarvis's scythe accidentally caught his leg. I'm glad you were here. You acted quickly and knew just what to do."

"I've helped Mama some, and she knows healing, almost as well as Grandfather. She knew some, when she went to the mountains, but she learned more from Granny Em, who learned it from Hawk's mother."

When Rachel got back to the house her knees suddenly felt weak, and she grabbed hold of the porch rail. Patrick helped her into the house and sat her in a chair.

"What's wrong, honey?"

"I'm sorry. Thoughts of the huge gash and all the blood just hit me, and I grew weak."

"I remember you once saying you could deal with emergencies, but then you were often shaky afterwards. Is that what happened?"

She nodded.

"It's okay, sweetheart, you were great. You just sit here and collect yourself."

"Could you move one of these chairs to the kitchen for me? I'm already beginning to feel some better, but I'd like to sit with you men while you eat."

Annie handled the serving, and when it came time for dessert, Rachel had recovered enough to help.

The men had finished eating and were getting up when Uncle Sam returned. The hurt man wasn't with him.

"I took Jarvis home," he said. "The doctor treated the wound, stitched it up, and put a heavy bandage on it. He said you did an excellent job with your temporary bandage, Rachel, and the tourniquet may have saved his life."

The four remaining workers looked at her in admiration and nodded their appreciation. Patrick looked at her, and she almost lost herself in the depths of pride in his eyes.

"Patrick, if you'll take these men and go back to work," Uncle Sam said, "I'll get something to eat and be on out to help you."

After the workers finished in the fields, Patrick stayed and helped his father for a few more days. Near the end of October, he and Rachel packed their things into the wagon for the move.

Besides the basics that they'd taken to the mountains with them, Rachel packed their winter clothes, her chest of linens she'd retrieved from the mountains, a few canned goods Mama had sent, and their books. They took some basic furniture that Aunt Ivy didn't use anymore, but they wouldn't need much for the small house.

She'd also brought back some of her personal things from the mountains, like the doll Hawk and Granny had made for her before they died. He had carved the head, arms, and legs and painted on beautiful features. Granny had made a cloth body and clothes, and they'd even added a set of leather Cherokee clothes. Mama hadn't let her play with it much before she got old enough to take care of it, so it was still in good shape. She hoped to pass the prized possessions to her daughter someday.

After loading the last of the produce from the garden they'd take with them, Uncle Sam looked over at Patrick. "Come back once you get settled, and we'll give you more of the root crops and canned goods from the garden. You helped produce them. I'll let you have some chickens, a milk cow, and the young bull too. We've also probably got some more extra furniture stored in the attic you could have when you build your other house."

They went by to check on the house first and found it nearly finished. She and Patrick unloaded their things into one of the bedrooms. They decided to stay in the hotel until the builders finished.

The next day they shopped for some other things they'd need. "We'll just get serviceable items now, and we can leave most of them for Annie and Willie," Rachel told her husband. "I'll need to do some more shopping when we move into a bigger house."

"You're easy to live with. Have I told you that, Rachel? I guess I'm used to Mama. I love her dearly, but she's not always so agreeable."

"Your father seems to deal with her well. They seem happy together."

"Yes, they are. I guess Papa knows how to manage her, but I'd much prefer to have someone like you."

"Well, that's good." She laughed. "Because you have me."

They bought a table, four chairs, and a bed. Rachel looked around for something to sit on in the sitting room. They loaded up their purchases, and took them to the cabin. The carpenters were just finishing up, and they helped Patrick unload everything.

"Tomorrow we'll need to buy a cookstove," Patrick said after the men had left.

Rachel nodded. "We'll also need to buy some staples to stock the kitchen."

Rachel knew something was troubling Patrick, but he tried to hide it, and that worried her all the more. He would sink into an uncomfortable quietness and look deep in thought, if not worried. She decided to be direct.

"What's wrong, Patrick?"

"What makes you think something is wrong?"

"Now who's answering a question with a question? What don't you want to tell me? I don't think there's another woman."

At first he looked shocked, but then he saw she was teasing, and he laughed. Both of them were so much in love, the thought of another love interest was laughable.

"It's nothing really. It's just the building and moving here is taking more money than I expected. I guess I neglected to count all the little expenses when you have to buy so much. We have enough right now, but I don't know when we start building the other house."

"We don't have to do all this, you know. I've always known it wouldn't be easy. It would require a lot of hard work from both of us to start a farm with nothing but the land. Instead, we could come here as a winter retreat and hunt and fish. We'd go to the mountains in the summers and stay with your folks and help on the farm in the spring and fall. Now wouldn't that be the life?"

He smiled. "You'd be happy being vagabonds with no place of our own?"

"I live in your heart, Patrick, as you do in mine. Wherever you are is my home."

He thought for a minute. "But we prayed about it and thought this was best. Besides, I wanted to have you to myself more than just during the winter."

"You had me to yourself quite a bit in the mountains. We can always find time to be alone. How bad is our financial situation?"

"We have money left, but we're not finished yet."

"If you want to stay here, let's just forget about the big house for now." Rachel looked him in the eyes, so he could see her sincerity. "This house will be fine. I don't need a fancy home or material things."

He shook his head with regret. "I thought we had it all planned out, but now I don't know."

"Let me look at the money issue with you." She saw his reluctance. "Mama has always shared the accounts with Papa. I'm not some Southern belle you need to shelter from the realities of life, and I'd be very unhappy if you treated me as such."

"I'm sorry, darling." He pulled her to him. "You're right. I was trying to keep any worries from you, and we should share the good and the bad. I'd certainly want you to come to me with any problems or concerns; therefore, I should do the same."

Patrick and Rachel looked over the numbers, then she asked, "Had you planned to have enough money to build the main house too?"

"No, I always planned to get a bank loan to cover part of it."

"Then this doesn't look too bleak. If we get only the bare necessities for the house, you'd still have enough for the tools and seeds. Perhaps we could buy some used tools."

"We'll need to build a barn too. I'd overlooked that at first."

"It doesn't have to be fancy. Get Moses and Ezra to help you build a log one for now."

He sat back and sighed. "This is nothing like I envisioned. I guess my dreams were too big."

"I think you've done well to save as much money as you have, and with the cash gifts from our wedding, we definitely have a start."

"Yes, Papa has paid me some from the farm profits since the time I turned eighteen, and I've saved most of it, but it's going fast."

"Let's stay here this winter and see how things go. We can make a definite decision just before time for spring planting."

"I guess we'll go back to my parents' for Thanksgiving and get the things Papa offered. We worked in the garden there and you did a lot of the canning, so I don't feel bad about taking some of the food."

"We'll hunt and fish here. A deer would do us a long time. We'll have a cow for milk and chickens for eggs. We'll be fine. God will provide."

"I just wanted to give you so much."

"Patrick, you've given me what I need, your love and devotion."

Patrick heard of a man who had fallen on bad times and had to sell his small farm. They bought an almost-new cookstove and some farm tools from him.

"Come get the rest of the hay and feed and anything else I leave that you can use," the man told them. "The new owner isn't moving in until spring. He didn't pay me nearly enough for the place, so I have no desire to leave him anything extra."

Mrs. Suggs, a sweet little widow from church, found out they were furnishing a house and gave them her everyday dishes. "At my age, I decided I want to use my good china," she told them. "I'd might as well enjoy what I can."

The dishes might be her everyday ones, but they were still pretty. They were solid white with a small, elegant raised fan design on the edges.

"I'll be happy with these," Rachel told Patrick. "They will go with everything, and I wouldn't want anything nicer."

"God is providing, isn't He?" Patrick smiled.

They bought some groceries and moved into their house the day they picked up the dishes. Patsy, Moses, and Ezra met them there. Patsy had cooked a stew and baked bread, and she'd brought it over for dinner. The younger children were in the colored school.

"I know it won't be as good as your mama's," Patsy said, "but she did teach me to cook, so I do all right."

"What a nice surprise! It'll be our housewarming," Rachel told her.

"I have a favor to ask," Patsy said as they finished eating, "I'm not happy with the education my children are getting. Aquila and Callie like school and would like to be taught more. I used to help them some when they were younger, but I never learned to read or write at higher levels, because your mama taught me after we moved to the mountains. I was wondering if you'd have time to tutor them for an hour after school this winter. It would be the younger four. Ezra wouldn't be included. Moses and Ezra will help with whatever they can to repay your time."

"I'd be glad to help them, but you don't need to pay us," Rachel said. "I taught school a month at Big Lick, and I found I enjoyed it. I might have to work on supper while they study, but I'm sure I can do both."

"Let them help some with supper, and the boys can get in wood or something. I don't want people to know you're teaching them. If they do a few chores, we can honestly say they're working for you."

"Okay. Give us a few days to get settled here, and I'll start next week."

*I wants to hep,* Moses wrote on his pad.

"As you can see," Patsy said, "Moses insists on helping you here. I'm sure you have something he and Ezra can do. We know it's a lot of hard work to start a farm."

"I do need to build a barn or a shed for the animals before we go to Big Lick for Thanksgiving," Patrick said. "I'm planning to fell the trees and build it out of logs. I sure could use your help on that."

Moses grinned and nodded his head. He must be in his late forties now, but he still looked strong and healthy.


After Patsy and Moses left, Rachel made the bed and unpacked the things they'd need first. Before he started working on the barn, Patrick planned to build a bookshelf in the sitting room. At least the pantry already had shelves.

She and Patrick ate a simple supper, and he smiled and laughed as they talked. Rachel was thankful Patrick had shed most of his worry. They had their devotion and thanked God for His blessings.

The evening felt special to them. They appreciated being alone together in their own home, and they went to bed with childlike excitement.

CHAPTER TWENTY-THREE

# Blessings

RACHEL FOUND AQUILA TO BE very smart and eager to learn. Although a good student, Callie was quieter and shyer than her sister. The two boys were cooperative, but they'd rather be outside than sitting at the table doing lessons. Overall, however, they were easy to teach.

Moses, Ezra, and Patrick worked hard to build a six-stall barn. They would have the four horses and a cow right away. In addition, the men would attach a shelter for the wagon.

Patrick had already built a chicken coop with scrap materials left over from building the house. He'd only had to buy some nails and wire.

By Thanksgiving, the men had finished the barn. When he and Rachel returned, Moses and Ezra would help Patrick clear a garden plot and some fields for spring.

Rachel and Patrick left for Big Lick on the Monday before Thanksgiving. Rachel wanted to see Annie on Tuesday, and she would do most of the baking for Thanksgiving on Wednesday. Despite the fact they liked being on their own, they both looked forward to seeing the family.

"We're still hoping you can come in the spring," Rachel told Annie, "but Patrick doesn't want to start the big house until we have more money. He's afraid something will happen and we won't be able to make the payments on it. We've decided to wait until after the first harvest is in to start building. If you come, you'll have to live with us until we can finish the other house. The one we're in now has two bedrooms, and it would be yours when we move."

"I's wouldn't minds dat," Annie said. "We be livin' wid Willie's family now, and dat house's crowded. I'll ax Willie, but I's thank it be jus' fine."

"What do you think about Charles?" Hope asked Rachel when they were alone. "You seemed to like him."

"Patrick and I both did. I think he's a fine young man. What do you think of him?"

"I think he's quite wonderful." She grinned. "I'm hoping he'll propose to me soon. You and Patrick will have to come to the wedding if he does."

"As long as it's not during planting or harvesting."

"Are you kidding? With Papa and Charles both being farmers, there'd be no possibility of that."

The full spread on the table at Thanksgiving looked wonderful after trying to stretch their meals on few groceries. They laughed, talked, and visited well into the night.

Because his family begged them to go to church with them, Patrick decided to stay until Tuesday. That would allow them to go to church Sunday, then pack up the wagon with things they were taking back on Monday.

No one had heard any more rumors about Rachel, but she still went to church with some trepidation. At least Blanche and Julius wouldn't be there.

Rachel saw she'd been wrong about the couple as soon as Patrick helped her from the surrey. She noticed Julius right away, and she clutched Patrick's arm tighter.

Julius had been talking with some men, but started toward Rachel and Patrick. She couldn't read the expression on his face.

"Could we talk in private?" he asked, then the three of them walked off from the others. "I need to beg your forgiveness."

Rachel didn't know what she'd expected, but it wasn't this. She listened attentively.

"I did you a great wrong, Rachel. First, I was so angry when you decided you didn't want to marry me, Blanche and I started horrible rumors about you. I also had the KKK scare you. I was trying to get back at you for rejecting me. Can you ever forgive me?"

"But since my Cherokee heritage bothered you, you didn't really want to marry me either, Julius."

"I'm not sure of that, but you didn't give me a chance to think things through before you jilted me."

"And, it's natural to want what you think you can't have," Patrick added.

"It was you that night I was tied to the post, wasn't it?"

He turned very pale. "You knew?"

"I suspected as much. Although I'd been blindfolded and you never talked, there was something very familiar about the man."

"Blanche and I went to a tent revival in Asheboro. We both were saved that night. Now I know what you meant when you were asking me those questions about my faith. I had many sins for Christ to forgive. How I treated you that night was one of the biggest. I regret my actions more than words can say. Can you possibly forgive me?"

"I forgive you. Unforgiveness would hurt me more than anyone else."

Julius looked at Patrick. "I hope you can find it in your heart to forgive me, too, Patrick."

"I don't know. You wronged the woman I love. That's much harder to forgive than if you'd wronged me. Do you have any idea what we went through that night?"

"Patrick," Rachel pleaded. "Remember Matthew 6:15. 'But if ye forgive not men their trespasses, neither will your Father forgive your trespasses.'"

Patrick breathed in deeply and closed his eyes in thought. "You're right, darling." He put his arm around her waist. "I do forgive you, Julius." And he extended his hand.

The people in church were very friendly and went out of their way to make Rachel and Patrick feel welcome. Some of them seemed to be trying to make up for taking part in gossip or for believing it. Others had never gotten caught up in the mayhem at all.

Blanche went up to them after the service. "Julius said he told you about what we did. I want to add my apologies. I knew most of the things I told about you were untrue, Rachel, and I beg your forgiveness."

"Of course, you have it," Rachel said and hugged the pretty blonde.

"Well, that was an unexpected turn of events," Patrick said on their way home.

When they were alone, Patrick asked Rachel, "How do you feel about knowing it was Julius that night and seeing him again today?"

"I'm relieved to finally know and not just be guessing, but I'm not sure what you mean by the last question. I hope Julius and Blanche will be very happy together. I experienced some uneasiness when he first came up to us, but after that, I had very few emotions. I certainly wasn't overjoyed to see him, but I didn't loathe him, either."

"No regrets?"

"Patrick Whitley! How could you even ask me that? After loving you so completely and having that love returned, I would never have a regret about marrying you. There has never been and will never be another man for me. It's sometimes hard for me to believe any two people could be as perfect for each other as we are. Have I done such a poor job as your wife that you're unsure of my love?"

"No, you're everything I hoped for and more, and you're a fantastic wife. I guess I was so jealous and so scared of losing you when you were seeing Julius that I let those uncertainties start to creep back. It'll never happen again."

When he wrapped her in his arms and gave her a kiss that left her soft as clay in his hands, she forgot everything else. Afterwards, she knew the ghost of Julius had been expelled from both their lives.

Packing up took more time than Rachel expected. They loaded up enough potatoes, carrots, and onions to do them through the winter. They also took back enough turnips for a couple of months. They packed up cases of canned fruits, vegetables, pickles, jams, and jellies. They even took some kegs of apple cider, hams, and bacon.

"I'll give you a couple of spring pigs,if you come back when they're old enough to wean," Uncle Sam told them.

"Are you trying to bribe me to come home more?" Patrick teased.

"If that's what it takes." Uncle Sam laughed.

Tuesday morning, Patrick strapped four chicken crates full of chickens and tied the cow and young bull to the back of the wagon. He and Rachel would have to travel slowly.

"I don't want you to go," Sammy said. "I've missed you."

"We've missed you too," Patrick told him, "but we'll come again, and you'll have to come see us too. Maybe you can come and stay with us a few weeks this summer."

"We have much to be thankful for, don't we?" Patrick smiled as they crept along in the wagon.

"Indeed we do." Rachel spread her quilt over his legs and snuggled in closer to him. "This has been a good Thanksgiving too. I'm thankful for so much."

They got home and unloaded everything. She gave Patrick a quick hug, then they started unpacking.

"I just realized this is beginning to really feel like home to me," Rachel said, "and it's good to be home."

"Yes, it is," Patrick agreed as he pulled her into his arms and kissed her.

The bounty from Stanly County added variety to Patrick and Rachel's meals. Having milk and eggs was especially welcomed. With the milk, she could also make butter and cheese.

It amazed her how fast Patrick, Moses, and Ezra could clear the fields. She went out and helped them some. Patrick protested at first, but she reminded him she liked to work outside, and she liked working alongside him.

"Since these were cleared fields until well up into the war," Patrick said, "it's not as hard to clear them as it would have been if they'd never been used as fields. Also, sitting without crops for a time should make them more fertile. I'm not going to clear all of them now. It would be too much for us to work."

The weather stayed mild until the first of December. Of course, winters here were mild to Rachel all the time, since she was still more used to Watauga County.

"Are we going to go to your parents' for Christmas?" she asked her husband.

"Papa asked me the same question, and I told him I didn't think so. What do you think? Would you rather have Christmas with the family, or have our own Christmas here?"

"Have our own Christmas here."

He grinned and his eyes danced. "That's what I thought too. We'll cut a tree from our property and decorate it."

"I'd like to suggest we don't try to surprise each other with a gift this year. Instead let's buy something we need, like a sofa and chair."

"If that's what you want, it sounds fine with me. We should go order it tomorrow, so it'll be here by Christmas."

After the couple returned from church and ate their Sunday dinner, they walked around the property to determine where they wanted to put the main house. Rachel thought she saw a piece of metal sticking out of the ground near the foundation of the old plantation house, and she went to investigate.

"Stop!" Patrick shouted, and instantly a loud bang followed.

Rachel froze and her heart did too. She looked and Patrick held the pistol she had given him for his birthday. He ran toward her and took her in his arms.

"What happened?" she asked.

"Look." He pointed to a large copperhead he'd shot. It had been sunning on the bricks, and in a few more steps, she'd have been within its striking range.

Patrick pulled her close. "I was so afraid the snake would bite you that my heart almost stopped. I'm glad you gave me a revolver I can carry in my jacket pocket. Did the shot scare you to death?"

"Almost, but being scared is better than getting snake bitten. I would've thought the snakes would be hibernating by now."

"Normally they would, but it's warmed up enough today this one decided to lie in the sunshine."

"I was so intent on seeing what that piece of metal is, I wouldn't have seen the snake at all."

"They're usually hard to spot. They blend in too well. Come on." He put an arm around her waist. "Let's see what almost got you in trouble."

"It almost looks like some sort of handle," she said as she stooped over the object. She reached out and gave it a pull, but it didn't budge. "It's stuck."

"Here, let me see." Patrick couldn't get it up either. He took his hands and started moving some of the dirt from around the object. Soon they could tell it was attached to a larger piece of metal. Rachel used a nearby stick to start digging on one side as Patrick used his hands to dig on the other side.

"This red clay sure packs hard," she said.

"That's why they make bricks from it. Look, it's a box." Patrick gave a tug, and the metal box broke loose. "It's heavier than it looks." Since it wasn't locked, he opened the lid.

Twenty-dollar gold pieces gleamed in the sun. They looked at each other in amazement.

"Let's take this home and see how many are here," Patrick said. "You've found a treasure, Rachel. There's probably enough here to build our house, and if not, it'll be a good start."

"Do you think it was hidden during the war? Do you think Lawrence buried it?"

"I don't know. It makes sense it was buried because of the war, but it doesn't seem like something Lawrence would do without telling Mama. It could have been his mother or someone else."

"I don't guess it really matters."

"No, what matters is that you found it. Are you as excited as I am?"

"I am, but I'm having a hard time believing it."

Patrick lugged the metal box to the house, and they spread the contents out on the kitchen table to count.

"All of them seem to have been minted before 1860," Rachel commented.

Patrick nodded. "Yes, but they could have been saved and stored later."

There were close to two hundred coins, nearly four thousand dollars' worth. It would be enough to build the house.

"You told me God would provide, but I didn't realize how abundantly." Patrick shook his head in amazement.

"I didn't either." Rachel laughed.

They sat and made plans for the new house. It would have a parlor, kitchen, pantry, dining room, library, and a room for bathing downstairs. There would be five bedrooms upstairs with two being larger than the other three. There'd also be room for storage in the attic.

Rachel had first wanted a larger kitchen and no dining room, but Patrick thought they might want the more formal dining room someday.

"Do you think we'll need so many bedrooms?" Rachel asked.

"I'm hoping we have several children, and we'd also have room for our families to visit. We can use them for other things, until we need them for bedrooms. I'm sure you'd like to have a sewing room. I want this to be the last house we'll ever have to build."

Monday, Patrick and Rachel went to see the man who'd built the little house. He wasn't busy and could start that week. They'd decided to place the new house near where the plantation house had been. It was a lovely spot on a knoll with huge shade trees already there.

Agreeing to stick to their original plan, they ordered parlor furniture for their Christmas present to each other. Now, with the money they'd found, they could buy much nicer furniture and more of it. Their first anniversary drew near too.

They joined hands and trekked to the edge of the woods to find a Christmas tree. They chose a pretty cedar that smelled marvelous when placed in the corner of the sitting room. They strung popcorn, added stems of holly, and Rachel made some small quilted ornaments from colorful scrapes of folded fabric. She even rolled out some cookie dough, then hand cut simple shapes, such as bells and stars. She sewed a string into the top of each before she baked them, so they could be hung on the tree.

"The tree is lovely," Patrick said as they put the ornaments on one evening. "But why didn't we buy some ornaments and save you the trouble of making all these?"

"I want us to choose one special, store-bought ornament each year," Rachel said. "If you don't mind, I'd like you to help me choose it."

"Now, when have I ever minded doing anything with you?"

She smiled to herself at the truth of his statement. If she wanted to drag Patrick to a sewing circle, he'd probably be willing to go. He loved being with her, and that took precedent. Where they were or what they were doing didn't matter nearly as much as their being together did.

December 14 was their anniversary. Patrick had offered to take Rachel to Wadesboro for supper, but she preferred to spend the evening at home. She cooked a special meal, including a cherry-chocolate cake for dessert. The children didn't come for tutoring, so she had plenty of time. Patrick did the outside chores a little early. That way they could spend the time together from supper on.

Rachel had bought Patrick a horse-drawn mower to harvest the hay fields more quickly. Moses had picked it up for her and stored it at his place. He and Ezra would secretly bring it over while they were eating supper and put it behind the barn.

Everything went according to plan. They ate supper by candlelight, and with the fireplace burning in the sitting room, the atmosphere was romantic and special.

"Can you believe we've been married for a year?" she asked.

"No. Although I feel like I've known you all my life, the time since we were married has flown by. How do you feel?"

"This year has been the fastest of my life, but in some ways, it seems we've been married longer. I feel I know you better than I should, since I really met you less than two years ago. You may remember me as a child, but I had little memory of you."

"It's been the happiest year of my life, except when you were abducted. Those were the worst hours."

"Getting to know you has been wonderful for me. You were my best friend ever and meant the world to me, even before I recognized how much I loved you."

"I fell in love with you almost the minute you walked through the door. But I had some tense moments. I was so afraid you would never grow to see me as more than just your friend. I had to constantly caution myself to be patient and give you time. It was hard when you ate dinner at Blanche's with Axel, but I was so relieved when you refused to see him again. When Julius started courting you, my heart nearly broke. I had no doubt he'd ask you to marry him. What man wouldn't fall in love with you, given half a chance. I tried to school myself to accept whatever God's will was, even if that meant losing you."

"Then, I told Julius good-bye."

"Yes, and I was overjoyed, especially when you didn't seem all that hurt, but I dared not think you'd ever love me as I wanted. The fall festival made me long for you all the more. When you snuggled up to me and put your head on my shoulder in the hay wagon, I could barely hold my love. I went home convinced you must love me too. I thought I was going to tell you how much I loved you the next day, but when the morning came, I was afraid I'd misinterpreted everything. I decided it would be safer to preserve our friendship and wait."

"The hayride was special to me too. I wanted to share my love for you, but I decided to say nothing until I talked with my parents. Then, if you didn't love me and I had to return home with them, I'd at least have had a few more weeks of your friendship."

"What if they'd disapproved and made you go back with them?"

"I didn't think they'd do that. I knew they wanted my happiness, and they'd at least listen to how I felt. They'd have had a hard time keeping us apart once I knew you loved me too. As much as I love my parents, I would have defied them for you. I love you that much."

"That's good to know. I love you that much too. I thank God every day for you, but come, Mrs. Whitley. I want you to see your anniversary present. I didn't try to wrap it."

"That's okay. I didn't wrap yours either."

Patrick led her to the spare bedroom. They'd set up the second bed, but they never went in there.

It didn't take her long to spot the sewing machine. "Oh Patrick! I love it! You don't know how often I've wished I had one here. Now I can make curtains for the new house and everything. Thank you!"

She jumped into his arms, and their embrace turned into a long kiss. She would never get tired of the feel of him and the thrill he gave her every time he touched her.

Patrick was almost as excited over his mower as she had been her sewing machine. He examined it carefully. "This is perfect. Papa will be so jealous. Just you watch. He'll buy him one before getting in the spring hay. How did you manage to hide this without me seeing it? I thought keeping you from finding the sewing machine was hard, but this is even larger."

"Moses helped me."

They went inside to sit in front of the fire. They held their devotion and then talked and cuddled. They even lit the Christmas tree for the first time, and the candles made it sparkle. They wouldn't light them again until Christmas Eve.

Rachel lay in bed that night overwhelmed with love for her husband, and it was multiplied knowing he loved her that much too. He reached for her, and she lost herself in his embrace and kisses.

# CHAPTER TWENTY-FOUR

# Fair Oaks Farm

IT WAS EXCITING TO WATCH the house being built. Mr. Culp, the builder, brought two other workers. Patrick, Moses, and Ezra helped also. They worked three weeks before Christmas.

The store sent word by Mr. Culp that Rachel's parlor furniture had arrived, and she and Patrick planned to pick it up on the twenty-third. That way, everything would be in place on Christmas Eve.

On the twenty-second, they went hunting. Even after her going out with him at the farm, Patrick still seemed astounded Rachel knew how and wanted to hunt. She couldn't help but laugh.

They each shot a wild turkey, and Patrick said they would take the biggest one to Patsy. Rachel had made Christmas presents for the Morgans, and they took those too. They brought back three packages, so they'd had gifts under their Christmas tree.

They returned and cleaned their turkey in the backyard, taking turns picking the feathers off the scalded bird. The unpleasant task seemed more fun with them working together.

"Do you think it will keep if we hang it in the pantry?" Patrick asked. "I wish we could order an icebox, like your grandfather talked about getting, but I don't think anyone will be delivering ice in the country. They are a new thing, and it'll take a while for the idea to spread."

"Little heat gets in the pantry, and it's below freezing most nights, even though it warms up some during the day, it should keep until Christmas. I'll start roasting it early Christmas morning."

That night the weather turned colder. She and Patrick wore their heavy winter clothing as they drove to Wadesboro the next day to pick up their furniture.

The sofa and upholstered chairs looked a little too nice for the small house, but they would look great in the new one. It would crowd their small sitting room now, but the parlor of the new house would be more spacious. Rachel liked the set. They placed the sofa facing the fireplace, and it was much more comfortable than what they'd had.

On Christmas Eve, they lit the candles on the tree, and Patrick read aloud the Christmas story. They sang some carols, and Rachel wished they had Papa to play his fiddle.

"I enjoyed dancing with you at Hope's birthday celebration and at our wedding," Rachel said after they'd stopped singing. "I wish we had more opportunity to dance to music like that."

"I do too. At Hope's party, I told you to waltz only with me, unless there was someone there you wanted to hold you close, hoping there wasn't, and I'd get to hold you close on every waltz. It worked." He grinned. "And I loved it. Dancing with you at our wedding was even more special, because I knew you loved me too."

"Perhaps we'll get to dance at Charles and Hope's wedding soon."


Rachel and Patrick woke up to snow Christmas morning, so they stood at the window in the kitchen and watched it float down. Rachel hoped they would have a blanket of white for Christmas, but it didn't materialize. The flakes melted as they hit the ground, and it later warmed up and turned into a light drizzle.

Rachel cooked way too much food, but they could eat the leftovers. They opened their Christmas presents from the Morgan family after dinner. Patsy had made Rachel a brown calico dress and white apron. She'd made Patrick a flannel work shirt. Callie had sketched them a picture of a scene on their property by the river. Rachel hadn't realized the girl had so much talent.

They played two games of chess. Patrick won the first game, and Rachel won the second. Afterwards, they read some and talked more. They went to bed happy.

The following day was clear, and the sun had warmed up things by midday. About three o'clock they heard a wagon pull up. Uncle Sam, Aunt Ivy, Hope, and Sammy emerged from under quilts and climbed out of the wagon.

Rachel and Patrick ran to meet them, but hurried them in the house. The day was above freezing, but it was still cold for such a long drive.

"We all missed you so much yesterday, we decided to come for the day today," Ivy said. "Charles said he would check the farm and milk for us this evening if we didn't make it back until late."

At the mention of Charles's name, Hope smiled and stuck out her left hand for Rachel to see. Charles had given her the ring and proposed yesterday. They had asked Uncle Sam together, and he'd given his permission.

They'd planned the wedding for Saturday, March 5, at Mt. Olive Baptist Church. Hope wanted Rachel to be her matron of honor, and Charles wanted Patrick to be his best man.

"We bought you a Christmas present together this year," Aunt Ivy said.

It was a beautiful mantle clock. Rachel felt badly they had no gifts to give, but she boxed up cookies she had baked for them. They seemed pleased.

"We really didn't come expecting presents," Uncle Sam said. "We just wanted to see you."

They had a wonderful visit. When they'd warmed up enough, Rachel and Patrick showed them over the place, especially where the new house was taking shape. Rachel could tell it brought up some good and bad memories for Aunt Ivy, but she said nothing about it.

Aunt Ivy wanted to see Patsy, so they visited there for a while. Patsy and Ivy reminisced about times past.

They talked the family into spending the night, and Rachel cooked a ham for supper. With potato salad, beans, corn, biscuits, and cherry pie, it was like having another Christmas feast.

Aunt Ivy and Uncle Sam slept in the spare bedroom. Hope slept on the sofa and Sammy had a pallet on the sitting room floor. It was crowded, but it worked out.

The guests ate an early breakfast and left at first light. The morning was cold, so Patrick filled their warming pans with coals and placed them in the wagon at their feet. It would help for a little while, and the day should warm when the sun came out. They had brought the quilts in, and they were warm too.

Eighteen and eighty-one came in with a cold blast, and the workers didn't come for a week. Patrick and Rachel kissed in the new year wrapped in each other's arms. If there were revelry or celebrations elsewhere, they didn't hear them.

Patrick took her to the inn in Wadesboro for supper on Valentine's Day. She had made him a Valentine's card, and he gave her a beautiful card with a personal note added telling how much he loved and adored her.

She knew there would be something else from the way he was acting, but she didn't know what until they started to bed. She found a beautiful white iron bed with brass accents sitting in their bedroom.

"Happy Valentine's Day, darling," Patrick said to her surprised look.

"It's beautiful, but where's the other bed?"

"I had Moses move it into the empty barn stall and set this one up while we were out. When we move to the new house, we'll take this one and put the other one back in here."

"You have very good taste, Patrick. I like this better than any bed I've ever seen."

"I do have good taste," Patrick teased. "Look who I picked to marry."

"But I didn't get you a present."

He looked at her with a glint in his eyes. "I assure you, darling, this is just as much for me as it is for you."

She couldn't help but laugh.

For Rachel's birthday, the afternoon was pretty enough they decided to ride to the river. Patrick put on his coat and Rachel donned her riding skirt and warm jacket, and they headed out. It was cooler in the shade of the woods, but the ride invigorated Rachel. She loved to get out like this with Patrick. Most days he, Moses, and Ezra were helping with the new house.

They stayed out later than she'd expected and arrived back at the house near suppertime. As they entered the house, Rachel smelled the aroma of hot food.

"Are you hungry?" Patrick asked.

"I am now after smelling this food. What is it?"

"I had Patsy cook a pot of chicken 'n dumplings for us, and she baked you a birthday cake too. We just ate at the inn for Valentine's, and I wanted to do something different for your birthday."

He sat her down and served them. The food was especially good. Maybe the ride had whetted her appetite. She ate plenty, and Patrick seemed pleased.

"I hope you aren't disappointed in your birthday present. Patsy suggested this, and I know you are very practical, so I thought you might like it."

He had her a home canning set with everything she'd need and five dozen more jars. In addition, he'd bought a large set of spices.

"I love it," Rachel said. "And I can use it all. It's a perfect birthday present. I do like practical things, and I'm glad you and Patsy thought of this."

The shell of the main house was completed by the time Rachel and Patrick left for Hope's wedding. The men were working on the inside now. There hadn't been too many days when the weather had prevented them from working. Patrick said the work helped keep the men warm.

Rachel had made Hope a quilt. She'd pieced the top on her new sewing machine, which made the process go so much faster. Patsy, Aquila, and Callie helped her quilt it.

Moses and Ezra would take care of the chores while they were gone. They planned to be away only for a few days.

After the songs at the wedding, Patrick walked Rachel down the aisle and then took his place beside the groom. Rachel wore a mint green dress trimmed in lace dyed the same color.

"You know the attendant isn't supposed to outshine the bride," Patrick whispered in her ear. "You are breathtaking, the most beautiful woman I've ever seen."

Charles watched Rachel as Patrick led her down the aisle to the front, and she feared he might still be infatuated with her. She had a sinking feeling, but when Hope appeared, his face lit up and he had eyes only for his bride.

Hope looked radiant, and Charles appeared mesmerized with her as she walked down the aisle on her father's arm. Guests had packed the church for the event.

After the short ceremony, the family and a few select guests went back to the farm for a reception. Annie had helped Rachel prepare the food and kept the table supplied as the guests helped themselves.

Charles was the youngest in his family, and his parents looked older and more worn out than Rachel expected. Hope would be going to live with them. Mrs. Hinson treated Hope tenderly. Mr. Hinson appeared to expect a lot from Charles, but seemed to approve of Hope.

When the musicians turned their instruments to begin the dancing, Rachel looked at Patrick, and he smiled his understanding. After the bride and groom led off, she danced every dance with her husband. When he held her close and their bodies moved in harmony, she felt transported to a magical realm. She even enjoyed the reels, where they parted, but rarely took their eyes off each other.

On Sunday they went to church in the morning. That afternoon they went to find Annie and Willie. They received many stares in the colored community, but the people were either friendly, or else didn't look up at them.

"Come in, come," Willie said with a happy grin.

Annie started to hug Rachel, but then looked unsure, so Rachel hugged her and said, "We just came to see if you'd be ready to go back with us when we leave for home tomorrow." Like her, Patrick had noticed how small this house looked, and it already seemed full, so they stood and talked beside the wagon.

Willie nodded. "Dat sound fine. It won't be no problem atall."

"I hope this isn't too short a notice for you," Rachel added.

"No, no," Annie assured her. "We only have a few clothes to take, so dis'll be jus' fine."

"Our big house will be finished soon," Patrick told them, "but all four of us will stay in the cabin until then, like we talked about."

They both nodded, their eyes full of excitement. Rachel realized they had been looking forward to the move.

Uncle Sam gave them three small pigs to take back. They would keep two and butcher one in the fall. They put them in a large wooden crate in the wagon bed. He had also given Patrick some seeds for the garden. They would buy the rest they'd need.

They left at first light and picked up Annie and Willie. The couple were ready and waiting on the porch with a sack of clothes each. Annie sat up front beside Rachel, and Willie sat in the wagon, just behind the front seat.

They made good time and stopped only to eat. Rachel had packed a dinner for the four of them. They arrived home midafternoon.

Annie and Willie liked the house very much. They said it was as big as their family's, and three couples and four young children had been living in it.

Rachel and Annie started a stew for supper, and Patrick and Willie quickly built a pigpen.

The next morning the men walked over to help on the house. Both of them were excited when they came back for dinner.

"Willie is as good a carpenter as any man there," Patrick said. "He's going to be especially good on the detail work."

"I's likes Moses and his boy, Ezra, too," Willie said. "I's can tell dey goin' ta be good friends ta hab."

The next day, Patrick and Willie started turning the soil to get ready for spring planting. They did the garden plot first and then started on the other fields. They were going to plant a large field of cotton, two of corn, and a small one of sugar cane this year. Next year Patrick hoped to add more.

The cotton and part of the corn would be cash crops, while the cane would be used to make them some molasses. Moses had a molasses mill, and they could make their molasses at his place.

On the rainy days, which came more frequently in the spring, they helped inside the house. It had a roof, so they could work there and still stay dry.

They'd planted some of the garden in March, but Rachel and Annie planted the rest of it in April. By then, Patrick and Willie were working in the fields.

Moses and Ezra had quit helping, because they were working in their own fields now. Rachel still helped Aquila and Callie after school. However, the boys had asked to help with the planting.

Annie wanted to learn to speak proper too. When Patsy was still a slave, Mama had taught her to speak proper English, so all of the children talked like her.

Annie could read and write enough to get by, but Rachel planned to let her join the children's tutoring sessions in the fall. School would soon be over for this year. In the meantime, they could work on her English as they worked around the house.

They celebrated Patrick's birthday in April. Rachel cooked him a special supper and a cherry-chocolate cake. He needed so much on the farm, he was easy to buy for. She gave him a team of mules that Moses and Ezra had picked out for her. This way, one of the men could plow and the other could use the harrow to break up the clods.

With all the hard work, the days passed quickly. Rachel and Annie helped the men with the seeding. They had most of the planting done by the end of May.

The house was ready a week later, and Patrick had the builders start on a large barn and some outbuildings. They moved the parlor furniture, their bed, Rachel's sewing machine, and the other things they wanted to take to the new house. They would leave the rest of the furniture for Annie and Willie, and they had some things they'd collected for the couple to replace the essentials they were taking.

"Are you sure you can handle things here?" Patrick asked Willie. "We'll skip going to the mountains this year if you want us to."

"We's be jus' fine," Willie said. "Iffin we be needin' mo' hep, I's ride a mule up and gets my younga brotha ta come. He'd be mighty glad ta stay in a nice place like dis. He's 'bout fifteen now and a hard worka."

"You do that, Willie, and if there's an emergency you can always go for Moses, and you know where my parents live in Stanly County too. We'll be back the first part of September."

"When we get home, we'll have the new house waiting on us," Patrick said as they traveled. "We'll buy the things we need then. There's enough money left to furnish the kitchen, what other pieces we need for our bedroom, and probably one more bedroom. We can wait until the harvest is in for the rest. I could take out a loan for the rest, but I'd prefer not to, if it's not necessary."

"I like that better too. You know, we could have stayed here this summer, since our farm is so new."

"And miss a summer like we had last year?" He looked at her with his eyes twinkling. "Not if I can help it."

She laughed. It was good to get away. They were leaving all the chores, all the work, and all the stress of farming. For a summer, they could honeymoon without a care in the world. What a blessing!

Rachel and Patrick spent just the one night in Big Lick. They got there in time for Rachel to cook supper, and Sammy rode over to invite Hope and Charles. Hope seemed very happy, whereas Charles was quiet, but looked content.

They stopped for three days in Salisbury. Like the Whitleys, her grandparents tried to talk them into staying longer, but they were eager to be on their way.

They stayed at the hotel in Jonesville and had a shorter trip to Wilkesboro the next day, which gave them more time in the lovely town. They made it to the farm late the following day.

The family was excited to see them. "You haven't written us as much as you used to," her mother said. "We've missed your letters."

"I'm sorry, Mama, but there's been so much to do. The house is finally finished, although we've only partially moved in. The garden and three huge fields have been planted. We left Annie and Willie to see to things."

"Well, it's wonderful to have you with us."

The summer went much like the other had. Patrick and Rachel picked plenty of cherries to can and take home. They helped on the farm, but spent half their time roaming the hills, frolicking in the creek, and enjoying each other. They stayed in the Cagle Cabin and climbed to their mountaintop, and the days passed too quickly.

They packed up and started back on August 27, reversing their earlier trip. They got back to Big Lick on September the first and stayed through Sunday the fourth.

Hope told them she and Charles were expecting a baby in February. Charles was so pleased he beamed. The news hit Rachel hard.

She thought she would've been in a family way by then, but she and Patrick had been so busy and they'd enjoyed each other so much, she hadn't let the fact she wasn't bother her. Now that

Hope and Charles were already looking forward to their baby, she wished she was having Patrick's.

After the congratulations were said, Patrick looked across the table with understanding. That man! He could read her mind much of the time. After the meal, he asked Rachel to go for a walk with him. They walked down to their place at the creek.

"Like both of us learning we loved each other, our baby will come in God's time," Patrick lovingly told her as they sat on the log with his arm around her.

"I haven't really regretted not getting in a family way until now. I'm happy for Hope and Charles, but I'm ready too. Don't you want a child, Patrick? We'll soon be married for two years."

"You know I do, but I can wait. Having a child will put you at risk, and I dread that thought, but I love you and want to have children with you. Can't you just imagine how precious our baby will be?"

She smiled at him. For a while they sat quietly and Rachel let the brook soothe her. Patrick was right. They needed to wait patiently, trusting in the Lord. "How many times have we come here to talk? How many times have you comforted me here? You always know what to say to make me feel better."

"That's not hard to do with you, darling. All I have to do is remind you of the God we serve. It's your faith that's your strength, not me."

"But I need you to remind me." She smiled. Then, she looked at him seriously. "I need you for so many reasons, Patrick. I don't think you understand how much I really depend on you."

"Well, you have me, sweetheart. You definitely have me."

They got back home on Monday, September 6. The white house with black shutters stood proud and tall to greet them.

From what they could see the crops looked good too. There must have been enough rain, but Willie had managed to keep the weeds down.

They went to the little house first. Willie and Annie were glad to see them. Willie's brother, Quinton, was there and had been helping. He wanted to stay and help with the harvest too. Annie had been canning fruits and vegetables to use during the winter.

Rachel and Patrick spent the rest of the week getting their house in order. Rachel loved the wash room. They had a small stove in it, so they would be able to take a bath comfortably in winter. They could get some warm water out of the reservoir of the cookstove and not have to heat as much. It was off the kitchen and very convenient. It could also be used for laundry in the winter.

Moses helped Patrick schedule the cotton pickers and hire three more workers to harvest the corn and sugar cane. Since Patrick had the mower, he, Willie, and Quinton planned to get up the hay. Annie and Rachel would cook dinner for everyone at the main house.

Since the corn was ready, they started with it. It took them two weeks to pick all the corn and cut the stalks for fodder in the two fields.

It didn't take as long to cut the cane, but it took some time to press out the juice and boil it down into molasses. After they got it started, Patrick left Quinton to watch and stir it until it cooked down and cooled enough to pour into jars. The other three workers were finished after the corn and cane were cut.

The cotton pickers came last. There were so many of them, it didn't take long to clean the field. They brought their dinner with them each day, so the women went back to cooking for only three men.

Annie and Rachel always cooked breakfast separately, but they had dinner and supper at the main house for everyone six days a week. They did separate meals on Sunday, because their schedules were often different, since they attended different churches.

It was good to have Patrick with her more after the harvest. They had their own fall celebrations and spent time fishing, riding, exploring the woods, and enjoying their new house. The three families celebrated Thanksgiving together at the Morgans' this year.

It was even more fun to decorate for Christmas in the new house. Rachel used cedar and pine branches, red ribbons, and candles throughout the house. The Christmas tree was even larger this year.

She and Patrick celebrated their second anniversary by going to Wadesboro and ordering a dining room table that would seat twelve. Most of the time, they planned to eat in the kitchen, but it would be nice to have the bigger table for special occasions. Afterwards, they ate supper in the dining room of the inn.

Christmas was only eleven days from their anniversary. One of the things they gave each other was a white sign at the start of the drive to the house. It read "Fair Oaks Farm, Rachel and Patrick Whitley."

# CHAPTER TWENTY-FIVE

# The Circle

AFTER CHRISTMAS DINNER WAS OVER and all the presents had all been opened, Rachel and Patrick sat in front of the parlor fireplace and held hands.

"I think we've been given another Christmas present," Rachel told him, watching his expression.

He raised his eyebrows and looked at her. "Oh?"

"We'll have to wait about seven more months for it to come, and it's from God."

He understood then. "A baby? We're going to have a baby?"

"Yes, Patrick. We're going to have a baby."

The look of joy on his face was indescribable. He took her into his arms and held her tenderly. He kissed the top of her head. "How have you been feeling?"

"Okay. Sometimes I feel a bit nauseous in the mornings, but it hasn't been too bad, and it wears off by about ten o'clock."

"Seven months. That means it should come toward the last of July. We'll need to cancel our trip to the mountains this year."

"I don't want to do that. If everything is going fine, I'd like to go to the mountains as planned. We'll take a wagon with springs, so it'll ride easier, and we can take our time. The roads are much improved over what they used to be, and I'll be only seven months at the end of May."

"I want to please you, darling, but I'm not sure this is best."

"Grandfather can check me out when we stop there. If he thinks it's a bad idea, we can turn around and come back. I just want Mama with me to help deliver our baby. Please, Patrick, this is important to me."

"I'm afraid such a long trip will be too tiring on you at that point, Rachel. I think you'll be miserable, and I don't want us to do anything that might harm you or the baby. Let's see if we can come up with an alternative. What if we go stay at your Grandfather's and have your parents meet us there? I know it's not as good as going to the mountains, but I do think it's wiser."

"Hmmm. I hadn't thought of having my parents come to me. I'd rather be in the mountains where it's cooler, but Salisbury isn't much better than here. Let's write and see if Mama and Papa will come here instead. I know Papa hates it here in July and August, but I think they'll come for their first grandchild. I know Mama will, and where she goes, Papa will go."

"Thank you, darling. I would've been so worried if we'd tried to go that far in your condition. I'm glad you're being sensible."

"Don't you know I listen to you, Patrick? I've never known you to give me bad advice. I want to please you too."

"You do that very well. You please me immensely."

Rachel wrote her parents the next day. She asked them to come down by the first of July and stay until the baby was born. She'd also ask them to bring down the silver baby rattler Papa had sent for her when he was away fighting in the war and the cradle she'd used. It had been passed down through the Moretz family.

*I need you here with me, Mama,* she'd written. *I want you to deliver your grandchild. Please come.*

Rachel was sure, with such a plea, they'd come, so they started furnishing a bedroom for them. She wanted to get as much done as possible before she became heavier.

Sure enough, a letter came telling that her parents would come. They'd bring the items she requested, as well as the rocking chair Papa had commissioned for Mama's Christmas present the December before Rachel was born.

The three men planted the fields, and this year they'd prepared another field of cotton. They had everything in the ground by the first part of June.

By then, Rachel had become uncomfortable and was glad Patrick had talked her out of traveling to the mountains. She felt awkward and unsightly.

The baby moved enough to let its presence be known. Patrick liked to sit beside her with his hand on her abdomen and feel its movements. He treated her so tenderly that it almost brought tears to her eyes. This would be one blessed child with Patrick for its father.

She and Patrick prayed for their baby. Rachel knew Patrick prayed for her health and well-being, also. It made her feel protected and cared for.

Rachel helped Annie do some of the canning in the little house, but she mainly sat and helped prepare the fruits or vegetables. Annie stood over the hot stove.

Mama and Papa came July the sixth. They'd spent the Fourth of July in Salisbury with Grandfather. They liked the house and the farm, but Papa didn't like the heat and humidity.

"You're about the only person who's ever been able to get me down here during the month of July," he told her.

Mama helped with the cooking and canning, and Rachel needed to do very little. She had already made some baby clothes, but she made more, especially diapers.

Papa got out early in the morning or late in the afternoon to help on the farm. He and Patrick had long discussions about possibilities on the place.

The baby wanted to take its time. By the last week in July, Rachel had grown miserable. Someone had to help her up out of a chair, and there was no way she could get in a comfortable position at night. Patrick spent half his nights fanning her or trying to help her get as comfortable as possible.

Her labor started on July 27 at about nine o'clock at night. Patrick got Mama right away, but both women assured him this was not going to happen quickly, and they had plenty of time. Mama gathered the things she would need.

When Rachel's water broke about midnight, Mama shooed Patrick out of the room. Rachel heard him pacing the floor outside.

"Everything looks good," Mama said.

But everything didn't feel good. The pain became intense. Rachel felt as if her insides were being ripped apart. She listened to Mama and did what she was told, but heard herself scream out before she realized she was doing it. Patrick was in the room in an instant.

"I wondered how long it would take you," Mama told him. "I'm used to Luke doing the same thing."

---

When Patrick burst into the room, Rachel lay in agony with sweat drenching her. His heart broke for her. How he wished he could go through this instead of her.

Leah handed him a damp cloth, pointed to a basin of water, and told him to bathe Rachel's face along. He did that and held her hand. She clenched his when the pains hit hard.

"It's going to be okay, darling," he whispered to her and held her hand. "It won't be much longer." He hoped not anyway.

He noticed dawn starting to break. "Why is this taking so long?"

"Some births do," Leah answered, "and especially the first one."

Leah looked exhausted, and he didn't know how long she could endure. *Lord, please give her the strength she needs and help her and the baby to be okay.*

Leah examined Rachel again. "Everything looks normal," she said when she saw his concern. "The baby is in the right position, and I don't see any problems."

"Maybe we should have had her grandfather or a doctor come as well," he thought aloud.

Leah gave him an indulgent look. "Her grandfather is getting about too old to make long trips, although I have no doubt he would have come if we had asked him. I've probably delivered as many babies as most doctors, though. Women usually prefer another woman at such times."

Patrick nodded and wiped Rachel's face and neck again. He rubbed her hair back away from her face, wishing he could transfer her some strength. If the baby didn't come soon, neither one of them would survive. He shook his head. He wouldn't allow himself to think those kinds of thoughts. God wouldn't let anything happen to Rachel. He had to believe that.

He could tell the pain was getting more intense. Rachel gripped his hand hard, but her strength was ebbing.

*Lord, help her. Please.*

Leah came to stand at Rachel's head. "Rachel . . . Rachel . . ." She had to say it twice to get her attention. "The next time a pain hits, I want you to push with all your might. Do you hear me? You can do this. One more big push, and I think you'll have your baby out into the world." Rachel gave a slight nod, and Leah moved back to the foot of the bed.

Patrick leaned over and kissed her forehead. "Come on, darling. Push this baby out and be finished with this pain. I know how strong you are. I know you can do this. Do it for me. I don't think I can see you like this for much longer."

Her eyes fluttered open, but another pain hit. He sat on the bed beside her and took both her hands in his. "Push, darling. Push!" Her face contorted in pain, but her grip seemed stronger. She let out a final scream, and the baby came.

"You have a beautiful baby girl," Leah said.

Patrick kissed Rachel's forehead again before he went to look at his daughter. "She is beautiful, just like her mother," he said and returned to Rachel's side.

"Her mother doesn't feel so beautiful right now," Rachel mumbled.

"So, I guess this is Rebecca," Leah said as she lay the tiny girl beside Rachel. They'd told her the names they'd chosen.

Leah looked over at Patrick. "Go downstairs and tell Luke the news. He'll want to come up to see her as soon as I get her gown changed. Then we'll need to let her rest for an hour or two before she has to feed Becca."

Patrick did as he was told. Luke came eagerly. Rachel had already fallen asleep, but woke back up.

"What a pretty baby," Luke said.

Rachel smiled and he kissed her cheek.

"I'm proud of you, sweetheart."

"Let's all leave and let her sleep," Leah said. "We'll leave the door open, Patrick, and you can check on them along."

"I'll just sit quietly in this chair." Leah started to move Becca to the cradle. "No, let me hold her for a while," Patrick told her.

She smiled and put Becca in his arms.

Rachel woke up when the baby began to whimper. It must be about time to feed her.

Patrick smiled at Rachel. "She's almost as precious as you are. God has really blessed me to send me so much love in my life."

"He's blessed us both. Fair Oaks really feels like home. Isn't it ironic? Mama left a plantation in Anson County and fell in love with the mountains and a mountain man. I left the mountains, fell in love with a flatlander, and ended up on plantation land in Anson County. I feel like we've come full circle."

He sighed in contentment. "Yes. A circle of love."

---

Leah heard Luke come up as she stood on the back porch looking out at the night. He stopped close behind her and put his arms around her. "You're not melancholic, are you?"

She leaned back into him. "No, not melancholic. Maybe reflective, thoughtful."

"Want to talk about it?"

"I'm not sure I was as prepared to be a grandmother as I thought I was." She paused, hunting for words to explain.

"I know." He put his chin in her hair. "I feel some conflicting emotions too. I'm elated, but it's hard to realize how grown-up your child has become. We remember their childhood too clearly, and it means another stage in our lives."

"Are we getting old, Luke?"

"Never." He laughed. "We're getting older but not old. I don't see you any differently than that first time you rode up the mountain beside me in the wagon seat. Besides, we're only middle-aged."

She chuckled. "Then maybe middle age has dimmed your eyesight." She thought a moment. "But I know what you mean. You're still the handsome man I married. You still take my breath away."

"Does it seem strange to you to come back to this area that used to be your home?"

"No. Everything has changed so much, and it was never as much my home as our mountain farm is. I'm glad we came, but I'm looking forward to getting back there. What seems strange is that Rachel has made it her home. I never thought she would leave the mountains for good."

"In a way, our family generations have come full circle. Granny came from this area too. I've always thought you and she had a lot in common. But despite some rough spots, we've had a good life, haven't we?" He squeezed her tighter.

"The best. The hard times all came from outside situations . . . like the war. Our relationship has never faltered. I guess that time of uncertainty, before we settled the situation Ivy created when she ran off, made us appreciate each other all the more once we were able to marry. I thank God every day for what we have."

"Uh-huh, and you know the best part? It isn't over yet. I think we'll have years to continue to love."

"Do tell." She turned around to face him. He slowly drew her close and gazed into her face. When his lips captured hers, she let his magic carry her away.

# Author's Note

Although I have used names common to the area, all characters in this novel are totally fictitious. There has been a book written about Jesse James coming to the Big Lick area incognito, but this is debatable. I used it in the book as rumored and never substantiated. Most of the places mentioned in Big Lick really existed at some time, but, except for the church, placing them in exact time periods was difficult despite extensive research.

An interesting sidebar is that when I taught at Oakboro School, I sponsored the Oakboro Junior History Club. My students in the club did history projects each year to take to the state convention of the Tarheel Junior Historians in Raleigh. One student did a model of the old town of Big Lick, which is now on display at the Oakboro Regional History Museum. I used this as part of my research.

All the profits from these books go to a scholarship fund for missionary children.

BOOKS IN THE APPALACHIAN ROOTS SERIES

# CLEARED FOR PLANTING

BOOK ONE

# SOWN IN DARK SOIL

BOOK TWO

# UPROOTED BY WAR

BOOK THREE

# TRANSPLANTED TO RED CLAY

BOOK FOUR

All the books are stand-alones, but they should be read in order to prevent spoilers.

For more information about
*Janice Cole Hopkins*
&
*Transplanted to Red Clay*
please visit:

www.JaniceColeHopkins.com
wandrnlady@aol.com
@J_C_Hopkins
www.facebook.com/JaniceColeHopkins

If you enjoyed *Transplanted to Red Clay*, please consider leaving a review on Amazon.com

For more information about
AMBASSADOR INTERNATIONAL
please visit:

www.ambassador-international.com
@AmbassadorIntl
www.facebook.com/AmbassadorIntl